I0582869

SISTER, LIAR, SUSPECT, SLEUTH

LISA NICHOLAS

BLOODHOUND
— B O O K S —

Copyright © 2025 Lisa Nicholas

The right of Lisa Nicholas to be identified as the Author of the Work has been
asserted by them in accordance with the Copyright, Designs and Patents Act
1988.

First published in 2025 by Bloodhound Books.

Apart from any use permitted under UK copyright law, this publication may only
be reproduced, stored, or transmitted, in any form, or by any means, with prior
permission in writing of the publisher or, in the case of reprographic production,
in accordance with the terms of licences issued by the Copyright Licensing
Agency.
All characters in this publication are fictitious and any resemblance to real
persons, living or dead, is purely coincidental.

www.bloodhoundbooks.com

Print ISBN: 978-1-917449-6-56

For Steve, always.

CHAPTER ONE

Susannah Wilson folds her paper napkin around the square of lemon drizzle cake she cannot possibly eat, as she cannot abide dry cake. The tea poured for her from the pot is lukewarm. She shifts on the hard plastic seat and shivers, a draft blowing in from the swinging door as people arrive and stand greeting one another, inconsiderately, in its frame. Susannah arrived promptly, and is sitting at the front, ready to share her news.

'Darling, how's the cake? Finished already? Another slice, dear?'

Susannah stands and gently puts her hand on Jenny's, her other hand a friendly admonishment. 'I couldn't possibly, though I'm so very tempted. You've outdone yourself yet again.'

Jenny beams. 'Oh it's nothing, must do my bit. Terrible business, terrible. How lucky we are to be in a position to help.'

Finally, the heavy red door to the Old School House bangs shut and the key is turned by Jenny's husband the Parish Councillor, to prevent it from blowing open once more. Fervent chatter dulls, whispers peter out, chairs scrape on the scratched and dented old wooden floor.

Lady Knutsworth clears her throat, somehow daintily yet

1

with unquestionable authority. 'Welcome to the parish refugee crisis appeal committee meeting,' she says, quietly, clipped, and with understated confidence.

Susannah does not begrudge Lady Knutsworth her self-appointed role of Parish Chairperson, but sometimes she did wonder if an elected committee – beyond the single Parish Councillor Keith Beard, who nobody would be rude enough to stand against – might help broaden the horizons of their little settlement. Susannah was brimming with ideas, and would be more than willing to pull her sleeves up. Her news today would surely prove her status as one of the leading beacons of the parish, and not before time.

Lady Knutsworth reels off the achievements of the committee, which had formed as an offshoot of the Parish Council to support refugees of the war. Names are mentioned and backs are patted. Lady Knutsworth, or Lydia, as she is known to her friends – such as Susannah, who has always been proud of her ability to assimilate – already knows Susannah's news, encouraged her in fact. Susannah knows that her dear friend is saving it for the grand finale. She wouldn't – *couldn't* – have forgotten.

In the excitement of applauding the five bin bags of children's and women's clothing that have been donated and are stacked in the corner of the draughty hall, a handful of mumbled comments are rising to a babble of opinion.

'I just can't believe there is war in Europe. Never forget, we said.' Mrs Bentham visibly trembles, and although it *is* chilly, Susannah has long suspected that the old dear is a bit of a drama queen.

'These tin-pot dictators, the bloody Tories have been propping them up for years, whatcha expect, eh, eh?'

'Now then, Harry, you and your boys were quite happy to vote them in when they promised farming subsidies.'

'How bloody dare you! I'm a bloody socialist–'

'Please do take a seat, Harry,' Lady Knutsworth requests without a question mark.

With several self-conscious coughs, the room quietens. Lady Knutsworth adjusts her glasses and looks at her handwritten notes, mouthing the names of items she has covered already. Susannah watches her long, bony finger as it reaches the last item on the list. Seeming satisfied she has completed her duty, Lady Knutsworth starts to stand, glancing at Mary who is seated at the piano. They always like to finish with a song.

Susannah doesn't like to interrupt, or challenge. So, she attempts to stare into the very mind of her friend, to catch her eye before the first chords are hammered out on the tuneless upright in the corner. When that doesn't work, she tries her luck at a dainty throat clear, which turns into a violent coughing fit and several offers of water.

That, at least, does the trick.

'Good lord! I almost forgot to mention our most important news,' Lady Knutsworth retakes her seat at the front, 'Our newest parish family–,'

'We've been here fifteen years!' Martin Wilson, sitting next to his earnest and now red-faced wife, chimes in, receiving a sharp elbow in his ribs.

Lady Knutsworth appears not to notice. '–The dear, charity-minded Wilsons, as discussed at our last meeting, have been accepted as a host family for refugees of this dreadful war.'

Uproar with mainly positive vibes ensues, applause, too. Some murmurings are ignored; embarrassed spouses shushing sceptical other halves, whilst silently thinking they may have a point.

'I'm just not sure we have the infrastructure to house immigrants,' one such husband, slow to take the hint, finishes voicing his concern as Susannah quietly tuts, just loudly enough to begin a subtle wave of compliant headshaking across the gathered group.

'We must do our bit, Dennis, it's a crisis. It's a humanitarian emergency,' someone says, using terminology they have quite recently picked up, to the sudden and shifty agreement of the group. They all know they should help, should *want* to, but the whole situation has thrown the world off-track, and their tiny bit of grass and rock is in a bit of a spin.

'I'm sure you'll all support Susannah and Martin in their endeavours to make their guests feel at home in our little community,' Lady Knutsworth instructs. 'Why don't you tell us a little more about our new arrivals, Susannah?' she adds, and Susannah tries not to hear it as an afterthought. After all, she's already stood from her chair and unfolded her notes.

'Her name is Mila Kiss, she's thirty-one years old, and a mother to two small children. Her husband is a war hero.'

CHAPTER TWO

Sofia scrambles on the dirty floor, fingers dancing between sensible, rubber-soled shoes. She reaches for the small rucksack she had dropped as the crowds surged towards the newly opened security desks. As her arm stretches long, skin taut, reaching, she feels the tattered nylon straps make contact with her fingertips. Someone kicks her in the head. She loses her grip as her arms autopilot to protect her skull, and the bag disappears into the forest of legs.

The gravity of hopelessness weighs her down, her perfect plans evaporating above, adrift in the shouts of women, the confused whining of children, the screams of babies. It's all over now. She has lost.

Someone pulls her up, roughly, against the coats, scarves, shoulders and bags of others. Crammed in like sardines, elbows everywhere.

Sofia is suddenly blinded by the airport lights, deafened by the sound. More than anything, she is startled to be standing, her bag in her line of sight. It isn't over yet. She doesn't plan to lose.

'This yours?' Friendly eyes smile at her, an old man – the

only kind of man here today, aside from the soldiers – but strong-looking. He removes his hand from her arm, his leverage no longer required.

She takes the bag, mutters her thanks, tries to smile. Before she can show the gratitude she feels, the tide takes him one way, and her another. She's almost at the furthermost left desk and can no longer see him.

She breathes. She is saved. Back on track.

Her turn finally comes. She arranges her face into a neutral shape as she tells herself that she has nothing to hide and nothing to fear. Her paperwork is in order and she holds her passport. Her final destination is England. Manchester Airport, to be exact.

The pretty woman in uniform stares hard into the photo page, as if it is a Magic Eye puzzle with a hidden meaning, rather than the 800th passport of the same hue she's seen today, and yesterday the same. She types and mutters to her colleague as Sofia unwittingly holds her breath.

'Full address where you'll be staying please, and the names of your hosts?' the woman behind the desk asks, without looking up. She taps the passport details into her keyboard while she waits for an answer.

Sofia can't remember. She freezes, her mind blank.

The woman looks up, and Sofia clocks her matt immoveable red lipstick and lacquered chignon. The attendant smiles, flashing unnaturally bright white teeth, 'It will be on your forms,' she says pleasantly but firmly, her eyes giving away a hint of impatience.

Sofia starts to rummage in the rucksack. They were here, in the inside zip pocket with her ancient iPod. But the bag had opened in the scuffle, and the zip was already broken. Heat rises through her body, her heart thumps. Can the woman behind the desk hear her rasping breaths, see the flurry of panic engulfing her? She must leave today. She needs the forms. They cannot be replaced, not now, and certainly not by Sofia.

'Would you like to stand over there to find your papers and return to the end of the line when you do?' This woman cannot possibly live in the outside world, the city that shakes every hour, sirens echoing through the city reverberating from every corner, until the corners turn to dust. She's too calm. She's too in control. Sofia pulls out a hoodie roughly from the bag, desperate now, and a small tin box crashes to the floor. She quickly picks it up, holding it tightly in her grip.

'No, I, please – I have the papers.' But she didn't, did she? They were somewhere on the floor behind her, amongst the feet and the dirt.

Sofia feels a prod on the shoulder, and she turns around.

'You need to get out of the way, before we all miss the flight,' a middle-aged woman stares unkindly at her. Sofia wonders if she was always hard, or if she's been forced to discard her softer edges this last few months.

Sofia's shoulders slump as she realises that she may have to consider just accepting her fate, failure. Never before, surely not now. The beat of fear is replaced by a churning sickness in her belly: guilt, and a deep overwhelming sadness. She shoves the hoodie and the tin back into the bag and pushes them down. She glimpses it then: a corner of white paper, poking out from inside the ripped lining. Pulling the papers out, she pushes the passport back at the perfect woman behind the glass. 'My hosts are Mr and Mrs Wilson,' she tells her, handing over the papers with the full address in black and white, 'Low Beck Barn, Farlington, Lancashire.'

The woman barely checks the papers, and waves her away. 'Please go through.'

Sofia takes the passport and papers, and grips the strap of her bag. She doesn't look back. She pops her earphones in and turns on the iPod to maximum volume, roaring black metal to help her relax.

Fastening her seatbelt, Sofia ignores the steward's timeless mime on safety. Cheap suit trousers, grey-blue, appear in front of her. She removes an earphone as she looks up, conscious she is being tapped on the arm. Apologies are muttered in a gruff voice, a local accent. It's always awkward to be last on and in a window seat, but as they are on a small, old plane, at least they're only two by two.

'It's fine, don't worry,' she says more sharply than she means to, willing the propellers to turn, the wheels to leave the tarmac. No going back then.

'Ah! Serendipity!' the man in the cheap suit exclaims, as he clicks his belt into place and adjusts the wrinkles at his knees, smoothing the nylon neatly down.

Sofia turns and meets the same kind eyes she's seen only once before, not yet one hour ago.

She smiles. 'Serendipity indeed. I meant to thank you.'

'No need, why don't you make the time quicken? Humour an old man and tell me your story instead. Start with your name, wild child,' he chuckles. He is impossible to resist.

'Mila,' she says, 'my name is Mila Kiss.' And from now on, she will be.

Just like that, Sofia disappears.

CHAPTER THREE

'And so, you are all alone in the world, Mila,' says the old man, Nikolai, to the girl sitting next to him as the turbulence rattles them in their torn leather seats. She couldn't be more than twenty-five, he guesses, but there's a weight where there should be none on one so young, innocence snatched by war. 'Starting again in a new country, with strangers,' he goes on, 'you poor girl, you brave girl. When I first looked and saw you in the airport, crawling around, wild, I thought: she's a crazy girl.' His eyes glisten, but his laugh tinkles as he shakes his head; sorrow and disbelief, emotions he can no longer shake off. 'Your big, dark eyes,' he continues, 'something I couldn't catch within them. Fear: I see it now, poor little Mila.'

Nikolai had not wished to be on that plane today either, or any other day.

'My son, he made me come,' he tells Mila with a sigh, 'I would never have left my home. I wished to die at home, in my bed. Now what is home? Rubble? Pain. Soiled memories.'

'My sister died in her home. It isn't so romantic.'

Nikolai says nothing as he takes the girl's pale, slim hand.

She allows him to. She still misses her father after all these years. She misses them all.

'Let's drink, Mila, to new beginnings. My son tells me to bring waterproof clothes, it's always raining in Manchester, but he has gone soft. Mental in the head,' Nikolai does a swirl with his index finger against the side of his head, 'he thinks his old papa doesn't know how to cope with weather now? The boy has forgotten our winters, it seems, forgotten where he comes from, where he belongs! He lives in some place called Alderley Edge, where all his neighbours play football and the wives have plastic faces. He always did make odd choices.'

'You can't say mental in the head anymore. Or do that sign with your finger,' Mila tells the old man, as he presses his crew member calling button over and over until an exasperated woman in her fifties makes her way down the aisle, a frown already in place as she reaches them and leans over to switch the red service light off.

'People move, language changes, the young invent new rules to confuse us. But our origins stay the same, and I'll only sing one national anthem as long as I live. Ah!' Nikolai suddenly notices the perfumed presence above him, 'A vodka with ice, please, and some nuts would be nice.'

'Sir, this is an emergency evacuation service. A *free* service, may I remind you.'

'And Mila, what will you have, sweet girl?' Nikolai looks up and catches the tired eyes of the server. They are turquoise blue and her eyeliner is smudged. The lines deepen around them, highlighted by the cracks in her foundation. Her name badge reads Karen. 'Karen, are you from the States? Such a great country, supporting us, helping us flee, you must be making a lot of people very proud... and such a beautiful smile, I'd bet.'

Karen smiles then. The old man is a charmer, that's for sure. 'Well don't tell anyone, all right? You keep this quiet.'

Mila sips her warm white wine, and Nikolai drinks his miniature vodka in one go.

'Need something to calm me. My son – Peter – he's so clever, I'm told – a computer engineer. Though not a man's man, I'm afraid. They call them nerds on American television shows. He never stops telling me things; it's very stressful. He doesn't have a wife yet. Maybe I'll introduce you. He needs someone to tell things to. Though I don't think he can even change a plug, so maybe you'll find someone better in Lancashire, eh?'

Nikolai falls asleep for the rest of the journey, and Mila looks across him to the clouds beyond. When they disembark, he hugs her tightly and scribbles an address on a scrap of paper for her. Mila walks through the gate, nothing to declare, and searches for her name in the sea of anxious-looking couples holding small home-made banners. Some are in crayon, done by children. Others are in neat calligraphy, a few printed. She fingers the piece of paper in her pocket, Nikolai's son's address.

The sign bearing the name *Mila Kiss* is printed, with flowers hand-drawn around the border. It is held by a slim, petite woman with a shiny, swinging blonde bob who is standing next to a tall, broad-shouldered man, salt and pepper hair, T-shirt collar erect above his expensive looking jacket.

Mila slowly walks towards the couple. She notices subtle diamonds in the woman's ears, a fitted knee length coat, skinny jeans, a white blouse tucked in. Brown knee high boots give her the look of the countryside, albeit a hygienic version. Her silky scarf hides her neck, as women of a certain age so often like to do. Mila didn't used to care about such things, but now she thinks about the luxury of ageing a lot. The man looks uncomfortable, and is still searching the crowd behind her. Of course he is; she will not be what they expect. She pulls out her earphones, and the crashing drums fade to nothing, while the shredding of the thrash guitar stays in her mind, soothing her.

'Mr and Mrs Wilson?' Mila says in perfect English, her accent faultless. She has always excelled in languages, in most subjects, in fact.

'Mila?' The woman starts to offer her hand, appears to think better of it, and passes the sign to her husband, before awkwardly embracing the young woman before her. 'But where are the children?'

CHAPTER FOUR

Martin pours himself a second large glass of wine and switches on the television, stretching back into the depths of his favourite sofa. Susannah marches over to the set and switches it off at the mains.

'Martin! We haven't finished discussing the issue,' she says, a strained sort of shouted whisper, laced with irritation.

'There's nothing to discuss, Susannah. The whole process was so badly organised, like everything this bloody government does, it's no great shock to me that they got Mila's details muddled.'

'Muddled, Martin? Muddled? We're missing two children. Mila is at least five years younger than the Mila we picked.'

'We didn't *pick* her. She's not our new pet. She was *assigned* to us.'

'No, Martin, a thirty-one-year-old wife and mother with a little boy aged nine and a little girl aged seven were *assigned* to us. A grown woman with responsibilities, with a husband fighting back home. In the introduction pack she sounded so lovely. So *grateful*. Where's *that* Mila? *This* Mila,' she gestures, pointing to the ceiling indicating the room above in which their guest sleeps, 'is what, barely twenty-five? No husband, no kids, no manners!'

'She was just tired, and nervous, Susannah. What do you propose we do? Send her back? I wonder what their returns policy is.'

'It's not funny. What will we tell Lydia? She organised a place at school for each of them. Everyone is expecting a mother, not a five-foot-eight sullen supermodel with an attitude!'

'I see,' Martin replies, dangerously.

'You see what?' Susannah seethes, 'Because if you're implying I'm concerned about her being a young, attractive woman, you are very much mistaken. I didn't expect her to be a ray of sunshine, given the circumstances, but a smile wouldn't go amiss. And her clothing is somewhat provocative, so black, so clumpy – there were metal chains on her jeans, which were unfeasibly tight.' She glances at the photo of her own daughter grinning back at her, blonde waves flowing. 'I simply wanted to offer a home to someone we had things in common with, who would find it easy to settle in, make friends with the other mothers. As a mother, I could offer advice, support her, be almost like a grandmother to those poor displaced kiddies.' Susannah takes her gaze, more pointedly, to the photo on the fireplace: Chloe, sun-kissed on the beach, folded into a half embrace by Geoff. It had been almost a year since she married an Australian and moved to Perth. 'The disdain in her eyes!' Susannah almost wails, 'She practically scowled the entire evening.' She sighs as she picks up the photo in the pretty silver frame.

Martin pats the seat next to him, nods encouragingly. Susannah sits, and he pulls her close.

'I know you miss Chloe. I know Mila isn't the same person we thought we were getting. But look on the bright side. It's been a long time since we have had a house full of children's mess and noise and tantrums. How would we have coped?' Martin asks with a smile, and a raised eyebrow, trying not to let the relief reveal itself at the lack of small children at his feet, in his house, running mud over the carpets. 'Mila isn't much older than our Chloe. Like Chloe, she's out in the world without a mother in a strange country, and not even a nice reliable husband like Boring Geoff–'

'Do stop calling him that, Martin,' Susannah scolds, but with a smile. They had always imagined their pretty, vibrant, clever girl to be with someone a bit more handsome, more dynamic, very much less of an accountant. When Chloe had first told them she'd met an Australian, they'd imagined all sorts of horrors – ripped vest tops barely concealing tanned muscles, scraggly too-long blond hair – and found themselves sorely disappointed not to have anything at all to complain about. Until Chloe failed her first year at university and announced they'd decided to marry and emigrate, the UK clearly not being ready for Chloe's talents. Susannah was still in online therapy over the shock, though at least it seemed to be working out. Heavens, Chloe seemed almost like an adult last time they spoke; settled, their nest to remain empty.

'Mila needs you Susannah, I don't think she meant to be rude. You did ask a lot of questions. It was like you were interrogating her for not being the *right* Mila. As far as she'd been told, she was assigned to us, and now she may feel a little unwelcome.'

Susannah tips her head back and closes her eyes. 'Good God, Martin, you're right. I've been awful. That poor girl. It's not her fault she has been sent to us by mistake. I just don't understand!'

'We can get in touch with the placement team tomorrow. They've mixed up the details from another family with those of

Mila. She *is* Mila Kiss, love. The mother of two is clearly somebody else. She showed us her passport when you asked, didn't she?'

Susannah groans as she recalls her demands. Didn't her therapist keep reminding her not to allow her anxiety to rise when she is thrown off in social situations; not to panic?

'But if we tell them, they might make Mila go back into the system while they investigate. It could be weeks before they sort it out. The welcome party at the Old School House is set for tomorrow. Jenny has made a cake. Someone has put up bunting. They made a *"Welcoming the Kiss family"* sign. Oh no, they'll need to change the sign. I'd better call Lydia. Or perhaps Keith?'

Susannah picks up her mobile phone from the coffee table and begins to scroll.

'Darling, the party doesn't matter; we should straighten it all out first.'

Susannah doesn't register her husband's interjection. 'As you say, we didn't pick her, she was assigned, what difference does paperwork matter to the party? We can sort that out afterwards. We really don't want to spoil the party for Mila.'

'Or for the damned committee,' Martin grumbles, pouring more wine.

Susannah starts to compose a text, then the phone jumps to life and rings. Chloe. Susannah answers. Martin listens to one side of the conversation. Something is wrong. Muffled crying is audible.

'Of course you must come home,' Susannah soothes, 'We never liked him anyway. Far too boring for you.'

CHAPTER FIVE

Lady Lydia Knutsworth has never once imagined she has anything in common with Susannah Wilson. She has nothing against her, after all the woman is very community-minded, if prone to uncouth over-enthusiasm. Not that Lydia is a snob, she tells herself when she finds herself shrinking back from Susannah's over-familiar method of greeting her Ladyship, which for Lydia, feels like a strange hybrid of *la bise* and a minor assault.

Yet, that evening two absent children had called their parents, and both were coming home. Two mothers had started preparing. Susannah was making up the spare room, as Mila was in Chloe's old room, and Lydia was instructing her housekeeper to air Fabien's quarters. Both were making shopping lists of their child's favourite treats.

Lord Knutsworth, who had taken the call from his only son and heir, is less enthusiastic than his wife. 'He'll want money,' he tells Lydia, who is looking for flour, leaving every cupboard door open, and a trail of destruction as she drops and spills various baking goods she has not once previously set eyes on. 'What *are* you doing, Lydia?'

'I'm baking Fabien a welcome home cake, isn't that obvious, Gregory?'

'There is nothing the least bit obvious about you baking a cake. Why don't you ask Anna to do it? That's what we pay her for, isn't it?'

Lydia stops what she is doing, and places a bag of out-of-date raisins on the kitchen table. She sighs, and composes herself, readying herself to explain a very simple concept to what is currently appearing to be a very simple man.

'Darling, Fabien is a *woke* now. He doesn't believe in staff, these days. He says it's exploitation. Besides, I'm his mother, and I'm–'

'He's not bloody woke, he runs a hedge fund!'

'An *ethical* hedge fund,' Lydia reminds him.

'He only says that stuff to wind me up and to pretend he's not itching for me to drop off my perch.'

'What a thing to say about our only son!' Lydia begins to pour flour into a mixing bowl, and crack eggs over the top.

'Besides, I've never seen him lift a finger. He may not *believe* in staff, but he's obviously far too polite to say.'

Lydia ignores her husband's sarcasm, and starts to whisk the mixture, creating a sticky snowstorm.

'Do you know the recipe?' Gregory enquires, with uncharacteristic trepidation. He has never seen Lydia cook or bake, or even so much as make a sandwich.

'Oh, I used to watch my old nanny do it all the time, and I'm practically glued to the television when *Bake Off* is on.'

Fabien arrives to applause. Literally. As his shiny off-white, top-down 1951 Jaguar XK 120 pulls up the vast tree-lined driveway, Lydia calls Anna the housekeeper, and Danny the gardener, and her begrudging husband to the front steps. Even their younger daughter Elodie meanders up the driveway from her studio-slash-home, the gatehouse, in her paint-splattered overalls with Offal, her scruffy rescue dog – so named because most people had rejected him, but she knew with the correct ingredients of care and attention he was the most delicious, lovable creature anyone could wish for. She was right; he is smitten, and pads dutifully alongside her everywhere she goes.

'Good God woman, I feel like I'm in a bad period drama,' Gregory complains to his wife.

'Don't be ridiculous,' Lydia says, 'there *are* no bad period dramas.'

She embraces her son, still after all these years surprised by him towering over her, his hard body so unlike the one she occasionally held years ago, surprised he is a man now.

Fabien accepts his father's handshake and tells the staff how much he's missed them. He ruffles Offal's head, who rolls over to expose his fluffy, white belly.

'You are a very naughty boy, how long has it been since you last visited? Christmas, I think. Over six months! How I've missed you,' Lydia titters in a baby voice as she pinches Fabien's cheek, much to the amusement of her son, and the bemusement of her husband, who never did fully understand her soft spot for Fabien. Usually, she was more composed.

'Ah, but Mummy, one of your offspring must make a proper career, and I suppose that falls to me. Sold a painting yet, Elodie? Apart from to Granny, Uncle Richie, or that gallery Daddy basically props up with free rent in town?'

'Get stuffed, wanker-banker,' she retorts.

'Boho tramp,' Fabien sticks his tongue out.

'Come now, inside, tea will be ready,' Lydia instructs, as Elodie marches back towards the gatehouse without a word, Offal skipping behind her happily.

The remaining Knutsworths sit in the drawing room, and Anna goes to fetch the tea. Danny resumes his work in the gardens. A quiet descends. Lydia goes to fill it. 'Of course, we have planned your favourite for dinner, but first we must attend the party for our new refugee girl. I know you'll be tired after your journey, darling, but it is so important to be supportive during these challenging times, don't you think, hmmm?'

'You shipped in a refugee girl? Is she to work the land?' Fabien teases.

Gregory winks at his son, smiling despite himself, before reconfiguring his face under the heat of his wife's glare. Fabien may be a spoiled, entitled brat, Gregory considers, but he and Lydia are no doubt to blame, and the boy does have a wicked sense of humour.

'We did not ship her in, Fabien!' Lydia straightens herself, and knits together her eyebrows. 'She's staying with the Wilsons. Chloe's in Australia – of course you'll remember the scandal – so they have the room. She was supposed to be bringing children, and apparently that's all fallen through, though goodness knows how one misplaces two children. We had to remake the welcome sign.'

'You have a few spare rooms, Mummy,' Fabien looks up through his lashes, coy, 'shall we be getting our own refugee family?'

'Over my dead body,' declares Gregory. 'It's a frightful war, but nothing to do with us, and the last thing Britain needs is a new generation of immigrants crippling the economy.'

Anna clatters into the room with the tray of teapot, milk jugs, and china cups. A plate of biscuits and a last-minute shop-bought lemon drizzle cake are arranged on the stand. Lydia's effort was buried in the bin, along with her aspiration to ever bake again.

'Thank you, Anna. Here, let me help,' says Fabien to the blushing housekeeper, scowling at his father, who admires a chaffinch, bobbing on a swaying branch just outside the window. Anna and her mother had been immigrants from Poland, years ago.

'No, no, please. Don't get up, sir.'

Gregory sighs, and rolls his eyes. Fabien needn't be embarrassed on his account. *Obviously,* he didn't mean Anna. She's a great worker, he couldn't live without her. He clears his throat and whistles a few bars of his current favourite record, while admiring the red leaves of his beloved Japanese maple fluttering in the breeze. He tries to recall the lyrics, something about an Irish girl and a fiddle. Anna seems to be taking an awfully long time to serve the tea.

Lydia reaches for a large piece of cake and fills her mouth, rendering herself unable to speak for the time it takes Anna to pour the tea and exit the room. Gently dabbing her lips with the napkin, Lydia looks at her son. So handsome, so wise in so many ways, but slow to learn the ways of their world.

'It wouldn't be proper, my dear Fabien. You have such a good heart, but this home, it belongs not only to us, but to every generation before and yet to come. It belongs to the community, to history. It cannot be open as a public house, for lodgers, no matter how much your father and I dearly wish it to be possible.'

'Well said, well said!' exclaims Gregory, who has no intention of welcoming anyone, refugee or otherwise into his home, other than at the ghastly annual community ball. Even then, he insists on carriages at ten. He only tolerates Fabien's infrequent visits because he is obliged to on a number of levels. Elodie choosing to live in the gatehouse in the manner of a squatter was a godsend, although the girl was more tolerable than the boy.

Gregory claps his hands. 'Now, drink up, eat up, and then we can get ready for the party. We should only have to stay an hour. It starts at 5pm, isn't that correct, my dear?' Lydia nods, and sips her tea, happy to have the subject changed. 'Well then, we have an hour to bathe, read, nap, whatever you like. Right-ho?'

Finishing up, and leaving the tray behind, Lydia leads the way from the drawing room to the hallway, and starts to ascend the wide, winding staircase.

Fabien, behind her, and ahead of his father, slows, almost tripping Gregory up, and waits for his mother to turn the corner onto the landing, her back disappearing from view. He stops abruptly. 'Father, I wonder if I might have a word in private?'

'I thought you might,' Gregory sighs. 'Come into my study.'

CHAPTER SIX

Mila drips with sweat, another nightmare broken by the calls of the birds outside, so happy to have made it through another night. Lucky them, Mila thinks. Lucky me, she adds, not quite convincing herself.

It's been nine days since her sister died, five days since she ran, and just one since she boarded the plane, safety in sight. Distance and the unfamiliar comforts of a room that isn't really hers, in a strange house in a strange country, has not lessened the constant throbbing of memories.

During the days of the last week, relentless planning took up all the space in her mind, pushing down the visions determined to block her view of the future with a force Mila has always possessed. Mila knows what she is capable of, but what she doesn't know is how to find what she came here for. Not yet, anyway.

Mila stares at the childish light fitting that hangs above Chloe's bed. The bed is a strange halfway point between a single and a double, designed for the grown-up child who will never be permitted to bring a boyfriend home to stay. Mila can understand that. Her parents were strict too. They'd pushed her, and she'd delivered, though rarely in the way they'd hoped for.

Mrs Wilson – *call me Susannah* – is nothing like Mila's mother. Mila's mother never fussed. She was too busy working, fighting for what she believed in. Now it's Mila's turn to fight. But she isn't fighting, is she? She's lying in the bed of a spoilt English princess, satin covers and feather down pillows.

She remembers the blood coming from her sister's body – on the floor, on her hands. She can almost hear the sounds of the wailing emergency vehicles, loud at first, fading as her feet thumped on the tarmac as she ran. She ran. She only returned once to find what she knew was hidden, what Janos had been looking for too. By then the body had gone. The murder investigation had begun. Witnesses spoke of the dead girl's sister fleeing the scene. Mila puts her earphones in and turns the volume up loud to drown out her thoughts.

It is quiet in Farlington, which should be nice, Mila supposes. Just the noisy birds, the distant rumble of tractors, the odd car, and late yesterday afternoon the bleating and mooing. Mr Wilson – *call me Martin* – had explained when Mila asked, that they didn't really know why the animals were moved with some regularity, but he assumed it was something to do with keeping the grass healthy. Also, he had chuckled, it gave the farmers something to do. Susannah had slapped his arm playfully.

So, they are townies too, Mila had concluded silently.

Mila is a city girl. She loves her home city. Watching it burn and crumble made her heart burn with rage. No one had believed they would be invaded. *Idle threats,* everyone had said six months ago. She'd warned them; her group had campaigned for years for action. Prevention before cure. Mistrust before complacency. Where had the rest of the world been then? Spare rooms are one thing, MQ-9 Reapers are better.

Her friends left. Everyone left. Except for people like her, her family, and Nikolai. Those desperate to fight, those waiting for somewhere to go, and those insisting they'd rather die at home. And now, people like them, Nikolai and Mila – strangers to one another, separated by years and ideology and probably everything else as well – both afraid they may never get home. Both determined to, one way or another.

Mila doesn't dream of the bombs or the burning buildings. She doesn't dream of bodies in the street. She dreams of her sister, dead on the living room floor, and of her sister's children, Konstantine and Karlie, who are out there somewhere. The face of the man they all trusted, once, a long time ago. Their world is changed forever, and not only because of war. She wonders if *she* is changed as she lies here in Farlington, the gentle sounds of a household stirring, sunlight seeping through the gap in the curtains, visions of monsters, the voice in her head telling her they all think that she is one too. That he, Janos, will tell them so.

She throws back the covers and pulls open the curtains to let the day in. The view reminds Mila of a cheesy hotel wall print of somewhere unnamed, by an artist unknown. Green and blue for miles, not an inch of character. Mila opens the drawer in her bedside table, painted a girly white, with an expensive-looking oak top. Her small tin box is there, within it her passport, paperwork, photographs, evidence. Also, the address Nikolai will be staying at with his son. It seems strange to keep her most important documents in the drawer belonging to a girl she has never met.

What would her hosts make of her padlocked box? She knows the Wilsons will not snoop; they're too polite. Mila understands English polite society. She visited London several times with school, and those at partner schools more interested in history and culture than skiing visited her great city.

Sometimes they had hung out in bars. Where did that life go? All the promise.

There is a gentle knock on the door, which Mila doesn't hear above the rising waves of a chorus wailing in her ears, but the banging that follows finds its way to Mila's consciousness as the song begins its fade to end. She removes the earphones, pauses the album. The next song is so riotously angry, she doesn't want to miss a beat.

'Yes, I'm awake. I shall get up.'

Mrs Wilson's voice is soft, and kind. 'I thought I'd heard movement, so I brought you some tea. I'll leave it here, no rush, you should rest.'

'No, please, come in,' Mila says, feeling uncomfortable to be the gatekeeper to any room in another's home, yet she takes the dressing gown from the back of the door she had been told was hers – a welcome gift, brand new – and pulls it tight around her.

They perch together awkwardly on the bed.

'Did you sleep well?' asks her host, who Mila realises is already dressed in smart clothes and is wearing full make-up. Her hair is smooth, freshly blown dry.

'Yes, thank you.'

'I assume you'll want to rest today, or Martin can take you for a walk, show you around the village – where the shops are, and the like?'

'Yes, thank you.'

'The little welcome party is at 5pm, is that okay with you, Mila?'

'Yes, of course, thank you.'

'Do you have something to wear?'

'I have clothes, thank you.'

'I understand you left in a rush – I don't know what you managed to salvage, you just brought that one bag, and well, you could borrow some of Chloe's old things if you like? You're a

SISTER, LIAR, SUSPECT, SLEUTH

little taller than she is, but we might find something,' Susannah didn't wait for an answer, and was already walking to the door. 'The clothes she left behind are in this spare room, more of a study now really, Martin's workplace from home. I moved them before you came. We put bunk beds in the other one, for the children, it's a yoga suite usually, these days. Not that that's important. I'm rambling, sorry dear.'

'Thank you, but I will be okay with what I brought from home,' Mila hears the stone-cold quality of her own clipped responses and tries to smile, 'But, thank you again,' she adds, willing Mrs Wilson to leave her alone with her mess of thoughts.

Susannah stops and turns, takes a breath, her hand to her heart. 'I'm so insensitive, Mila. Forgive me. You need as much familiarity as possible. You must wear what you like. Let me wash everything for you, freshen it up after being crammed in a bag for hours.'

'Thank you. If you show me the utility room, I shall wash the items myself.'

Susannah's face reddens, a slight glisten appears on her forehead. Mila feels a little bad.

'Mrs Wilson,' she begins.

'Susannah, please.'

'Susannah, I only mean I don't wish to cause you any more trouble than I have. The misunderstanding with the information you were given, taking up room in your home, eating your food. I will contribute as soon as I can. I have some savings.' She just can't access them: her phone is in pieces at the bottom of the river, her bank cards are all cut up. There will be no trail.

'Nonsense. No need at all. Focus on settling in for now. We are happy to have you.' Mila looks as if she might protest. 'But,' Susannah continues, not leaving space for argument; she's a mother to another feisty young woman and knows the drill, 'if it would make you more comfortable, I'll show you where everything is when you're dressed, dear.' Susannah smiles, grateful that the end of the conversation is in sight, and thinks not for the first time how impeccable Mila's English is, and wonders how she manages to make "thank you" sound so rude.

Martin tells her that Mila is nervous, tired, and explains it must be difficult to communicate complex emotions in a second language. Susannah sees the look in Mila's eyes, though, and it is positively icy. The villagers will be in for a surprise, she thinks, as from previous conversations and news reports one would be forgiven for thinking all people fleeing any war were constantly draped in headscarves, speaking pidgin English, gushing sentimental thanks, and praying.

'What is it you do back home? The information sheet said you are a librarian, but it also said you have two children, so I think we can probably assume it got that wrong too.'

'I'm a lawyer, human rights,' Mila replies, 'or I was.'

Susannah pauses, mouth slightly agape, before turning towards the door as Martin passes in the hallway, offering up fresh coffee, and a walk later. 'Oh. I see. Lovely,' she says to Mila.

Mila watches as Susannah closes the door behind her, and listens for the inevitable hushed debrief as the Wilsons descend the stairs. She cannot make out any words.

She wonders what they are saying back home. What stories Janos is telling them. He has the children, no doubt, and she has what he's searching for. What she doesn't have is much time.

Mila puts her earphones back in and presses play. The beat starts with a muted electronic thud, thud, thud. Mila closes her eyes and she thinks of the children. She promises her sister she will save them, she will expose Janos, and she'll do it all before they find her.

CHAPTER SEVEN

There is a nervous energy in the village hall. The sign has been repainted to welcome their solo refugee guest, the cakes look divine, and Mary is playing the piano. People sit, then stand, unsure of their roles. Is it a welcome party akin to when a local dignitary visits? It certainly doesn't feel like one. They doubt Mila Kiss will expect or enjoy standing applause as she enters their little building, new and foreign to her.

They wonder how to arrange their faces. Sympathetic, welcoming, sombre? Perhaps a clever combination of all three. They wish they had practised in the mirror before they arrived. They are all beginning to regret that they did not pay more attention to Susannah's endless village WhatsApp chat group messages, in which she shared links from government websites about how to welcome refugee families into the community.

Jenny worries she is overdressed and will make the poor young woman feel uncomfortable should she only have war-torn rags to wear. Her teenage daughter Lottie thinks she is an out of touch patronising old lady, and told her so, which didn't help. The child has threatened to move to Australia to live with the ever-enviable older girl Chloe twice already today, and it's all

Jenny can do to remain calm and pour the tea. Lottie is only sixteen, and Chloe was always trouble, in her opinion.

At least now Elodie is exerting some good influence over her, Jenny muses, and helping her learn to paint. In return, Lottie walks Elodie's funny little mongrel when Elodie is *"in the zone"*. Not that he needs walking, Jenny has pointed out to Lottie once or twice – as he has acres and acres of gardens to roam – unlike their own family dog, who Lottie refuses to look after. Jenny passes her daughter, slouched in a chair furiously tapping away on her phone, and hisses in her ear to sit up straight and look more engaged.

Lydia notices a tension between Fabien and Gregory as they drive to the hall, squeezed into the tiny back seat with Elodie, who complains that the red leather sticks to her bare legs as her skirt rides up each time they whizz around corners too fast. Lydia reminds her daughter she should be wearing tights. Fabien seems on edge. His mood doesn't improve when the car starts to emit strange fumes accompanied by even stranger sounds, and she wonders if it will start again after the party.

Gregory had offered to drive, but Fabien was quite insistent, muttering about being independent and not in need of anything from his father. Lydia had ignored them, assuming he was making another criticism of his sister who was also ignoring them, lost as she always was in her own thoughts, a walking daydream. Both women, different as they are, are used to the competitive sparring.

Susannah is anxious as they pull up and squeeze into one of the last spaces on the road outside the hall. All day she has typed, erased, retyped, and erased again, group messages informing them of Mila being an entirely different person to the one she has told them about. In the end, she said nothing. It had been embarrassing enough having to explain the missing children mix-up to Lydia, although she is entirely blameless.

To proactively explain that Mila was a university educated, beautiful, bilingual, assertive young woman with a keen interest in heavy metal who had not long begun her career in law before war broke out would be to also admit they had expected otherwise. Which could be construed as patronising, racist, or worse – behind the times. Susannah Wilson, a fusty old-fashioned bigot.

The contrived enthusiasm for the *Farlington Support for Refugees* campaign had been powered by guilt and a deeply ingrained community-spirited obligation that they must help those less fortunate. Having her home blown to bits did still give Mila the edge on being less fortunate than anyone in Farlington, but Susannah doubted she was entirely what they'd signed up for.

Stay-at-home mother of two with a war hero husband away fighting while she struggles to make ends meet as the economy collapses, my backside, Susannah keeps thinking, before reminding herself to be a better person. Mila, too, is blameless. Stupid government, stupid online matching system, broken like everything else in this country. Susannah inwardly sighs again, remembering to count her blessings. Her country isn't at war, and *she* isn't lodging with a strange family far from home.

Mila is two heads taller than Susannah, at least. As she enters behind her, her eyes dart around, meeting a sea of faces, staring and trying not to, smiling, not too big. Waiting. Martin is not with them, and Mila feels uncharacteristically untethered. There is a calming weight to Martin's presence that stills the whirlwind around his wife, and even in such a short time, he has helped Mila breathe slower, and find brief respite from her thoughts. He is currently trying to book his daughter flights home, as she can't bear to stay in her husband's country a moment longer than necessary. He promised to be along a little later.

When they told Mila, a few hours ago, that Chloe would be returning, Mila had offered to leave. That quickly put to bed, she had offered to vacate Chloe's room and take the room they had originally set aside for the children that hadn't arrived.

They wouldn't hear of it, explaining Chloe wouldn't either. Her return was unplanned, and not one of them would dream of putting their guest in bunk beds after what she had been through. Chloe is a few years younger than Mila, and in the midst of a marriage break up, having, from what Mila could gather from Martin's remarks, *"refused to listen to sense when she rushed into things"*, and being, from Susannah's sympathetic replies, *"far too devasted and embarrassed for anyone – including Martin – to remind her of that"*.

Mila does not think this bodes well, and is already planning how to firstly vacate the room, and then quickly find what she is looking for so she can put an end to this once and for all. So far, her searches on the iPad the Wilsons have lent her have been fruitless.

A hand grasps Mila's, and she is hit by a wave of heady perfume, something like Chanel No 5 but not quite. 'Good afternoon, Miss Kiss. I am Lady Lydia Knutsworth, and on behalf of the whole village, I'm delighted to welcome you into our community.'

'Thank you,' replies Mila, feeling a slight nudge she assumes is from Susannah, but not sure what she is expected to do. She searches through her memories of books by Jane Austen, a favourite of her mother's, though not her own. Should she curtsy? Surely not. She remains still, does not remove her hand, but continues, 'Lady Knutsworth. I am very grateful to be here.' Mila swallows the truth with a smile.

Her hand is released, and the sea of faces comes closer, teeth showing, offering hands, and pushing small children forward with wilting handpicked flowers from the roadside. Mila is given tea and cake. She is quickly relieved of it too, as the villagers introduce themselves with handshakes and smiles, and well-meant personal questions.

'Human rights lawyer, blimey, well done,' says Jenny.

'But just begun your career and had to leave, how terribly difficult for you,' adds Mary.

'Did you work for a big firm?' asks Councillor Keith Beard.

'No, a small lobby group, you might say,' Mila answers.

'Such excellent English, better than my daughter's!' Jenny remarks, as her daughter reddens next to her, narrowing her eyes at her mother.

'Politics and law, eh? Can't have been easy, given the circumstances,' Keith goes on.

'No,' Mila replies.

He appears as if from nowhere. He's taller than her, though she hadn't noticed him until this moment. She can feel his warm breath as he gently touches her arm, and says, 'Let me get you a fresh drink,' and leads her away. She is grateful, truly, this time. 'I'm Fabien,' he tells her. Something about his interruption has calmed the swarm of people, who are now talking amongst themselves.

He is beautiful; a cliché of manhood, like a doll or a Disney character. He has a cocksure smile, and an entitled swagger. Mila dislikes him immediately.

'Mila,' she offers her hand, and in it he places a saucer and cup, and pours.

He's looking deep into her eyes, but if he notices the glare breaking through the polite expression Mila has tried to cultivate since her arrival at the party, he doesn't let on. Mila looks away, through a small window, where a squirrel darts up a tree. Fabien makes a small amused noise, not quite a laugh but nicer than a snort. He gestures to the room full of people, who are all starting to make for the tea trolley.

'The rabble is back on our tails; what do you say you and I make a run for it?'

Mila's expression must give her away, and for a moment Fabien looks embarrassed. Like everyone else, he is afraid of phrases that mock the reality of war, of refugee life.

He recovers well, does not apologise, and Mila's eyebrow inadvertently rises at his lack of sensitivity, which makes her relax, as now she doesn't have to pretend to be nice to him. She allows the scowl to escape onto her face and immediately feels a little better. The fury inside her needs a release.

'Let's just get some air. There is a bench outside, and soon the birds will start to roost, and although some might say their song is beautiful, it is quite the racket, but rather fun, I think. I like to imagine what they're calling out to one another. I always assume they have filthy mouths.'

The man's an idiot, Mila thinks. What an easy existence he must have to concern himself with such inane thoughts. She follows him outside all the same, desperate to breathe, and be in the company of someone she is sure is so dim, she can drop her pretence, for at least a moment or two.

CHAPTER EIGHT

Fabien is lying in bed, thinking about Mila. Beautiful Mila, like no other woman he has met: utterly uninterested in him. Fabien knows he is a catch, but Mila clearly hasn't got the memo. The fact is, he is getting tired of fawning girls with aspirations, and he wants something more. The trappings of wealth and beauty are trappings all the same, he'd tried to explain drunkenly once or twice, to the tune of no sympathy whatsoever.

On the evening of the party, or, as Fabien liked to think, the evening that would change both their lives forever and be the perfect anecdote to regale jealous friends with smugly when they asked, *"However did you two meet?"*, he and Mila had sat on the bench for a full forty minutes outside the Old School House. Eventually, Susannah had told him off for not allowing Mila the chance to enjoy her welcome party, and ushered her away.

Elodie had appeared then, cigarette dripping lazily from her fingers. 'What was that?' she'd said, smirking.

'Were you smoking behind the bush? How old are you?'

'She looked bored senseless.'

'She was in awe; the stony expression's just a thing over there.'

'My brother, the cultural guru. You know stereotyping isn't really okay anymore, right? Maybe they don't teach that in ethical banking.'

'Piss off,' Fabien said, 'I'll meet you in the car.'

'You know?' Elodie called back over her shoulder, 'I'd go further than bored. She was positively seething.'

He'd called over with flowers the following day. Susannah had dragged him inside to wait for Mila who was in the bath, but after an hour of being talked at and three cups of tea later, she had not appeared, and was not answering calls shouted up the stairs. In the end, Martin had suggested that she most likely had her earphones in, as she tended to listen to very loud music.

'Dreadfully awful stuff,' Susannah had muttered, having politely asked to listen as a way to get Mila to open up a little.

Martin had suggested Fabien might like to get home, as he probably had things to do.

Susannah had protested, and offered to fetch Mila herself, glaring at her husband, but Martin had urged her to let the poor girl rest.

'Let me see you out,' he'd said to Fabien; an instruction.

'Would you mind if I telephoned, Martin? I'd like to ask Mila if I could show her around.'

'Of course you can telephone, Fabien!' Susannah called from down the hall, behind her husband, who Susannah suspected had been thinking of ways to say no. He'd never forgiven Fabien for the incident with Chloe, leading her on like that, humiliating her.

'She probably needs time to settle in,' Martin had told him, opening the front door.

'I'm sure she'd be delighted,' Susannah had said, an edge to her voice.

But first, Fabien needs another yes.

The dancing butterflies in his stomach transform into caged birds fighting to get out. He feels anxious, and he doesn't like it. His father told him he would think about it. He will talk to him again today, once he has looked through his affairs.

Fabien slides out of bed, his big feet landing heavily on the wooden floor, which is cold, as always. The heating is a constant battle in the big old creaky house. He might turn it into apartments one day, with underfloor heating and en suites. He leaves his childhood bedroom and walks down the breezy corridor to the nearest bathroom. The window hasn't properly shut for years, and double glazing is not an option, according to his stingy father.

He turns on the shower, and after ten minutes the trickle of lukewarm water has made it all the way to his floor from whatever ancient unit it is pumped from. Another ten minutes, and the flow is just about fast enough, the temperature warm enough, to stand beneath. The pipes rattle as he scrubs. His penthouse apartment's luxuries flash into his mind, quickly replaced by a violent urge to be sick, as he is reminded of all he stands to lose.

His mother is drinking tea in the breakfast room when he goes downstairs. He kisses her cheek, and takes a seat.

'I do hope you've given some thought to our conversation Fabien,' she says, eschewing her usual morning greeting.

'Mother, Mila is a lawyer, she went to a good school, she speaks four languages.'

'You barely know her, Fabien. And I sincerely hope you are not suggesting that I am in some way invoking some old-school aristocratic snobbery. She is a refugee, and I am head of the refugee committee – there isn't a person more attuned to her needs and her best interests than I. Mila is recovering after loss and grief, and in a new place. She is in no fit state to be wooed. Especially not by a man who is visiting only briefly, and will no doubt leave her heartbroken. It's not on Fabien,' Lydia stated her prepared and well-rehearsed argument commendably.

'You're getting ahead of yourself, Mother. I'm simply going to show her around, provide friendship, give her a breather from that ghastly woman!'

'So rude,' Lydia tuts, 'Susannah is doing her best, and in such difficult circumstances, having a completely unknown lodger, a different person to the one she had readied her home for.' Lydia sips her tea, and places it down on the table. 'Odd though, isn't it dear?'

Fabien is helping himself to cold toast from the rack in the middle of the table, never an early enough bird to eat it warm, unless he bothers to make it himself, which he never does.

'Hmmm?' he mumbles, his mouth full, raising an eyebrow in question.

'Don't speak with your mouth full, please. I mean, Fabien, it's just very strange that Mila is not at all the person the paperwork said she was. How does one get everything so wrong? I do hope it is just an administrative error, and not something, well, more *illegal*.'

'Wow,' Elodie is standing in the doorway, with Offal at her heels, Anna visible behind her. 'That didn't take long.' She moves further into the room, allowing Anna to come through with a tray.

'What on earth do you mean?' Lydia turns to face her daughter. 'Do sit down, eat breakfast with us.'

'You. And Daddy. Pretending to care about the people fleeing war.'

'Your father has not once pretended to care about people, Elodie. Please don't exaggerate.'

'People who, by the way, are fleeing war because the corrupt powers of the world have propped up neighbouring dictators for years, for their own political gain!'

Lydia fans her face with her napkin dramatically, making a show of being lost for words, and also feeling a little self-conscious that their young, Polish housekeeper may be forming unfair judgements as a result of her offspring's runaway mouth. Lydia is extremely proud of her equal opportunities employment policy.

Fabien waves his hand in a motion to quieten his sister. She takes a breath to protest and continue her point, but Fabien gets in first. 'I hate to admit it, Mother, but Elodie has a point. Whatever happened with the paperwork is irrelevant. You heard a little of Mila's story yourself; there is no doubt she is a genuine refugee. And let's not forget the hash the government has made of the host family project. It's all over the news. I highly doubt *their* government is on top of its administration either, right now, what with all the bombs and shallow mass graves they're having to dig.'

'Well, *you* can get off your high horse,' says Elodie, 'the banks are one of the worst culprits for letting the money men behind that invading lunatic off.'

'Elodie, enough! Fabien runs an *ethical* hedge fund.'

Fabien smirks at Elodie, forgetting his troubles for a second. She flounces into her seat, hunger trumping indignation; her gatehouse fridge is empty as usual. Elodie helps herself, while Offal sits staring up at them, hoping for some titbits.

Lydia continues. 'I still think the Wilsons should let the authorities know about the mix-up. Whatever has happened to the other girl seeking a host family? The one with two children and a war hero husband?'

'You're right, of course,' Fabien pats his mother's hand, 'I'm sure you'll advise them.'

'Naturally, darling.' Lydia gestures to Anna to come over. 'Anna dear, could you refill the pot, and put some more toast on? The children are like starving hyenas in the morning.' Lydia turns back to Fabien. 'It's my duty to advise our parishioners, and I've never been one to shirk responsibility, as you well know. Oh! Anna,' Lydia calls to the housekeeper's back, 'could you fetch the telephone?'

Fabien knocks on his father's door, feeling about ten years old again.

'Come,' his father bellows, and Fabien just knows he relishes the rituals of power.

He steels himself; he knows his pitch by heart. I do this for a living, Fabien tells himself. People give him their money willingly to invest, and he makes them more. Why can't his father see his talent? Have the faith his clients have in him? *Had* in him, until recently. He can earn their confidence again, with a little help.

Fabien is ambitious. His father is always telling him to stand on his own two feet, show more gumption. He thought outside of the box. He put all his chips down, left his comfort zone and branched out. He was brave, like Mila. Well, perhaps not quite. And, despite everything his evidently unreliable gut had told him, it had all gone terribly, terribly wrong. Fabien needed to repay what he had lost, and fast, before it all got out and his name was ruined.

Perhaps his father had been right about one thing: trust no one outside of the family, he'd often told his son. As well as insisting that Fabien's business partner was good for nothing, and the two of them together were a recipe for disaster.

'Hello, Dad.' Fabien is surprised to see his father sitting in his armchair, rather than at the desk, no evidence of recently reviewed affairs, no paperwork, no files. Most worryingly, no cheque book and pen.

'Sit down, son,' Lord Gregory Knutsworth instructs, 'this shouldn't take long.'

CHAPTER NINE

'You can't teach an old dog new tricks, you said,' Nikolai punctuates his point with a delicate swipe of his screen, followed by another.

'No, Papa, *you* said that. I gave you an iPad and said you will pick it up in no time, which, it would appear, was correct.'

'I've been underestimated my whole life,' Nikolai continues, 'I didn't have your education, but look at me now, a master of technology.' He continues to swipe, eyes darting intently but never leaving the screen. 'I always suspected this computer lark was a scam.'

'But you love the computer, Papa, you have been glued to it for a week. Though I'm not sure it's good for you, constantly scrolling through those news channels from back home. You should get some air, think of something else. Life is not all bad here.'

'The young pretending it is complicated, keeping all the information for themselves, using it as an excuse not to learn a proper trade. I knew you had time to help more, locked away in your room writing codes that make no sense. Besides, it's easier to read the news from home. It is in the right language, for a start.'

'As it turns out, Papa, they made quite a lot of sense, those codes of mine.' Peter grabs his coat from the hook on the wall, 'They paid for this,' he doesn't bother to gesture at the vast space around them; he has long given up seeking approval from the old man. Nor does he gesture to the glass bifolds looking out to the perfectly manicured garden, which Nikolai had admired before shaming his son for employing a gardener rather than getting his own hands dirty. 'I've got an investor brunch. You'll be okay?'

Nikolai starts to mutter something about brunch being for old rich ladies back home not grown men, without looking up from the screen, but as Peter shouts goodbye, he immediately forgets his latest despair at his son's strange, foreign life, because staring back at him on the news site from back home is the crazy girl from the plane, but this girl's name is not Mila Kiss. The news article calls her Sofia, and she is in a lot of trouble.

In the Wilsons' living room, Mila is curled up on the mahogany armchair, her long limbs folded beneath her in what appears to Susannah to be some form of yogic torture, but their young guest is very much at ease. Angry tinny sounds flow from the ever-present earphones, no doubt shouting hateful lyrics into the clearly troubled mind of their willing recipient.

'Mila!' Susannah repeats, louder, close to her now, slightly leaning over the girl as she stares at the screen before her, the old iPad Chloe left behind a way for Mila to privately connect back to the world, to feel slightly more independent, they'd told her. Until she got a smart phone of her own as – rather oddly, in

Susannah's view – she hadn't brought a phone at all. She'd never heard of a young person not glued to a phone before.

Mila jumps, presses the iPad to her chest, pulls her earphones out.

'I didn't mean to make you jump, dear.'

'No, sorry, I... I was reading the news. From home.'

'Are you all right? You look like you've seen a ghost.'

'I'm fine,' Mila replies, clutching the device protectively.

'Telephone, Fabien again. Did you not call back yet? I know you're adjusting Mila, but he's only trying to help. Would it be so bad to get out a little, perhaps take a break from looking at this thing?' Susannah reaches for the iPad, but Mila jumps up, almost knocking her host to the floor in the process. She keeps hold of the iPad.

Susannah stares, aghast; this is too much. She must say something. The girl is unbelievable. Who behaves like this? Has she got PTSD or some other syndrome off the news? All these young folk have something. Though Susannah acknowledges at least warzone survivors are *meant* to get PTSD. She thanks the heavens every day she had such a nice, normal child. Simple, uncomplicated Chloe. For the most part, anyway.

'Mila,' she begins.

'I'm sorry,' Mila says at the same time.

A car beeps outside. Not once but three, four, five times. Although all beeps have the same tone on the old Volvo, these are celebratory beeps; Susannah can feel it in their rhythm. The beeps of her daughter arriving home, collected by her father. She rushes to greet them.

Mila closes the news site and deletes the history. She places the iPad on the coffee table and slowly walks towards the hall. She watches as the family reunites, suitcases and bags thrown down, hugs and kisses, and a mother's tears of joy.

Good timing, thinks Mila. Thanks, Chloe.

'You must be Mila,' the pretty and petite young woman says, 'Chloe.' Chloe looks Mila up and down and doesn't smile until she feels her father's gaze, and suddenly her face is consumed by a toothy grin. Mila knows her type; her unwavering combative stare tells her everything. Chloe takes her hand in both of her own, and shakes it gently, like royalty.

Mila returns the gesture with her biggest smile, and bends to kiss Chloe's cheeks one by one. They lock eyes for a moment, and Chloe catches the truth; Mila isn't going to like her any more than she plans to like Mila. At least that might make it more interesting.

'Why's the phone off the hook?' Martin asks, lifting the handset from the hall table.

'Oh flip! It's Fabien.'

'Gosh, he didn't waste any time,' Chloe smiles ruefully, mock-rolling her eyes, as she takes the handset and brings it to her ear.

'No, darling, it's for Mila,' Susannah says, but Chloe isn't listening as she thanks Fabien for calling so soon. Then her face falls, and her eyebrows raise as she takes a breath and smiles sweetly. 'It's for you, Mila. Apparently.'

CHAPTER TEN

Mila folds her old hoodie and places it in the top drawer of the chest opposite the bunk beds. At first, Chloe insisted she keep her old room, but Mila insisted harder that she wouldn't dream of it. Chloe offered to help, but Mila explained she didn't bring much. The door to her new room is closed. Her small tin box is in her new bedside cabinet. She sits on the lower bunk and closes her eyes, imagines Konstantine and Karlie here, arguing over who should get the top bunk.

Where are you now? She silently asks them. Are you safe? Has Janos hurt you? Or just tossed you aside to fend for yourselves? Mila answers herself, her legal skills honed to make the winning argument. He can't, not yet. They are his leverage. He knows she will go back for them, and that she'll swap what she found that day in her sister's flat for their return. He is so sure of everything.

And if she doesn't turn up looking for her niece and nephew? He'll find her. He already has them looking for her. They'll believe everything he says, and the papers she carries with her are not enough to stop him. He knows it. He also knows there is more out there on him, here in England. The final pieces to nail the bastard. Captain Janos Byros, celebrated war hero. Criminal and traitor.

What lies ahead for Mila is not an easy path. She must avoid detection – hope the news from back home doesn't travel as far as the UK Home Office, and that the Wilsons don't figure out her true identity – before she has time to find the evidence she knows is here. Then she must make the case, expose Janos, and find the children.

She doesn't mean to rile Susannah. Mila imagines her sister shaking her head, trying to reason with her. *You won't get a chance to find anything if they find you out first; just try to be nice.* But Mila doesn't have the time for distractions, or small talk. She has, as she heard Martin telling Susannah, "a lot on her plate". Mila sighs at the stupid phrase and aches for home. Surely a lot on a plate would be a good thing.

She managed to make her excuses to Fabien again. After all, Chloe had just walked through the door; it would have been rude to talk, ruder still to meet him in the pub later. She said she would call tomorrow, tried to sound sincere as she thanked him again for his kindness, and replaced the receiver without saying goodbye.

Back home, the boys like Fabien didn't pursue girls like Mila, and that worked for her. She didn't look the part, and she didn't pretend to care. Even before the war, Mila didn't have time for distractions, boyfriends. There'd been one or two flings, a couple of guys and a girl, just sex: after a protest had got heated, or a victory in the courts, a digital campaign gone viral – the things that made her blood run hot, her heart beat faster. The adrenaline of seeing the fruits of the fight and her small part in creating a just world brought her to life like nothing else. You can keep your flowers; they belong in the earth. She takes a T-shirt out of the rucksack, shakes it open, and begins to refold it.

'Mila, hun!' Mila's closed door is now open, and Chloe leans in the doorway. 'You *have* to come to the Royal Oak with me. It's the Spanish Inquisition down there. I need to get out.'

'Royal what?'

'The pub. Down the road.'

'No,' Mila says without looking up, then, sensing Chloe's continued presence, adds, 'thank you.'

Chloe cocks her head. 'You're not cross about the room swap, are you? Because I did say I'd sleep in the bunks.'

'No.'

'Come oooooon, then,' Chloe whines. 'We need to get to know one another. We could end up like sisters.'

Mila looks up from the bunk to Chloe, stops folding the T-shirt.

'Mila. I am *so* sorry. Mum and Dad did say, you lost your sister just recently. In the war.'

Mila doesn't reply, and looks down at her hands.

'And your parents?'

'Dead a long time now. Nothing to do with the war.'

'I'm sorry about your sister. What was her name? Do you want to talk about it?'

Mila looks back to Chloe, who sounds almost genuinely concerned. To avoid answering the question she says, 'You're right, we should go to the pub. I'll be down in a minute.'

The pub is thronging when they arrive, and despite the July sun still being high in the sky outside, the innards of the sixteenth century inn are dark, its tiny windows almost entirely useless.

'Some things never change,' Chloe says, 'always packed on a Friday night, full of the young farmers. Bunch of animals, of course, but not always in a bad way, if you catch my drift. Here, white wine, probably shit, they only do one type.'

Mila takes her drink, and almost spills it as her elbow is knocked by someone trying to get to the bar. 'Thanks, can we sit outside?'

Chloe looks disappointed. 'Maybe just 'til the sun cools down.'

'Okay,' Mila replies, sure to be gone by then.

'Course, I'll have to mingle at some point. Catch up with everyone.'

As they gingerly step through the crowds towards the door, Chloe shrieks and raises her arms in a wave, splashing Mila with gin and tonic. 'Fabes, babes!'

Shit, Mila thinks. So this is the pub Fabien wanted to bring her to. Of course it was. There's unlikely to be more than one. 'Chloe, hold this,' Mila says, forcing the drink into her hand, which is still trying to get Fabien's attention, 'I'll meet you outside. I'm going to the bathroom.'

In the ladies', Mila takes her time. She checks her reflection. Her dark hair has its natural waves, and her make-up is minimal. She used to wear her hair bright red, her make-up heavy. Very unlike her sister, who followed convention and kept out of trouble. Or so she had thought.

Mila figures, if she gives it ten minutes, she can edge around the pub walls, avoiding the bar, and find Chloe outside. She can tell her she feels suddenly ill, and make her excuses. Of course, Chloe would have told Fabien Mila was here, but this way she doesn't have to face him with her own excuses. Getting-to-know-you flirtations are bad enough at the best of times, but a whole new level when your entire existence is a lie. Besides, the guy is clearly a spoiled brat, far too used to getting what he wants. He probably shoots foxes and mounts dead heads on his walls.

As she pushes the swinging door to the ladies' open, the pub seems even fuller than before, but she squeezes past, and finally steps into the fresh air. She notices the cows in the field across from the beer garden before she notices the altercation straight in front of her.

'I didn't mean anything by it! Look there's just enough pressure on the country as it is, people who live here can't find decent work, let alone–'

Mila's eyes find the voice, a man from the party. Dennis?

'You're a bloody bigot!' Fabien shouts at him, squaring up to who Mila is now pretty sure is Dennis.

'Oh, easy for you to say, with your inheritance. You'll never have to worry about the illegals coming here and taking your job. They ain't after the banking gigs, m'lord. Ask me, you just fancy giving her one, she'd look good on the end of your–'

But Dennis doesn't get chance to finish his sentence, as Fabien grabs him by his lapels and shoves him up against the wall, the crowd around them standing back, but somehow growing simultaneously. 'Mila Kiss is a war refugee. She is a human rights lawyer with more intelligence in her little finger than you have altogether. She wouldn't want your job, and how dare you speak about our guest in that way. You're lucky I'm putting this down to the drink talking, Dennis.'

'Fabien, stop!' Chloe shouts. 'Enough.'

Fabien releases Dennis, and looks around the crowd. 'Goes for everyone,' he slurs, and Mila realises he is a little drunk, 'show some bloody respect. And do some research before anyone starts banging their *Daily Mail* theories around.' He looks up and sees Mila. 'I'm sorry,' he tells her, lips forming the words, but the sound barely audible.

Someone ushers Dennis inside, who is cursing the upper classes in general, quietly lumping them in with immigrants and socialists. The others follow, sending sideways glances to one another.

Chloe starts to walk through the door, and holds it open for Mila. 'Right, I'm going inside, thought I saw Lottie sneak in during the heroics, so I'm going to catch up. Fabien, I suggest you go home before you end up barred. Coming, Mila?'

Mila shakes her head and walks over to Fabien. He brushes the hair that has fallen into his face back, and he looks into her eyes. She sees they are glistening.

'I'm so sorry, I've drunk too much. Bad day. *Really* bad day. Bad week, actually. Didn't expect to see you. But I should have expected that kind of rubbish from that lot. I don't usually behave that way, I–'

'Fuck's sake,' says Chloe, as the door slams behind her.

'Thank you,' Mila says, taking his hand and squeezing it.

He looks at her, doe-eyed, and says, 'Fancy that drink?'

Mila shakes her head, drops Fabien's hand, and walks away, back towards the Wilsons'. He did a good thing, but it doesn't make him a good person.

CHAPTER ELEVEN

The crowds make Nikolai feel small, and the noise makes him feel deaf. He cannot hear his thoughts, and perhaps that is a good thing. He allows the swell of people to move him forward, down roads lined with tall red brick buildings like the streets of 1920s New York films.

He arrived early, and so he is near the front, with only ten or twenty rows ahead of him, behind him many hundreds more. He knows this because when they first met, moments ago, A.J. took a photo with the two of them in it, holding it high on a stick to capture everything behind them. Blue sky, corners of buildings, windows glistening, and a crowd of tiny faces going back forever.

A.J. is helping to carry a banner with the hand not in charge of his phone. Apparently, Nikolai's phone also has a camera, but Nikolai is afraid he will drop it and it will be stampeded upon, and then Peter will be even more irritated by him. Not that he cares; a son has no right to take umbrage with his own father, no matter how much the coffee machine cost. Not his fault the overpriced bit of plastic doesn't like granules.

The chanting picks up again, and Nikolai has remembered all the words. They sing together and it is glorious.

They shout for peace and demand an end to war.

His legs are aching now. It seems they are to tour the whole of Manchester before they reach the town hall where, A.J. tells him, there will be speeches, and bands, and donations.

'We will make a difference today, in Albert Square. At least 100 other cities in their own squares will come together on video link, and we will demand change, demand an end to the despotic reign, to corruption the world over, to inequality, to racism, to homophobia, to misogyny,' A.J. tells Nikolai, and the world, via his screen.

Nikolai wonders if A.J. and his friends may be biting off more than they can chew for one day, and isn't sure that all their plans relate specifically back to the war in his country, but he says nothing as it's nice to be popular for once.

'An end to plastics,' A.J. continues, 'and the war against the trans community.'

'But first, an end to *The* War?' Nikolai is compelled to clarify.

'Of course! An end to the war, that monster, and everything he believes in... but we must come together, no discrimination, and save our planet in order to make the world fit for peace, and peace fit for the world.'

Nikolai thinks about this, but before he can make sense of it, A.J. holds his hand and squeezes, and as he does there is a force from behind that nearly knocks him off his feet. Except it doesn't, as suddenly he is pushed against metal railings. He starts to panic. It feels like jail, like death, like his nightmares.

'We're here! We did it!' A.J. and his friends are whooping and waving their enormous banner high, unperturbed by the cage made of people and noise and grey steel. 'Front row!'

Nikolai looks up to a stage in front of a large old building, the town hall, he guesses. They are here. A man with big black hair that's tangled and dramatic, dressed in lady's jeans, a frilly blouse, and jewels is holding a microphone and shouting slogans that are hard to make out.

'Are you okay, Nikolai? Do you need air?'

Everything happens so fast. Dizziness, the dark, a push, a lift, a leg stuck, a tumble, an embrace. He is out of the crowd and in the small space between the railings and the stage. Nikolai takes the water offered to him by the burly security man with the tattoo on his neck and the kind smile. His name is Headlock – merely a nickname, he assures Nikolai, and nothing to do with the upstanding citizen and father he is today – but, he explains, these things have a way of sticking.

Nikolai can't disagree. From his chair he can see A.J. craning his neck, talking to the tall man on stage, the one in lady's clothing with the microphone, who has dropped to his knees to listen to A.J.'s enthusiastic appeal. Nikolai catches his own name as A.J. gestures towards him.

Yes, it all happens so fast. One minute he is chatting to Headlock, holding a plastic bottle of cold water, and the next he is agreeing with A.J. that he does indeed have a very important story to tell.

'Best get rid of that plastic bottle, Nikolai, the world is watching.'

Nikolai hands the bottle to Headlock, and carefully mounts each enormous black step up to the stage, one foot at a time.

Mila is in her favourite armchair in the Wilsons' living room, with its high arm rests creating a cocoon slightly further away from the main sofas in a comfortable corner beneath a reading light, and too small to have to share, unlike the oversized chair opposite. She realises, contrary to how it feels, it looks like a normal family scene.

Martin and Susannah are sitting together on the sofa, watching the six o'clock news, commenting quietly to one another occasionally, while Mila taps away, searching for the woman who has the evidence she needs so desperately. She has only a first name to go on, and a married name she's sure the woman would never use. Mila employs everything she knows about her: rough location, her children's ages, her previous spouse. Search results: nothing, over and over. Occasionally, she switches to the other tab, the article telling her they still would like to question her back home. There's no news on the children. Janos has probably pulled some strings, told them she was a danger to them.

The newsreaders' voices create a calming background noise, the words melting into nothing.

'Oh! Martin, switch over!'

Mila is alerted to the pictures on the screen by Susannah's shrill instruction. Tanks, smoke, the old factory on fire.

Martin reaches for the remote.

'No!' Mila bellows the word, to her own surprise, and Martin's too, who knocks the remote to the floor. 'Please leave it. I watch daily from here anyway,' gesturing to the iPad, 'it would be good to see from another perspective.'

Martin and Susannah exchange a glance, and Martin's knee clicks as he retrieves the remote, but he replaces it rather than pressing any buttons.

'I thought she'd use it to stay in touch with friends, watch movies,' Susannah whispers into Martin's ear, and Mila pretends she doesn't hear.

Martin shakes his head almost imperceptibly. Mila notices from the corner of her eye. She also notices the couple stiffen.

The air turns oppressive.

Mila ignores the atmosphere and refuses to feel bad for making her hosts uncomfortable. A stifling summer climate and awkward exchanges are starting to be a bit of a running theme in this village. She perseveres, her expression unmoving, her breath uniform, her limbs relaxed, her innards taut with the effort.

The scenes from home are filtered and clean compared to the ones she finds from her own sources: home movies, raw and angry, no hygiene in the narrative, objectivity be damned.

They don't last long, panning back to the anchor behind his desk, a thumbnail behind him showing mass demonstrations across the world. Mila had not known they were happening. All her efforts have been focussed on the news from home, her own research.

'Joining our team on the ground in Albert Square, Manchester...' Mila hears the presenter say, as the enormous flat screen in front of her is filled with a big open-air stage and that annoying British singer turned activist who had recently infiltrated the charts back home.

He is holding a microphone and standing next to a small, strangely dressed old man. 'Please welcome on stage... a survivor! A refugee! But most of all, a man with a story to tell!' he excitedly shouts as he hands over the microphone to the sound of cheers, and the camera zooms in on a very familiar face.

Mila drops the iPad to her lap and she leans forward, checking and double checking the sight before her. On the screen, Nikolai takes the microphone and clears his throat.

CHAPTER TWELVE

Fabien is due at the Wilsons' in a few minutes. Susannah places a bowl of olives on the kitchen island, and pokes a few with cocktail sticks, her good ones with the rose gold handle nubs. She refolds the napkins.

Mila enters the kitchen.

'You're a vision!' Susannah has persuaded Mila to borrow Chloe's purple dress with the lace sleeves, and as Chloe wore it too long, some fashion that had passed her mother by, it sits perfectly just above Mila's knees. Her clumpy black boots somehow work. Susannah suspects one would need Mila's long legs to pull it off.

'Do you want to borrow some shoes?' Chloe asks, helping herself to another olive, still miffed that Mila refused any help getting ready for her hot date she keeps insisting is no such thing. She's even invited Lottie over to make it a real girls' afternoon, but Mila has spent the whole day glued to her stupid iPad, listening to her crappy music, and has put basically no effort in at all. At least it should mean that Fabien's ridiculous infatuation will wear off even more quickly than anticipated.

'Chloe! Stop eating the olives!' says Susannah, rearranging

them to cover the gaps, sighing, and moving to the fridge to find some more as it simply won't do.

'It's just Fabien's rather... old-fashioned, likes girls to be ladies,' Chloe adds.

'That's why he wouldn't go out with Chloe,' Lottie quips.

Chloe glares at the younger girl, who is supposed to worship the ground she walks on. She's impressionable, according to her hysterical mother. If only, Chloe thinks; if anything, Lottie is getting far too big for her cheap teenage boots.

'Right then,' says Susannah pointlessly, checking her watch and tucking her hair behind her ear. She is delighted. Not only was the party a success, but Mila seems to have mellowed over the last few days, although she keeps herself to her room and still spends too much time on the old iPad they loaned her. That aside, now she not only has a friend, but a male friend, perhaps an admirer – who is the future Lord Knutsworth. If that isn't a success story in quickly integrating her refugee into British society, she doesn't know what is. Daydreams of MBEs and OBEs pop into her mind daily, though are often interrupted by her husband's naysaying.

'Is it really appropriate for her to be dating?' he had asked yesterday, while yet more hold music blared from the phone in his hand, 'especially that scoundrel?'

'Scoundrel!' Susannah had replied, laughing. 'Don't be such an overprotective daddy; Chloe's silly crush was years ago, and he let her down very gently – it wasn't Fabien's fault she got herself so upset. Besides, I believe he is simply being neighbourly, and isn't that what this is all about?'

The growl of Fabien's engine alerts the household to his arrival. Kisses and offerings are distributed in abundance, while Mila looks on, saying little, questioning her decision to finally call him back and agree to be taken out on what is very much starting to look like a romantic date. She mustn't allow herself to become distracted. She shouldn't lead him on. And, just because he isn't as right wing and self-absorbed as first suspected, doesn't mean he isn't a privileged aristocratic brat. But if it gets Susannah off her back, and makes her look normal – whatever that is – maybe he could be useful. She's still found nothing, but when she does, she's going to need to move freely, without an inquisition. She may need a cover.

Fabien declines another olive, and throws the remainder of his glass of iced water back down his throat, withdrawing his car keys from his trouser pocket, a statement of intent.

'Have a wonderful time, Mila, I'm sure Fabien will look after you,' Susannah calls to their backs. Mila turns her head and smiles. Susannah gives Mila a headache, but her kindness is catching.

Martin appears from nowhere, a door slamming behind him, and knocks into Chloe, barely noticing, as he is already midway through his rant to nobody in particular. 'Twenty-two minutes on hold, and then another ten when I was put through to the wrong person, blasted call centre, not a bloody clue, not a brain cell between them, *now* I've got to write a flipping letter to the Homes for Refugees Office. A LETTER! What bloody century are we in?! Oh,' Martin realises he is basically shouting into Fabien's ear as their baffled guest helps Chloe to her feet. Mila freezes. Susannah looks murderous, heat coming off her cheeks, eyes like lasers on her husband. 'Sorry, sorry, I was on the phone so long I'd have thought you'd be long gone,' Martin adds quietly, the rant abruptly completed.

'They're going now,' Susannah informs him from behind gritted teeth, using her body to push them down the hallway towards the front door. Shutting the door, she turns to face Martin. 'What are you thinking? Couldn't you have been more discreet? She'll think we don't want her.'

'I'm so sorry,' Martin says genuinely. He likes Mila, and he feels strangely protective of her. 'They just drive me mad. You know, I only want to report the admin error, just in case there's someone else lost in the system. And to put an end to Lady Lydia's constant complaining. Even Gregory was badgering me the other day. Convinced it could be something fishy. Told him that was utter nonsense. Mila's hardly some illegal, is she? She didn't arrive in a dingy! The woman's a lawyer, for heaven's sake. And she is welcome, so welcome. Do you think she picked up on what I was talking about?'

'Yes, Martin, I do.'

CHAPTER THIRTEEN

Mila is distracted as Fabien tells her about the history of the church and points out his family vault. They are taking the scenic route to the pub, while it is still light enough.

She had been sure it was going well with the Wilsons. She had been trying to be nice and normal, and grateful. But it is never enough, she thinks. Nothing ever is. She checks the internet every day, ha – every hour, more like. Mila uses the same website Nikolai is glued to, and there she has seen her image staring back from the screen, her name next to it, the one she must forget.

It isn't likely anyone in Farlington will visit her native news channel. After all, foreign languages are not a strong point in the UK. Frequently, she erases her search history. Then logs on again, unable to help herself. Refresh, erase, refresh, erase. What are they saying about her? The lies, the threats. They know nothing. The grieving husband, a war hero, seeking the truth, seeking Sofia. She wishes she could erase Janos.

How long, Mila keeps asking herself, before the Wilsons successfully report the discrepancy in their paperwork, and how long before the pieces come together? Given Martin's impatient tirade just now, she knows she is running out of time to put things right.

'Fancy a drink?' Fabien asks, 'I love the warm nights, orange seeping through the trees, don't you? We can sit in the beer garden?' He grimaces at his clumsy poetic words, but Mila doesn't notice. She has said almost nothing the entire time they've been out, driving to Fabien's favourite spots, parking up, and strolling gently into dusk.

'Sorry?' They seem to have arrived at The Royal Oak without Mila realising. How far is the church from here, she wonders?

'A drink. Would you like one, Mila?' Fabien sounds embarrassed; she knows she's being rude.

'I'm sorry,' Mila says, and she is, 'I was miles away.' She half smiles, shrugs, trying to be casual, unsure if she looks apologetic or insouciant.

Fabien leaves Mila at the table outside, and goes to fetch drinks and menus. Mila tries to focus. She'll ask him about his work, his family. Hopefully she hasn't just missed his entire life story.

Looking around, Mila sees familiar faces she can't put names to. People from the welcome party, people who were here last time she was, when it transpired she wasn't as welcome as the homemade banner suggested. She knows enough about the world to not be surprised. They have those types back home too, just as much as they have good people here. Right now, she can't tell which is which, and to give them a little credit, in fairness, their suspicions about her paperwork aren't entirely unfounded. Mila keeps her head down. She listens for her name, whispered, but she hears nothing.

She just needs a breakthrough in her search. Dead end after dead end. If only she could get access to records, without anyone asking to look at hers. She wonders, not for the first time, if Nikolai could help. She still has the address he is staying at. He has a son who is a British citizen, and could walk into a council office and request information.

'Mila?' a voice asks.

Mila looks up. A mousy-haired woman, nose covered in freckles, stands opposite. A slight breeze lifts, and she pulls an old too-large wax jacket closed. On her legs she wears loose denim cut-offs. Her lower legs are muddy, her walking boots well worn.

'I'm Anna,' the woman says. 'I work at the hall.'

'Hi,' Mila says, 'you work for the Knutsworths?'

'Yes, I'm the housekeeper. And a keen walker.' Anna gestures to her attire and laughs. 'I can't stop, I just wanted to introduce myself, and say, well, if you need a friendly chat, you can call me. Don't worry about the paperwork; they make it sound much scarier than it is. I know because my mother went through it all. I suppose I did too, though I was shielded by my mum. We were originally from Poland, you see. Anyway, I can help you, if you'd like, you know, with forms and stuff.'

'You know about that? My paperwork, the mix-up?'

'Well everyone was expecting someone else, so yes, but I hear things, too. Lady Knutsworth seems to think she's in charge of all village life, so she'll badger Martin and Susannah until everything is in order, and Lord Knutsworth, well he can be a bit—'

'Of a racist old twat.' Another woman has appeared next to Anna from nowhere, a wet little fluffball of a white dog jumping up at her own mud-splattered bare legs.

'Elodie!' Anna exclaims, looking surprised to see her standing there.

'You're Fabien's sister, we met at the party,' says Mila.

'Yes, pleased to meet you properly, but we must dash. You didn't see me, Mila; Fabien thinks I'm finishing my masterpiece

– supposed to be doing a portrait of the family for Mummy's birthday, and I'm woefully behind. Come on, Offal.' Elodie marches back down the beer garden path.

'I'm sure it will all be fine, Mila, and I don't really think they mean any harm in their interfering, they're just a tad overconcerned with appearances and fear scandal more than God himself.'

'Anna!' Elodie's voice comes from behind some bushes on the roadside, and Offal barks, backing up his owner.

'Coming! Mila, I'll give you my number.'

'I don't have a phone.'

'I'll call the Wilsons' landline, give it to you that way, when you have a pen and paper. And get a phone Mila, for goodness' sake!' Anna turns, waves, and runs down the crooked little path.

'Was that Anna?' Fabien asks, placing down the drinks. 'And I'm sure I just heard my sister's dreadful little mutt barking. Was she here too?'

'Just Anna. So, you live in London, usually? What brings you home?'

'It's complicated,' Fabien sighs, 'I know what you must think of me – living in the hall, the title... but I went away to make a difference, to prove I'm not just a trust fund brat, and now, well, I'm not sure if I'll succeed after all. So, here I am, living up to expectations, cap in hand.'

Mila takes a sip of the amber liquid, a dirty froth for a hat. He informs her it's a local brew, as some splashes onto the table.

'Are your parents not supportive, then?'

'My mother is,' Fabien replies, ruefully, 'but my father seems to have rather taken a dislike to me, and refuses to help. I don't even know if I blame him. It's my mess.'

'Want to talk about it?'

'I won't bore you, Mila.'

'Maybe you could embellish your disastrous business

failings and make my life look better. Do a poor refugee girl a favour.'

Fabien's eyes widen. 'Oh my God, I'm so sorry,' he starts.

'I'm kidding,' she says. The boy who has everything – his family, a home, an inheritance, and all the great and the good on speed dial – looks crestfallen. More to lose, she thinks. 'Go on, tell me. I'm interested,' she lies, wondering if some free legal advice could buy her a favour or two.

'I have a business partner, and he's made some investments my fund contributors don't approve of, didn't agree to... Now they want to withdraw their money, but the money is tied up, investments in companies that have gone suspiciously quiet, and my partner has gone AWOL. My father and I are at a bit of a stalemate. He wants me to file for bankruptcy, take the fall, and come home and do my duty. In fact, it's less stalemate, more checkmate. He never liked Hugo, and he never thought it proper for me to work in the city. He's delighted, secretly. I don't stand a chance.' Fabien looks up into Mila's beautiful pale face, dark eyes framed with long, unpainted lashes, and takes a long drink.

'So, you've been stitched up?'

'Yes. Maybe. Not really. I should have known what he was doing. I'm an idiot, my father's right there.'

'What's the problem with the investments? Why did the fund contributors object?'

'The war, actually. Lots of businesses are clawing funds back, cutting ties with certain suppliers. There's a bit of a panic.'

'You don't say.'

'Ah shit, I just can't help it, going on about myself like any of it matters.'

'I can look into British law around this sort of thing, help you figure out what your options are, if you like.'

'Really? Mila, that would be amazing!' And, he thinks, a

great reason to spend more time together. 'I'm going to try and stop being a total dick, now. Please, let's forget my problems for now. Let's talk about you. Is there anything you'd like to do while you're here?'

'Actually, there is, and maybe you can help me.'

'What? Anything, I'll be your guide. It's about time I put someone else first.'

'I'd like to find someone. A woman my sister knew. Her name is Xristina.'

CHAPTER FOURTEEN

'Papa, how could you?' Peter raises his head from his hands, where it has been bowed almost touching his knees in despair, as he sits across from his father.

Nikolai is still on a high from his successful day of protesting, and making friends who feel as passionately as he does about ending the war and ending the leader of the opposition in as gruesome a way as they can imagine. Though to be fair, Nikolai seemed more creative in that department than A.J. and his gang, who had a bad habit of skipping over the details. They were a bit squeamish for revolutionaries.

'How could you?' Peter repeats. 'I don't think you realise what trouble you have caused.' Nikolai does not like Peter's tone. It reminds him of his own disappointed voice when Peter always came last in school races, and was never picked for the first team. He remains sullen and silent, and inwardly curses himself for the role reversal occurring before him. 'I don't know where to start,' Peter sighs. 'Do you even know who those people are? Why would you bring them to my house?'

Nikolai finds his outrage, finally, and through it his voice.

'*Your* house? I thought I was welcome! You never said I could not invite my friends.'

'Friends? They're a disorganised semi-militant group of trouble causers always graffitiing their crappy logo on public property, and getting arrested for pointless ineffective antics. They are anti-*every*thing, including wealth or power unless it is transferred to them, and you bring them here!'

'A.J. is a lovely young man, with principles. He causes what you call *trouble,* only to fight for what is right. Which is what I was doing and what you should be doing too. Besides, I didn't invite him here; he helped me find my way home. I got confused.'

'Oh Papa, he is not a revolutionary! He's a silly, directionless boy with questionable taste in friends, and now you – and me, by extension – are associated with him, and he knows where I live. He knows the code to the gates. I'll have to change them. We may need extra security.'

'Nonsense. You're being a snob. A gated-community snob, afraid of the young and their ideas. A.J. is a sweet boy; he saved my life. I passed out, you know?'

'You wouldn't have passed out if this A.J. person hadn't seen fit to exploit you for his own gains and put you in a crowd like that. A man of your age! He doesn't give a damn.'

'He gives a damn, all right. He gives a damn about my home. *Our* home. Unlike you, sitting here in your ivory tower playing computers and counting your money while our kin burn and die.'

Peter suddenly rises, fast and furious like a geyser. His fists clench, and he keeps them by his sides. His body is rigid, wound, a coil ready to come undone. For the first time, Nikolai sees a man in his son. Taller than he looks, broader and stronger, too. Yet he does not cower, instead he rises to meet him.

'You are a stupid old man stuck in the past!' Peter barks.

'Wars are never won by student protests and banners, no more than they are won by bombs and guns. They are won by knowledge, intelligence. What the hell do you think I do all day?'

'I don't know what you do, but you tell the people lying in rubble that bombs don't matter, you pompous young fool! You think every answer lies in the computer, and you are wrong. Wrong, wrong, wrong. You should go home and fight like a man!'

Peter deflates, slumps into his chair. Nikolai picks up his iPad, and turns away, making for his room.

'Are you sure that's a good idea?' Peter's voice is soft now. Nikolai turns, raises his eyebrows. 'The iPad, the internet. It seems to only lead you to despair and trouble. What if something happened to you? Why didn't you at least tell me where you were going? I love you Papa, despite our differences.'

Nikolai clutches the iPad closer. 'I am going to read the news, if I am permitted?'

Peter shakes his head, sadly, and Nikolai walks away.

To his back, Peter pleads, 'Just please promise me not to contact A.J. or his cronies again, Papa, *please*. They are not good people.'

The wonderful thing about the iPad, thinks Nikolai, is being able to watch it, talk to people, find out what is happening nearby, all from the comfort of bed. He plumps up his pillow and shuffles back into it. His legs still ache, but the feeling of the soft mattress and goose feathered duvet on top is heaven.

He spent the first few days in England scrolling through the online news channels from home, but he has now discovered Facebook, and a whole new world. Facebook is where he found

out about the protest, and even directions to the start point.
Sadly, it did not include directions home from the end point.

A.J. taught him how to connect with friends. He and A.J.
were officially friends now, though of course they were before,
when they met in real life. He has two friends on Facebook:
Peter and A.J. He had wanted to connect with his friends back
home, but nobody he knew used it. Yet. He resolves to email
them to persuade them that social media isn't all bad after all.

A red note pops up in the corner. A.J. told him to watch out
for the little red numbers; notifications. He clicks on it – a
message! A.J.!

Typing.

Odd message, Nikolai thinks, but then a paragraph pops up,
with a link and instructions. Makes sense to Nikolai. His over-
cautious son set him up with some kind of child safety feature so
nobody can find him and befriend him, and he asked A.J. how to
remove it. Stranger danger; it's insulting. Peter says Facebook
steals your data and people can manipulate you, find out your
passwords and exploit you. The boy is paranoid. He uses a
funny name on it so only his trusted contacts can find him. Sad
to think people must live in fear of everything when they have
such luxury, and peace. They don't know what danger is, here.

Completing the task, he clicks back to his profile.

He checks to see if there are more notifications, expecting
none, and readies himself to get back to the difficult business of
searching for dear Mila.

Nikolai blinks, rubs his eyes. The number cannot be right.
342 friend requests. As he starts accepting each and every one
with joy – tap, tap, tap, he almost forgets his argument with
Peter. Another message from A.J. pops up.

I looked up your friend for you. Used Google translate and
the article was right about what they think she did – she's

wanted for questioning, and that girl's photo is everywhere over there, but she isn't called Mila Kiss. If that's the girl you met on the plane, she was lying to you. But don't worry; she's a hero. She used to campaign for human rights over there, was always in the media, and in cuffs a few times. Don't believe what they're saying. She must have her reasons for lying.

CHAPTER FIFTEEN

The Farlington Women's Institute always meets in the Old School House, but not today. They sit around Lady Lydia's coffee table, being served tea. All eyes are on Mila, who is today's special guest speaker.

Meanwhile, Gregory is grumbling to Fabien in his study about being banished from his own drawing room.

'They have a wasps' nest in the Old School House,' Fabien tells his father. 'The council is over there now, taking their lives in their hands.' He leans back in the chair across from Gregory's desk. He sounds calmer than he feels.

'We may as well take this opportunity to finalise this business Fabien, without prying eyes.'

'You mean without the female voice of reason?'

'Your mother may be blinded by maternal longing, but I'm sure Elodie would sit firmly with me on this one. *She* doesn't require handouts. Never has.'

'She lives here for free, and earns no money whatsoever, so presumably she eats for free too. And at some point, some wealthy heir to something will marry her and she'll transform from penniless boho to eccentric lady. Her life is made.'

Gregory clears his throat. 'You are too old for histrionics, particularly of the sibling rivalry type. Perhaps this immaturity is behind your senseless risk taking, hmm?' He pulls a newspaper from the rack, and opens it. 'Today's *Financial Times*. I presume you haven't seen it, or you wouldn't be manspreading.' Gregory smirks, pleased with the modern lingo he picked up from Elodie's latest feminist rant, which he had pretended not to listen to.

Fabien reaches for the paper, glimpsing a bad shot of his sunglass-adorned face, a smug look, his Patek Philippe watch peeking out from beneath the sleeves of an expensive suit jacket. He looks like a prat, and he knows it. His car is in the background. It is the kind of photo that if featured in *Tatler* would have had him invited to every opening in the city. It is also the kind of photo that if used with the headline they have chosen, will have the world wanting his head on a spike.

Before he can take the paper, Gregory lifts it up, and shakes it gently to de-crinkle the pages.

'Shall I read it to you?' he asks Fabien without looking up, or pausing for an answer. 'Reckless Banker's Tankers Go Down – Along With His Ethical Reputation.' Gregory glances over the paper to see his son squirm in his seat, his legs now crossed, hand tapping his knee, and continues to read the article. 'The heir to the Knutsworth Lordship and Farlington Estate once appeared to be untouchable, his family and schooling networks opening doors before he turned twenty-five, setting him up as one of the most ambitious modern hedge fund managers of our time.

'His fund's unique selling point was ethical diversion, and an insistence that investing in the future of the world was the key to wealth for individuals as well as environmental and moral wealth for the world.

'In 2018, he told a press conference at the opening of his

new penthouse offices in the heart of Canary Wharf, "There is no excuse, no profit, no gamble worth taking if it poses any risk to our children's futures. I will prove, contrary to centuries of assumption, that more money can be made from good than it can from bad."

'The poster boy will now be eating his words as it transpires he has invested millions in tanks and warfare in countries currently on the wrong side of history, without the knowledge of his clients. His so-called ethical investors have pulled out, demanding their full investments are returned immediately, afraid for their own reputations and potential government sanctions on profits given the ongoing war.

'The young Lord Knutsworth is likely to face a criminal investigation, the consequences of which will no doubt be influenced heavily by his response to the explosive situation. If he complies with the repayment, he will surely have to admit defeat and file for bankruptcy.

'We contacted Knutsworth's office for comment, but received no response.'

Gregory closes the paper and places it back on the desk. 'So, no response? Hiding here, asking for help, and allowing the papers to drag our name through the mud.'

'It's not like that; they've got it wrong. I just asked them not to go to print, for more time. Bastards! Hacks. The *FT* is no better than the *Daily Mail* these days Dad; you know that.'

'I know no such thing Fabien, but what I do know is who reads it, which is everyone that matters.' Gregory's fury was starting to escape from beneath his aloof demeanour, 'And to think that sitting across from me in that very chair just days ago you told me it was a *temporary blip*, a *short-term loan!* A *misunderstanding!*'

'Look, as I explained, I can fix this. I need to pay some back, yes, but I have new investors lined up. I can turn this around, I know it, I–'

'Whoever was *"lined up"*,' Gregory makes bunny ears to express the quote, 'will, I think you will find, have had a sudden change of heart this morning.'

Fabien closes his eyes. His father cannot be right.

'I cannot possibly fill the hole in your finances. Even if I wanted to – and I do not want to, not at all – we'd have to sell the estate to make that sort of money. You know full well we are not cash rich. But, and to be perfectly clear in case you are still entertaining notions that this is yet another scrape you can charm or buy your way out of, you cannot. Your reputation is ruined. You are a financier of war.'

'Mila thinks Hugo could be culpable alone, that if he deceived and defrauded me too, then–'

'Mila thinks!' Gregory roars with cruel laughter. 'She knows, does she? The whole truth, or last week's version of it?' Fabien slumps in his chair, and the leather squeaks unceremoniously. 'As I thought. You know you will be seen as supporting the invasion of your girlfriend's country? Just wait until they get wind of that bit of salacious gossip. It is an unprecedented disaster for this family, far worse than your earlier appeal suggested, which only compounds the situation. A *dishonest* coward to boot! I have never been so ashamed.'

'Are you quite finished?' Fabien asks. 'Because, if you would only listen to my plans, my insight–'

'I have *not* finished, but do not fret, this last bit will only take a moment more of your time. You will file for bankruptcy. You will then issue an apology, taking full responsibility and vowing to return the funds. I assume that dreadful boy Hugo is still AWOL? Never trusted him, as I told you at the time. Now listen, I have spoken to Harrop, and he thinks to a degree you can deny knowledge of precisely where the funds were going, and distance yourself from that particular side of the war. You will then withdraw from public life until one day this episode is forgotten, during which time I shall mentor you for your future role as Lord of Farlington, and you will finally learn to be the man you were born to be, and you will be where we can keep a close eye on you.'

'But—'

'But indeed, Fabien. But: if you fail to take this generous offer of a fresh start, and this opportunity to make something of your life, then you are on your own. Cut off. Finished. I shall leave the entire estate to Elodie. Or a bloody cat's home. You will not drag it down to the level to which you will fall if you continue on this trajectory.' Fabien stops breathing for a moment. 'You have one week to give me your decision.'

Mila's head is down as she closes the downstairs loo behind her, labelled *cloakroom* for no discernible reason, and quick-steps down the wide hallway. She smells him first – that overpowering musk men think reeks of power, but only milliseconds before she feels him crash into her.

'Sorry, sorry, Mila!' Fabien holds her by the shoulders, creating space between them, looking at her, trying to find her eyes.

Mila takes a moment to look up. When she does, she looks furious. 'I can't do this anymore.'

'Oh Mila, oh Mila, I'm sorry,' he tells her. She knows already. She will never forgive him.

'It's not your fault,' she says, to Fabien's surprise. He looks at her, questioning. 'It feels like an interrogation. They think I'm a history source, but the war is now, the dead are barely cold.'

There is a fierce look in Mila's eyes, this girl he thought was softening, her words and insight unsettling him.

'Bloody beastly WI! Poor Mila, I am sorry. You don't deserve any of this.'

'I am not just some war refugee, and I do not want to play the part any longer!'

'No one expects you to play a part.'

Mila shakes her head. 'You sure?'

'Let's go somewhere else, escape for a while.'

They sit on Silver Hill looking down onto the valley. The hike to the top has cleared their heads, burned off some of the anger coursing through their bodies.

'Let's talk about happier things,' Fabien instructed as they powered upwards, and so they had. All the way up, five kilometres of grass and scree and rocks. It was hard and sweaty and just what they needed.

'What's on your headphones all the time?' Fabien asks now, as they sit on a smooth rock on the edge of the bank. 'Let me guess: Metallica.' He gestures at her rock boots, teasingly tugs on the chain. 'Not very fitting clothes for a lawyer.'

'I'm not that kind of lawyer. Yes, sometimes Metallica. Though mainly gothic metal. I recently got into a new band – Inver? I saw them live back home, shortly before the invasion'

'Never heard of them.'

'Not at all surprised.'

'I love Chopin, personally. I used to play the piano, but I could never find my way past grade five. His greatest creation: the nocturne.'

'Which one? Besides, he didn't create the nocturne. John Field did.' Fabien turns to look at Mila, raising his eyebrows. 'I know the classics. I know Chopin well, actually. My father played him constantly. Had you down as a Coldplay guy.'

'Outrageous!' Fabien plays indignant, 'Though my father is, rather, and he's Ed Sheeran's number one fan. Also, and tell no one, or the family name will be ruined – I once found a Best of Dolly Parton CD behind his Puccini collection.'

'You're kidding.'

'Nope.'

They look out at over the views beneath them. Fabien touches Mila's face, and she turns towards him. She is everything he is not. Brave, clever, authentic, and full of integrity. She makes him want to be a better person. He kisses her, lips only just brushing, and she doesn't pull away.

Mila feels a need stir, for just one moment outside of herself and her thoughts, dewy grass on skin; *skin* on skin. Their eyes open, a message sent between them, and then they are kissing, and tugging at each other's clothes.

It is Fabien who stops. 'Mila, first, there's something you need to know about me. I'm so sorry.'

CHAPTER SIXTEEN

He is stupid and selfish and driven by greed. He didn't think about the consequences because they'd never mattered before, so why should they now? Mila hates him. She thinks of the strength of the army that invaded her country, their modern weapons, and how they turned desperate men into corpses, or worse, something else altogether, their true selves buried in the blackness of the living nightmares that played and played again.

Mila stood up on the top of Silver Hill and raged. Raged for everyone she had lost and everyone Fabien had inadvertently played a part in hurting. He'd told her his investors were pulling out, demanding money, that his partner had landed him in trouble. He hadn't told her the real reason why.

'And for what?' she had screamed at him, pulling on her T-shirt. 'You lost everything anyway!'

She lies on the bottom bunk now, staring at the slats above. Her face is red and blotchy, her things spread around her. She studies her own documents, and theirs. Those beautiful faces, those beautiful names, and only one she can still say out loud. *Mila.*

She can hear Chloe stomping about on the landing outside.

Mila prays she does not knock and expect to come in. She starts to tidy her things, just in case, and blows her nose, brushes her fringe across her eyes. As she places the final pieces in her little tin box, without knocking, Chloe barges in. 'Have you still got my purple dress?'

'It has been washed, but I wasn't sure where it went. I gave it to your mother.'

A darkness flickers across Chloe's face. 'Oh, right, I'll ask my mother then. No problem. I'm sure it will turn up. How are things with Fabien?' Chloe smiles sweetly, though not sweetly enough to counter the sharpness in her tone.

Mila doesn't answer.

'Oh,' Chloe tilts her head in an attempt at sympathy, 'if I'd been home sooner, I could have warned you. He did the same to me, to all of us, actually.' She laughs, girlishly. 'You just forget him, and focus on you, as I am. Men! Us girls need to stick together.'

Chloe moves to sit on the bed, an act more familiar than Mila has been led to expect from the prodigal daughter since her return home.

'What's all this?' Chloe grabs hold of the tin, but Mila pulls it back, hugging it protectively. The padlock lies on the bed.

'Nothing,' Mila replies, eyeing the padlock, but not relinquishing her grip. She knows how strange it looks. How suspicious. 'It's private family things. Precious memories.'

'Show me, if you like, it might help to talk?'

Mila quickly locks the tin box. 'I'm tired, another time.'

'Well, I just wanted to say, I'm going into town with Lottie at the weekend to get a new phone, so you can have my old one, seeing as you forgot yours, apparently. And you still can't access your bank accounts? Right?'

Mila swallows her response, fury and fear at the implied suspicion. 'There's no need.' But there is, actually. Mila could really do with a bit more independence if she's ever going to find what she's looking for. She really needs a phone.

Chloe takes a breath laced with indignation that reminds Mila of Susannah. She stays seated on the tiny bed for a moment longer, making the room feel smaller than it is, and then stands and leaves without a word.

Lying back in bed, Mila closes her eyes. She'll apologise later, get the old phone over the weekend. One thing Mila's sure of is that Chloe will enjoy Mila's pathetic neediness more than any lasting annoyance at her lack of gratefulness.

Mila sighs at the absurdity of it all. She thinks about home.

She thinks about her parents and how they suffered at the hands of their own government, long before the war. She recalls how hard they worked to create a better world for their children, and give them as many opportunities as possible. Mila wonders what they'd make of this mess; their own daughter, a refugee, with nothing of her own – not even her real name.

Would they be proud of Mila's capabilities to understand the system well enough to circumvent it? She doubts it. They'd begged her and her sister to take an orthodox route: law school, academia, marry, have a family, stick to the rules. Her sister had done as she was bid, and look where that had got her. Mila had decided to carry on fighting. She decides the same thing again, every single day.

Mila had got her law degree, and taken it to where she felt it was most needed – a small left-wing lobby group known as CC – disliked unanimously across the political spectrum for their uncompromising policies and creative guerrilla tactics; never illegal (Mila was too smart for that), generally harmless, but they did a good job of exposing hypocrisy. If it hadn't been for the war breaking out, Mila and her colleagues had begun to dare to hope they could become mainstream. The young people were coming around in droves.

Her tin box is centimetres away, containing everything she is and was and has today. All her beautiful memories. All her secrets and lies, and most of all, her desire for justice. She is still fervently passionate about the law. Perhaps her parents would have some pride in that. She had started off doing it for them, and for the country they loved. Now she was doing it for her sister, her niece, her nephew too.

She powers up the iPad. Nikolai's five minutes of fame has slowly trickled from the news, but if Mila knows anything about social media he'll be a meme already, and inundated with fans. She doesn't dare check. She closed down her social media before she left. She wonders how he's doing. Did his computer geek son put him up to it? Mila smiles to herself at the ludicrous hand life has thrown at a tech-shy old man and a girl who was once heralded as a beacon for change. In some circles, anyway.

Now Nikolai is the face of the future, while her face still sits on that same website, headlines getting angrier each day she remains hidden in plain sight.

She reads the article again, and her heart pounds in her chest. She puts her earphones in, hits play on the new Inver album, and turns up the volume. Soaring guitars on the opening bars of "Lost Traveller" relaxes her as the lyrics come in, building in volume and righteousness.

Before, she was a pain in the neck, a nuisance, one to watch. Banners and protests and subversive articles were no real threat in a modern country. Even mild disruption, the odd bit of damage was largely batted away, like adults irritated by next door's child going over the wall and damaging the border flowers. But she knew they were headed for bigger things.

Yesterday, Fabien had pleaded with her. 'I think I'm falling for you,' he had said, swallowing his shame. She had simply turned and walked away.

Now, she was considered dangerous; wanted.

Fabien lied, but so did Mila. The difference is that Fabien is sorry, and Mila is not. She will do what is necessary.

She rereads the latest headline next to the photo she can't stop going back to, the one with her name next to it. *Wanted For Murder*.

Mila is livid with Fabien. She never wants to see the treacherous fool again. But she needs to find Xristina before it is too late. Fabien said he'd look into it, but so far he's come up with nothing. Has he even tried, or is he too busy trying to save his own skin? He thinks she's looking for an old family friend; maybe if he knew who she really was, he'd do something.

Mila thinks Fabien is the last person she should trust with anything, let alone the truth, but he's also the only person who owes her something.

CHAPTER SEVENTEEN

It is only eight in the morning, and the telephone is ringing in the Knutsworth household.

Anna picks up. 'Farlington Hall, how may I help you?' She listens; it only takes a moment. 'Okay, stay there, don't open the gates.' Anna rings the bells, shouts up the stairs, and dashes from room to room.

Lord and Lady Knutsworth eventually appear on the stairs in dressing gowns.

'What on earth?' Gregory is muttering to his wife.

'The press,' says Anna, 'Elodie called, they're waiting outside the gatehouse. They're all here, and according to Elodie, they're baying for blood.'

Lydia will not be a prisoner in her own home. After breakfast, she jumps into her old Defender, scarf around her hair, and sunglasses covering her face. She has errands to run, people to see, and coffee planned with Mrs Bentham to discuss the petition for a new fountain in the village green. As she crawls down the driveway, she can hear the noise build. Excited voices, shouts, calls to colleagues, the rattling of gates as they clamber for a better view. She clicks the remote, glad the gates open outwards, as the sea of journalists is parted – but not for long.

They crowd her car, and she worries she will run over a toe and be sued, to add insult to injury. She has never courted the press. It's outrageous. The family just quietly performs its roles. Social work, charity, the running of a successful, happy village.

'Lady Knutsworth! Will Fabien be making a statement?'

'Care to give your view on the scandal, ma'am?'

Lydia shudders. She is neither royalty nor police, so ma'am is an entirely unsuitable form of address.

'Lady Knutsworth! Lydia!'

The impertinence, Lydia thinks, as she tries to restart the engine, which had stalled as she slowed to a stop forgetting to change gears.

'Will he be filing for bankruptcy?'

'Have the police interviewed him yet?'

'Your local paper recently reported you were the first village in rural Lancashire to provide a home for a refugee – a Ms Mila Kiss? How does your son's involvement in funding the invasion of her country sit with that, Lady Knutsworth?'

Bugger, she thinks. The trusty old Defender takes its cue, and grumbles back to life. Lydia drives, knuckles white on the wheel. Bugger, bugger, bugger.

News travels fast in Farlington. Jenny Beard decides to take a detour on her walk with Archie her little terrier, feigning surprise as she passes the gaggle of reporters, and blushing when microphones come her way. Luckily, she has done her hair this morning, and is wearing her best Barbour walking jacket. Archie just so happens to be in his smart matching coat, as it is a bit nippy first thing, and he's getting on in years.

'Lovely boy,' she tells them, 'I've known him since he was in nappies.'

Mary is coming from the other direction, arms full of flowers.

'I'm just on my way to do the arrangements for church,' she tells Jenny. 'The, um, usual path is all flooded.'

They both try not to look up at the blue sky.

'Drains, I think. I'll let Keith know,' Jenny tells her magnanimously.

The conversation is interrupted by the noisy chugging of Harry's tractor, and reporters start to dash for their vans as he veers dangerously close to them, unfeasibly quickly for a vehicle of that size on a single-track lane. The smell is terrible, and brings a sense of foreboding.

Leaning out of the cab window, he shouts down, 'Get off the bloody road! Be gone, you bleeding vultures, I'm muck spreading and you're in my way!'

Chloe's phone beeps for the eighteenth time that minute.

'For the love of God, Chloe, put it on silent at least.'

'Sorry,' she says, distractedly tapping away so fast her fingers are a blur.

'Who are you talking to anyway?' Susannah asks. 'Because I doubt it is anyone who can help you find a job. Look at Mila, she's been sitting there all morning with those forms, trying to get set up for work.'

'I'm talking to Lottie. And I am still in shock. I need time to grieve for my marriage.' The phone beeps, and Chloe gasps with delight, then laughs. It beeps again, then again, beeps coming in so fast they overlap like a particularly tense and annoying birdsong. 'Oh. My. God.'

'What? What now?' Susannah asks. 'Spit it out.'

'You will not believe this.'

Mila glances up from her papers at the occasional table by the window, where she works away at baffling papers she knows she can't submit. A repeat episode of some absurd reality show plays on television, and Susannah is tidying things that don't need tidying, while Chloe sprawls on the sofa in her loungewear-not-pyjamas.

'Well, you heard about Fabien, right?'

Susannah shoots a warning look at her daughter, who ignores it.

'It's okay, I'm fine,' says Mila quietly, going back to pointlessly filling out forms, while listening intently.

'Literally the entire press has turned up at the hall, including the *Daily Mail*. Even *The Sun!*' Mila stops pretending to write. 'So Harry goes and threatens them, being all like, *"Gerroff my land you vultures",*' Chloe is dissolving into hysterics, struggling to release the words, 'and, and, so they say they have every right to be there, it's in the public interest especially as apparently we are all a bunch of posh hypocrites housing refugees while funding the war against them. So Harry, who obviously won't hear a word against Farlington, is true to his word, and he, like,' Chloe is clutching her stomach now, the spasms of laughter too much to bear. She can barely breathe. 'He, like, actually starts spreading muck all over them!'

'Oh, dear God.' Susannah sits down.

'Now the police are there too! Elodie says the family line is for everyone to stay away and say nothing. Me and Lottie are heading over there now.'

'Absolutely not! I forbid it.'

'Mother, I'm twenty.'

'Then bloody act it. I'd expect this sort of thing from Lottie, but from a grown married woman? It won't do.'

'Divorcee,' Chloe corrects, leaning back, stretching her arm behind her head, 'a young Joan Collins – jaded, but still beautiful.'

'You're separated, not divorced, which you should be taking more seriously. It isn't a joke. It's not an episode of Townie.'

'TOWIE!'

The doorbell rings. Chloe uncharacteristically jumps up, shouting that she'll get it, barging past her mother, keen to be the first to receive any further developments directly rather than funnelled through diplomatic channels such as her parents.

Susannah looks to Mila, who has gone white, one hand gripping the pen, the other, previously resting on the paper form now inadvertently crunching it into a ball as her fingers retract into her palm, making a little white fist. Susannah mouths, keen not to miss what's happening down the hall, '*Are you okay?*'

'Muuuuuuum! It's Lady Knutsworth.'

Susannah sprints down the hall, and shoos her daughter away.

Chloe, back in the sitting room, silently beckons Mila to the door, which she holds open ajar, just an inch. The two young women stand together, straining to hear the hushed conversation.

Snippets of sentences slither down the corridor. 'No, I won't come in properly. This shouldn't take long. I must get back, you see, poor Fabien is...'

'Of course.'

'Just wondered if you'd managed to sort out the mix-up? The paperwork is important now.'

'... difficult, passed around... pillar to post, on hold, no answer...'

'Of course, darling... expedite the paperwork, get your house in order... make sure Mila Kiss is...'

'NOT A SERIAL KILLER ON THE RUN!' Chloe

finishes, laughing at herself, and giving Mila a friendly push. 'Honestly, these people. You'll get used to them; they're so dramatic. You'd think anyone actually cared outside of Farlington about the grand lady and lord. They definitely won't care about us, or you! So full of self-importance, really. It's only the golden boy they're interested in, and that's only because he's always flashing it about in the city with his famous friends and *"people in high places"*. Throw him to the wolves, I say, right Mila? Devil he is, ha ha ha, we love him really though, can't not, am I right?'

Mila doesn't reply, even as Chloe turns to her.

There is a sharp snap, and two halves of a plastic biro fall to the floor.

CHAPTER EIGHTEEN

When Peter was a little boy, Nikolai and his late wife had once caught him and his friend looking at a dirty magazine. The boy's poor mother was a traditional woman, religious too, and had never seen anything like it. She almost collapsed on the spot, but instead opted for screaming blue murder and crossing herself.

Nikolai had dragged the two boys outside and clipped them both around the head, several times for good measure. The friend – Nikolai forgets his name – had been banned from the house, as it was easier to think of him as a bad influence, than of his twelve-year-old boy of having such thoughts about women. Though, Nikolai remembers some relief at the woman part.

Peter had been a quiet, strange boy, and for a while Nikolai suspected he might not be *normal* in that department. Now he understands there is no normal, and everything is fine whatever you do and whoever you do it with (though his own parents would not have understood, God rest their innocent souls)... but still, the old normal was easier on everyone, plus they'd always dreamt of grandchildren. Not that Peter had delivered on that, regardless of his heterosexual persuasion.

A week or two later, he had received a phone call from the

friend's father. Furious, he was, having just caught the friends in his shed, a whole collection of magazines between them.

As Nikolai sat in A.J.'s pokey bedsit, he thought of this. He had told Peter he was going for a walk in the park.

'The way I see it, the person in the article is a rebel, like us. They could be making up the charges, using the war as a way to crack down on enemies of the state.'

'Mila.'

'Yes, well they don't call her that. But I do think that's the name we should use in the appeal.' A.J. is standing next to a flip chart and drawing arrows with felt tips.

'Appeal?'

'Yes Nikolai,' A.J.'s girlfriend Rain replies, 'you want to find her, don't you? She's your friend; she needs us.'

'Of course, but I don't want to cause her more trouble. It could all be a mistake. Such a nice girl. Clever, beautiful girl. Bit crazy,' Nikolai twirls his finger around his ear, then stops suddenly as A.J. and Rain's mouths gape, remembering the tips Mila gave him. 'Bit, er, sick in the head, yes?'

'Um.'

A.J. waves his hand to dismiss Rain's interruption. 'Sure, we know what you mean. She's different. She's misunderstood. Like us.'

'All of us, for sure.' Nikolai shakes his head, declining the spliff being passed around the small group. Most of them, he recognises from the march. There's a Pop, a Benj, and a Bananas ("with an s at the end", he explains at each introduction, because Banana singular would make him an idiot, whereas Bananas plural means he is intentionally unpredictable and difficult to define). They are an odd bunch, but then they are young and British, so what would Nikolai know.

He knows they are the friendliest faces he's seen since he landed, and they want to help Mila. Well, *mostly* friendly.

Monty, who wasn't at the march, but was temporarily crashing with A.J. and Rain, barely says a word. He mainly keeps glued to his laptop, scowling and retreating to the box room whenever A.J. and his friends start, as Monty puts it, 'talking absolute biscuits'.

'You see, if we use the name she gave you, rather than the one in the articles, she can respond safely. We use no photo, just her name. In the UK it is such a rare name, so we have a chance of finding her. We'll just post in local groups. You say she's staying in Lancashire, right? And if anyone who knows her in the UK sees it, they'll just think it's a nice old friend looking to get in touch. Nothing weird or suspicious about that.'

———

A text lights up Fabien's screen from the corner table. Damn journalists must have got his mobile number too, now. The home phone is off the hook, his curtains remain shut. He has only days to convince his father to help him. He tries to open the message and hit delete without even reading it. Although they'll never know, it feels like a small victory. Impossible though.

It's Mila. I finally got a phone. Can we meet?

He types back quickly, she responds.

Hood up, he grabs his car keys, and takes the footpath at the back of the house, where he has parked his car, tucked in an old outbuilding near the back gates hardly anyone knows are there.

Mila is waiting on the corner of the lane when he arrives. She slides into the passenger seat wordlessly, and the car gets going on the third try.

'Not exactly inconspicuous, is it?'

'I think you may have just articulated one of my biggest mistakes – generally speaking – in life.' Fabien risks a sideways glance, a half-smile.

Her lips move slightly in return, though not fully committed to warmth.

'This is it,' he tells her, as he opens his door, telling Mila to wait as he always does. She ignores his request, violently swings open the door, and jumps out unassisted.

Fabien tries not to visibly wince as she slams the door shut with a bang.

'Mila, I'm so glad you are here. I'll try to explain; I'm not who they say I am.'

Mila doesn't answer. Will she allow herself to listen, to believe? Does his ignorance make it okay? Not at all. Not for Mila. Careless, entitled man-child. And who is to say he isn't lying right now? She has no idea what he is capable of. She barely knows him, and she knows better than to trust a man with power, money, and lies on his side. She also knows that she needs someone who can keep her secrets and help her track down Xristina – someone who, in this moment, would do anything for her. It feels dangerous; a precarious balancing act. She could fall and crash at any moment.

'Walk this way,' Fabien says, trying and failing to take her hand, a rolled-up picnic blanket under his arm.

Mila follows, shoving her hands in her pockets, fingernails digging into the flesh of her palms.

They thrash their way through an overgrown, narrow path, stumbling over tree roots, nettles stinging their legs even through light trousers. Summer leaves make an awning over their heads, a tunnel to God knows where. To paradise. Mila hates to admit it, but the soft curves and colours of this strange new landscape have started to grow on her.

A clearing contains a waterfall splashing into a lagoon. The grassy verge is scattered with dandelions and daisies. It's warmer here, not a whisper of a breeze. The sun pushes through gaps in the trees, creating patches of golden grass. Fabien throws down the blanket and they sit.

'Can I explain, a little? I know I was wrong. And greedy. I didn't know about the companies behind the war supplies. My partner's still out of contact, totally vanished, the bastard. I should have known, though; I should have studied the firms he brought to me and told me were ethical. I wasn't thinking what these businesses were all about – just that they meant we were succeeding, that maybe I'd pulled it off, and my father was wrong, for once. I'm stupid, and so, so sorry, I don't know what to do.'

Mila doesn't ask many questions. She sits on her hands, and starts to gently probe, as Fabien tries to rebuild the trust that unravelled so quickly. Fabien keeps trying to explain; he knows by doing so he makes himself sound reckless and stupid. He tells her he is reckless and stupid, with a terrible head for detail. Lazy to boot.

Mila agrees that he is reckless and stupid. 'My argument should still stand if you can prove, or get him to admit, that he defrauded you. It's possible to bring a case against him, if you can find him, and dig out some evidence. Still, you may lose money in the meantime – money you may not get back, as there are no guarantees – to refund the investments that your fund contributors didn't agree to. So, you'll be bankrupt, but your efforts to repay could help to repair the damage to your name. Would that be so bad?'

Fabien wishes he could be more like Mila. It would be awful to be poor. But worse, it would be unthinkable to fail like this, to be cast out. Even with a woman like Mila by his side, could it be enough? Would he be the same? Who would want him? He's not sure Mila would, or does. 'I can't believe you're still trying to help me. I–'

'I will help you, but first, I have something to tell you. I think I might be in trouble myself, unless I find that woman I told you about: Xristina.'

They talk, and she tells him enough, but not all. Not yet. He takes it all in, and for a while they lie, the low sun warming their faces. When Mila stands and silently strips, wading into the lagoon, Fabien follows, and this time they allow themselves to forget everything, heads thrown back, the sound of the waterfall mingling with their moans.

Afterwards, the sun dries their skin, until it slowly dips. 'It will be okay; we will fix it. I don't know what I can do right now, nobody with any influence will take my calls, but I'll try, Mila. I promise.'

'I know I lied. I didn't have a choice.' Mila shivers as she thinks about her sister's still, white face, set against the blood. About Janos' threats, about the children.

'Are you cold?' He moves off the picnic blanket so he can wrap it around her slender shoulders. 'You did what you had to do; you're amazing.' He pauses, and looks at her; into her. 'I'm falling in love with you.' In the silence that follows, Fabien feels his heart almost stop.

'You don't know me,' Mila tells him.

'*Could* you feel the same?'

Mila cannot answer – moments ago, she needed him, or at least the release his body could offer her. Right now, there is no room for romance, only for the rage of vengeance and the promises she makes to herself every day: I will find Xristina, I will expose Janos, I will save Konstantine and Karlie. I will be free.

CHAPTER NINETEEN

'Are you sure we should be doing this?' Lottie is used to being a ringleader at school, having finished her final year, and about to go up to the sixth form, but Chloe makes her feel like she is still twelve.

Chloe shushes her as they close the door to Mila's room behind them.

'What if she comes back?'

'She'll be gone for hours; she's out with Fabien. Love's young fucking dream.'

'Are you all right, Chloe? Are you upset they're together?'

Chloe glares at the younger girl. 'Don't be so childish, Lottie. Honestly, I thought you'd grown up while I was away. I'm not upset about Mila and Fabien, that's ridiculous. Fabien and I had a childhood fling, I barely remember it.'

'A fling? I heard you tricked him into a date pretending to be older online and then he bought you a Happy Meal and drove you home. My brother said everyone was talking about how embarrassing it was, and you didn't come out for the rest of the summer holidays.'

'Your brother is a sodding liar. He was always after me.

Madly jealous.' Chloe opens the wardrobe, and starts rifling through the top shelf. 'Actually, if you haven't noticed, I'm in the middle of a crisis. My marriage is over, I've had to leave my job and travel halfway across the world to come home to live with my parents. And if that isn't bad enough, they've moved an illegal immigrant into my home!'

'She's a refugee.'

'What?'

'She's not an immigrant, Chloe, or illegal.' Lottie's voice is quiet but firm. Chloe still intimidates her, just like in first year, when Chloe was sixteen and dazzling and cruel; all the things that high school popularity required, but Lottie is fierce when it comes to acceptable terminology around immigration, war, race, and sexism. She is even getting a good repertoire in veganism, though living in rural farming land, she hasn't quite worked out how not to eat meat with every other meal.

'We have no idea who or what she is, Loz,' Chloe's manner suddenly softens, and she smiles warmly at her partner in crime, picked for the job due to everyone her own age being long gone to the city or university or anywhere but this dump, apart from Elodie who appears to be a hermit these days, 'and I don't mean any harm by it. If we find nothing, fair enough, but she's clearly hiding something, and she is living in my house. She could be dangerous. Now, you start on the drawers.'

Lottie doesn't like it, she feels uneasy. She used to sneak into her big brother's room and steal cigarettes before he packed up and went to Oxford, her parents' pride and joy. She never felt uneasy then, just determined and delighted about catching him out. He could hardly grass her up for stealing contraband. She thinks about what Elodie said at her last painting lesson – about how brave Mila is, how Anna the housekeeper, had explained what it was really like to move to a new country, knowing nobody.

'Your mum and dad will kill us if they come back and find us here.'

'Oh God, tell me about it.' Chloe sighs dramatically, and imitates her mother's voice, *"She's our guest!"'*

'Did you see the article in the *Daily Mail?* Says we only took Mila in to make it look like we care, when we're secretly living off the land of warmongers. Mum says Lady Knutsworth has taken to her bed with shame. Fabien is going to be chucked out on his ear if he doesn't fix it. Kind of stupid though, isn't it, to think an entire village is in on some banker's conspiracy? I mean, Fabien is never here, and he never speaks to any of us these days.'

'Speak for yourself, Fabien and I are still close,' Chloe huffs.

'I thought you barely remembered him,' Lottie says, as she opens the bedside drawer. 'Oh, look, Chloe, it's a little safe like they have in the tuck shop!' Despite her reservations, Lottie fails to keep the excitement from her voice.

Before Chloe can correct Lottie's insolence about Fabien, she sees the battered old tin safe, fastened with a padlock. 'I knew it was here somewhere.'

'You did?'

'She says it's family photos. But tell me this, DC Lottie Beard, do *you* padlock your holiday snaps in a safe?'

The girls have turned the room upside down and are doing their best to make it look like it did when they first entered. Thankfully, Mila's possessions are few.

'She must keep the key with her,' concludes Chloe, 'which if you ask me is doubly suspicious.'

'Or maybe she's just got your number,' Lottie laughs, somehow relieved they haven't found it, and taken the only thing that Mila has of her own, rather than loaned, shared, or begrudgingly donated by Chloe.

'Just hurry up, my parents will be back soon. Maybe they've had more luck.'

'Where have they been?'

'Town Hall, Refugee Support Office. Dad can't get through, no emails or letters are answered, and now Lady Lyds is insistent that no further skeletons are to be uncovered by the tabloids, my parents have jumped to attention. They're trying to speak to an "actual human being in the flesh", as Dad says. He's convinced a face-to-face chat will have it all sorted out in five minutes.'

'Then why on earth are we doing this?' Lottie sighs deeply. The weather is nice, and they could have been lying by the boating lake with a couple of cool ciders and some crisps, watching Harry Postlethwaite's nephew Noah go by in his tractor. He is gorgeous, but about to go off to agricultural college. Lottie's window of opportunity to lose her virginity before the year end is slowly closing.

'Because my dad is an idiot, and he and Mum are too trusting. They're wrong. They'll get nowhere today at the offices. I reckon Mila's hidden her tracks better than that. She isn't who she says she is, Lottie; mark my words. You should have seen her face, white as a ghost, when she heard Mum and Lydia discussing her *"paperwork"*, like she has any. Not any she doesn't keep hidden under lock and key, anyway.'

'What now, then?'

'Facebook.'

Chloe and Lottie are sitting in the garden when they hear the tinkle of the front door being opened, and Mila shouting hello. Susannah and Martin shout hello back from the kitchen, where they are chopping herbs, and sipping wine.

Chloe turns to her friend. 'Say nothing, Loz, not yet. I need to check the facts, okay? We don't want to upset her. Right? She's got enough to worry about.'

Lottie nods, still wondering what it all means. What does this old famous-for-five-minutes bloke Nikolai want with Mila? What has he got to do with that awful group of loser vandals backing his appeal to find her? Who the hell are "CC", some group the schoolboy revolutionaries seem to think Mila can connect them to back in her country?

Lottie despises The Full Circle and their dumbass mouthpiece A.J., who gets the odd bit of social media space amongst the memes circulating at college. They give proper agents for change, like herself, a bad name. Some of the less well-read in her class think he's a rock and roll revolutionary. Lottie knows he's just a no-mark stoner, looking to cause trouble for a slice of attention.

They hear Mila chatting to Chloe's parents through the open bifolds, the sound travelling from the kitchen to the terrace. The girls sip their ciders, and stretch back on chairs in the early evening sun. Lottie was allowed only one, and only because she promised her mother permitted it at home. Susannah still insisted on telephoning Jenny to check. She had felt so childish next to Chloe.

'Mila!' Chloe calls, 'Come have a drink with the girls; tell us all about your date with Fit Fabien.'

'Chloe,' she hears her dad's warning voice, 'please don't embarrass Mila.' Martin's head pops into sight, and he shakes his head at his daughter, who's still as flighty as ever.

Chloe rolls her eyes at Lottie, who giggles.

'Would you like a cold drink, Mila? Sit with the girls?' Susannah chips in, as they hear the fridge door pop open, and a gush of fizz and bubbles is released.

Mila saunters outside holding her bottle of cider. 'Hey.' She pulls out a chair. 'How was your day, girls?'

Chloe looks at Mila stonily.

'Oh fine, good, love a lazy day, doing nothing. I just came here to hang out with Chloe, but we didn't do anything at all really, which was lovely, really good.' Lottie overcompensates for Chloe's silence, and her own guilt.

'Oh!' Chloe's face abruptly lights up, a smile breaks across it. 'I've just remembered, I've got to pop out, won't be long. Mila, stay with Lottie, get to know her. You'll stop for dinner, won't you, Lottie?'

'Um, sure.'

Chloe has already gone, is shouting hurried goodbyes to her parents.

'Be back for seven please, lamb chops and Greek salad, don't be late!' Susannah shouts.

'Where are you going, anyway?' Martin asks, but too late. The front door slams.

CHAPTER TWENTY

Fabien is swinging on the garden seat overlooking the duck pond at the back of the house, when Chloe approaches.

'Can I bum one of those?' Fabien offers her the battered packet of Marlboro Lights without turning. 'Didn't know you still smoked,' she says, taking one, placing it between her lips, 'got a light, too?'

He fumbles in his jeans pocket, then stands unexpectedly, rocking the swing chair, slightly unbalancing Chloe but not noticing, or caring. He manoeuvres his hand into the corner of the tight denim pocket, retrieves the lighter, and passes it to Chloe.

'Thanks a bunch,' Chloe mutters. She expects he would have lit it for Mila. He always has taken Chloe for granted. She really thought that her return as a sun-drenched experienced woman would have been the perfect eye-opener Fabien needed, and just the new start she was looking for. The whole situation is intolerable. A post-Geoff distraction would have been welcome, and would have shown her tedious, judgemental husband that he was lucky to have her. Chloe feels she has one more play, at least, thanks to Mila's shady connections. 'So, how are things?'

Finally, Fabien turns to face her. 'Pretty crap, actually.' He throws his head back momentarily and returns his gaze to the ducks, who dip their heads beneath the surface, bottoms up, over and over, happy as Larry. He envies them.

'Yeah, me too,' she says. 'Oh, don't raise your eyebrows at me. You're not the only one back at home being judged by your parents for your failure at adulthood. Hey, remember that time we all went night-swimming in here after the ball? After drinking all your dad's good port?'

At the mention of wild swimming Fabien thinks back to the lagoon, and Mila's pale skin, covered in goosepimples. He smiles.

'See? Still something to smile about.'

Fabien feels bad for the lie, though not bad enough to correct her. 'Yeah, though I don't think your parents are cutting you off and changing the course of your life forever because of Boring Geoff.'

'Boring–' Chloe begins, puzzled, and changes her mind. 'What are you going to do? Expect you wish dear old Daddy would just drop dead before he has the chance.' Chloe laughs and kicks back her legs, and they swing backwards and forwards, the thick ropes creaking.

Fabien's feet stop the swing with a soft thud on the grassy ground beneath. 'I should be going. I have a pretty difficult conversation to have, and I can't put it off much longer.'

'Things good with Mila, though?' Chloe calls to his back, and when he doesn't slow his stride, she adds, 'What do you really know about her, anyway?'

Fabien stops and turns. She has his full attention now. Only taken the best part of ten years. She will not squander it.

'What do you mean, Chloe?' Fabien asks, retaking his seat next to her.

'I'm sure you know about the mix-up.'

'I'm sure you know it is *just* a mix-up. There's no drama here Chloe, however much you may wish there to be.'

'Not what I've heard,' Chloe retorts, forgetting the calm, benevolent tone she'd hoped to convey. 'Did you know she's involved in some *very* dodgy so-called political groups? Basically terrorists.'

Fabien's face gives him away, his fists clenched. 'What the fuck are you going on about? What would *you* know about anything to do with Mila? You've hardly been a friend of the year so far.'

'Just call me *Poirot*,' says Chloe, tapping her nose.

'Chloe, why don't you stop looking for trouble, and leave the poor girl alone. You're talking absolute nonsense. Just grow up.'

'I'm trying to protect you, Fabes babes.' Chloe smiles. 'In your current predicament, don't you think adding *domestic terrorist girlfriend* into the mix might finish you off for good?'

Fabien marches away without a glance. No less than Chloe had expected, though she had hoped for more. Still, Fabien isn't the only one with an interest in Mila Kiss.

'Delicious, Mrs Wilson.' Lottie is helping herself to more salad when Chloe clatters in, throwing her bag on the floor, and pulling out a chair at the kitchen table.

'Sorry I'm late,' she says breathily, 'I lost track of the time.'

Susannah puts her own knife and fork down, swords crossed over her unfinished meal, and retrieves a plate of chops from the oven. She opens a cupboard and pulls out a side plate, and places both in front of her daughter.

'I've had to warm your plate to keep the chops from going cold, so use a side plate for the salad.'

'Thanks,' Chloe takes the salad forks from Lottie, and helps herself.

Mila is studying her food.

'As we were saying, Mila,' Martin says, ignoring Chloe's request for pepper, 'they weren't really much help today. It would appear there's no missing person without a placement that they can see, and there's no explanation for the incorrect details they sent before you arrived. They had nothing to do with that apparently, all done in London, and it would seem they don't really care. The upshot is, I think we can put it to bed.'

Mila smiles, and looks up. 'Thank you, Martin. But you should have told me you were so worried. I could have come; I have my paperwork in order. Perhaps I could have saved you some time and effort.'

Chloe snorts, and quickly covers it with an unconvincing sneeze. 'Hayfever, sorry, do go on.'

'No dear, we didn't want to make you feel uncomfortable,' Susannah tells Mila, 'and we know you have everything in order. We took the photocopies you gave us. It was all fine. You know you're welcome... and the people at the Town Hall, well, let's just say they are under a lot of pressure at the moment. Occasionally they have been known to cut corners; they don't exactly go the extra mile.'

'Unless they want to chase up a parking fine or block a planning application,' Martin teases.

'Lady Lydia is just in a bit of a tizz, and who can blame her?' Susannah adds, loyally.

'Well, really, darling, the only person *she* should be in a *tizz* with is Fabien, but as per usual she is looking for someone else to direct the negative attention to.' Martin catches Chloe's eye, and she returns a weak, grateful smile. Her father had been the only one to back her when she insisted that Fabien had offered to take her out then reneged at the last minute. Lydia had never liked her, and was always quick to blame her for anything she could. The woman had a permanent stick up her arse.

'Where were you, anyway?' Martin asks his daughter.

'Oh, I had something to show Fabien. Nothing important, just something I found online that I thought might be of interest.'

Mila looks up, searching for a clue, but Chloe is looking at Lottie. She winks.

Lottie drops her knife on the floor. 'Oh, I'm sorry,' she tells Susannah, appealing to Chloe with her eyes before scraping her chair back and bending to pick it up.

She wouldn't have stirred things up with Fabien, or worse, Lord Knutsworth? She'd overheard him talking to her dad, in his capacity as a parish councillor, in the kitchen just the other day, convincing him that if there was any uncertainty in her documentation it would be wiser for the village to hand her over to the authorities.

Lottie didn't want to be part of anything that got their enigmatic guest in trouble, or took her away. Mila was the coolest, most stunning woman she'd ever met. She didn't seem to care what anyone thought of her, and Lottie badly wished she could pull off the same air of nonchalance, peppered with disdain. She was concerned her friendship with Chloe had her on the wrong side of the debate. Elodie and Anna would think she was a *Daily Mail*-reading reactionary like her mum if they knew how Chloe spoke – and how she made Lottie go along with her – and she could think of nothing worse than that. Elodie definitely wouldn't approve of their snooping, and would be livid if she knew that the small crumbs of information they had found had made Chloe feel entitled to write Mila off as some kind of communist criminal revolutionary. She pictured them giving her a disappointed look, imagined them telling her perhaps she shouldn't visit the gatehouse anymore.

'In the end though, turns out he was a little distracted,' Chloe goes on. Mila continues to eat, quietly, delicately, her head down once more. 'Seems he's more upset than you might realise. A *lot* of people have been lying to him, you know?'

'Poor Fabien,' mutters Susannah, pouring more wine. Her husband glances at her, tuts, and turns back to his food. 'I can't imagine he knew what he was getting into at the time,' she adds.

Still chewing, Martin suddenly pipes up, speckles of feta flying from his mouth. 'Pah, poor Fabien. He brought it on himself. He'll have to do the right thing.' He wipes his lips with the napkin on his lap.

'Well, Daddy, he was very angry when I left, he said he had to go and have a *"difficult conversation".'*

'Let's hope he's gone to make things right, take some responsibility for his own decisions for once.' Martin drinks more wine, incensed more than usual at the mention of Fabien's privilege, and the way he treats people, in particular his Chloe. She may be a handful, but the boy is no saint.

'Maybe he's mature enough to fall on his own sword this time,' Susannah adds.

'Or he'll throw someone else under a bus,' Chloe says with a smirk. 'At this point, who knows what he'll do to talk himself back into Gregory's good books, and his wallet.'

Mila looks hard at Chloe. She doesn't know what she thinks she knows about her, but she knows she has been snooping; the spoilt brat is too lazy to put things back properly after ransacking her room. But the padlock is unbroken. She's goading her, she's sure of it, but better to be safe than sorry. She knows she must go to see Fabien. He's been trying to call her. She knows she may have to leave sooner than expected.

Martin's mobile phone rings. He looks at the screen, raises an eyebrow, and answers. 'Lord Gregory, old chap! Good to hear from you,' he says, and listens for a moment. 'I see. Yes. Of course,' Martin lowers his voice as he leaves the kitchen.

As they hear him returning down the hallway, Susannah gives the girls a knowing look, a finger to her lips. They didn't need to be told to be quiet, and strain to listen. Mila especially.

'No, no, I understand, some things are better discussed face to face. Though, really, I'm sure whatever it is, we can get to the bottom of it. I'm in the city tomorrow for a meeting though, so it will need to be later. No, I'm sorry, I really can't do any sooner, Greg old chap, the CEO's summoned me. Would if I could.'

Martin stands in the doorway, gesturing to Susannah, miming a scribble. She duly passes him the notepad and pen, and with the phone nestled between his ear and crooked shoulder, he starts to write.

'The Royal Oak, 7pm. See you tomorrow.'

CHAPTER TWENTY-ONE

The cold tap runs furiously into the basin, splashing the sides, the noise a shield to hide Mila's retching. She holds her own hair back. Someone is knocking at the door, but she ignores them. There are four bathrooms in this house. They can go somewhere else.

Martin had been coy, embarrassed. He couldn't look her in the eye. He'd made his excuses, and Susannah had followed him out of the room, instructing Chloe to clear up.

They know too much, but how much, Mila cannot be sure. Through Chloe, through Fabien, through their own connections; however it has come about, it's clear the lord and lady have been suspicious from the outset about Mila's mixed-up identity. With the tabloids on their doorstep, and Fabien's business connections to the war, Mila is now surer than ever that they've been digging – faster and faster – in the hope of quickly burying whatever is about to be found.

Frozen to her kitchen chair, Mila had been holding her breath without realising and when she let it out, she felt everything inside woosh up through her belly. She had run upstairs without a word, slamming the bathroom door behind her.

How much do they know?

'Mila, it's me, Lottie. Are you all right in there?'

'Yes, fine.'

'Mila, can I come in?'

Mila doesn't reply. Lottie is a sweet girl, but she's just a child. Besides, she is enthralled by Chloe, and Chloe is up to something. Mila does not know why. Her inner voice tells her it is jealousy. Because of Fabien? It all seems too silly. She doesn't understand. Maybe she is wrong, and it is Fabien who has betrayed her.

More knocking.

Still, silence from inside the bathroom.

Mila's phone starts to vibrate in her pocket. Anna. One of a few friendly faces stored in her phone. She cancels the call. Who knows where Anna's loyalty will lie? Why would it lie with Mila, a girl she has known barely two minutes, versus her employers of God knows how many years? Just because they both come from somewhere other than the UK? Mila is not naive, and besides, without a doubt she is close with Elodie, and surely Elodie will want to do whatever she can to protect her brother, and her family's reputation.

She knows she never should have allowed her guard to drop, especially with the entitled few she has spent her life rallying against to stand up for those who are forgotten.

'Please, Mila, there's something I need to tell you,' Lottie pleads in a whisper.

Mila wipes her mouth. She's about to answer, maybe even let her in.

But Chloe's voice comes now, and not for her. 'Lottie, I need a word with you.'

The knocking has stopped, footsteps patter away.

Mila flushes, and uses the rushing cold water from the tap to splash her face. She puts the lid over the toilet and sits, closing her eyes.

Her phone vibrates in her pocket. Anna again. Then a text.

> M, please call back, it's serious. Overheard conversation with Lord G, being fed lies about you I'm sure of it. He's on the warpath. Let me help. A x

Mila deletes the message. No one in Farlington can help her now, not if they know even part of the truth. They think it is simple, just paperwork and bureaucracy. Anna means well, but she also seems to think Mila's biggest problem lies with an administrative error and a few bigots in the village.

They don't know who or what they are up against, the power Janos Byros has back home, and the unwavering belief in this treacherous, lying so-called war hero. The murderer who currently holds her sister's children as leverage, and bays for her blood, or at least her ever-lasting silence. But Mila does not intend to disappear. Mila intends to win.

Mila Kiss considers her options. She still hasn't managed to track down Janos' ex-wife. All she has is a name – Xristina – and the letters and photos her sister had been hiding: the evidence.

She can't stay here now. At best, after meeting with Lord Knutsworth, she will be confronted by the kind, trusting Wilsons. Or they could go straight to the authorities. Perhaps the Knutsworths already have. Once they make the connections to her old name, it will not take long to link her to the police appeal back home. She will be deported, arrested on the basis of Janos' lies, and imprisoned. She knows he has connections that will allow him to produce the "evidence" to prove her guilt.

She unlocks her tin, and takes out a small, torn, folded piece of paper, just a name and address scrawled in pencil. It's the details of the only person left she can ask for help, or at least a place to stay for a while. She puts it in her pocket and packs her few belongings. Tonight, she will leave here, sooner than she had hoped. She will not stay hidden forever: that would be far too convenient for Janos. She will find Xristina, she will unearth the truth, she will rescue Konstantine and Karlie. She will make sure that Janos never hurts anyone again.

After that, they can do what they like to her.

CHAPTER TWENTY-TWO

The real Mila Kiss had been beaten black and blue for years by her husband. She was known as Mrs Mila Byros back then. The children witnessed half of it. He lied and cheated his way through life, and through the army. When there were rumours of drunken brawls at camp, or peacekeeping missions turning into bloodbaths, his superiors always questioned him, but they never proved anything. He was Teflon, some said. Others said he knew too much, but what and about whom, nobody could say.

His loyal wife didn't believe any of it, even though she knew what he was capable of, and she had felt it first-hand. He told her it was just politics, and she trusted him. She had to. He was all she had. He told her she was the only one who understood him. His bitch ex-wife never had. Took his children away to England – what kind of a mother would do that to a loving father?

Her sister Sofia told her to leave him. She told her sister to shut up. And when her sister refused to shut up, she stopped seeing her. Kept her beautiful children away from their aunty.

Except sometimes, if she was too ill to care for them, or too afraid.

Her parents were long gone, and she missed them terribly. Was it so wrong to want to be loved? To try to keep her little family together? All she had ever wanted was a normal life. Her husband was a patriot, a traditional man. She was a librarian. Her children were perfect. They all obeyed the law.

Unlike her little sister, who was always in trouble. She was brave and clever; a lawyer. But how could her idealistic sister ever understand real life, and the compromises one had to make as a mother and a wife?

Konstantin was seven years old when he received a punch to the face from his father. When his mother returned home from shopping, his sister Karlie was dabbing his bloody nose with a tea towel. She was five. It turned out her little boy had a broken arm, too. Janos was nowhere to be seen. He didn't come home for four days, though Mrs Byros didn't know that, because she left with the children that day and never went back.

Her sister helped her find a safe flat, one her group used sometimes, for meetings, or hiding when they'd gone too far. She returned to her unmarried self, and name. She became Mila Kiss again. She updated her passport. She started to make plans, not dissimilar to the first Mrs Byros. Because, like his first wife, Mila knew Janos wasn't the type to give up.

Only one or two people knew where she was. Janos raged around town demanding answers, pleading for second chances, confessing his love for his family and his failures as a man. Promising to change. Threatening to kill them all.

When the invasion came, and the evacuation began, her sister helped her fill out all the forms. She and her children were assigned a home in a rural village in Lancashire. The evidence she had been collecting was hidden. Only her sister knew of it; her insurance should anything happen.

Her few belongings were mostly packed, days before her flight was due to leave to safety. Then in the middle of the night the phone had rung. 'He knows where you are. You need to leave. I'm coming to get you.'

But when her sister arrived, it was too late.

The real Mila Kiss was dead, her children were gone. The flat had already been tipped upside down. Sofia had pushed an armchair aside, praying the tin box was still there, that Janos Byros had not found it.

A neighbour had appeared in the doorway. 'Don't move, the police are coming,' he told her, unsmiling, shaking a little.

The dead woman's sister moved towards the neighbour, bloodied hands outstretched, asking for help. 'Don't move I tell you, on the floor!' The neighbour was carrying a kitchen knife in one hand and his phone in the other. He pointed at the girl he had been told was dangerous. Political, unhinged, and looking for secrets she believed this patriotic wife and mother may be hiding for her heroic husband. Sadly estranged, a misunderstanding, the neighbour was told during the brief phone call; he understood, women could be so volatile. Captain Byros seemed very nice, respectful. Of course, the poor captain didn't really believe his wife was in danger from her own sister, but could he please check anyway, to put his mind at rest; who knows in these troubled times what the over-politicised young people might resort to.

The girl covered in her sister's blood had put her hands up, started to back away. 'Who are you? Help me,' she said, confused, tearful, and frightened. 'My sister, Konstantine, Karlie...'

The neighbour put his phone to his ear, and talked into it. 'She's here, just as Captain Byros said. I fear it is too late; the poor woman is already dead. She's looking for something. He said she would be. I'm so sorry I'm too late.'

Suddenly everything became clear. Sofia had been set up. She would be accused of the murder of her sister.

Rage coursed through her body, powering a strength through her, legs straightening, chest forward. She barged at the neighbour, grabbing the arm holding the knife as she pushed them to the floor and ran. She would only return once to the flat, in the dead of night, to retrieve her sister's little locked tin box from beneath the floorboards on which the tatty old armchair used to sit.

From that moment, she knew she must become Mila Kiss, and the new Mila Kiss was going to clear her name and rescue her sister's children. She would see that monster behind bars where he belonged, or better still, dead and buried.

CHAPTER TWENTY-THREE

Mila isn't answering her phone. After five or six attempts going straight to voicemail, Fabien resorts to text.

> Chloe trying to dig up dirt. She knows something, but think she's blagging mostly, as usual. No idea where she's getting it from. Call me, please.

Mila's phone is off, so it makes no noise in her pocket as she quietly closes the back door, treading carefully around the side of the house, trying to avoid triggering the security lights. She will have to dispose of it, she knows that. Not that it matters now; the only numbers she kept in her new device were people she can no longer trust.

Did Fabien give her secrets to his father? What does Chloe think she knows? Are Fabien and Chloe both against her, for their own gain? Another sharp pain runs through her body from head to toe, the ache of betrayal.

She has to keep moving. She can't risk waiting to find out who knows what, or why. Even just a scrape of the surface could jeopardise her plans to find Xristina, and to get justice for her family. The questions, the confusion, the complications of truth, of war, of men, women, and love. The fucking paperwork.

She'll find out what they know soon enough, she imagines, but for now, she is going to have to work faster.

Frustrated, Fabien fidgets, checking his phone every few seconds. He tries to call again.

She's angry with him, but why?

Chloe.

He thinks back to earlier, as she joined him on the garden swing seat. Had she come from the house, from Lord Knutsworth's study? She could have spoken to his father, determined to make trouble for Mila, with or without his help. No wonder she gave up so easily. He starts to type again.

> I know what you must think, but it isn't true. Chloe is up to something. She'll get nowhere, but I have a plan. I'm going to give my father what he wants. I'm

'Fabien!' Fabien looks up to see his father towering over the sofa he's slumped on. 'Please stop looking at your bloody phone for once, and come with me. It's time for our chat.'

Fabien obediently follows his father to the study, quickly concluding his text as he walks.

> I have to go, please call me later, or text, I'll come over. X

He's ready. He'd been hoping to speak to Mila first, but that is no longer an option. He's going to have to fly solo, wing it. He promised he would fix it, and he will.

'Drink?' Gregory offers, pouring himself a large brandy.

'No, thank you.' Fabien waits until his father is seated opposite him. This is becoming far too frequent an occurrence, Fabien thinks, feeling inadequate, then sitting taller, remembering his purpose.

'Well,' they say together.

Usually, Fabien would stop and allow his father to begin, but not today, 'If I may?' he enquires.

Looking put out, Gregory replies, 'There's a complication, Fabien. I need you to listen.'

'I know, Dad. I think I can explain.'

'You know?' Gregory's demeanour transforms instantly, from controlled disdain to his well-known fiery temper, best known by his son, the one he deems wayward and unworthy. 'You know, do you? That your girlfriend is linked not only to a domestic terrorist group in her homeland, but is now linked to one here? So, whilst you are investigated for funding the invasion of her country, she is a known traitor and revolutionary trying to bring her government down from the inside! How the hell do you imagine this is going to play out, Fabien? And not just for you, but the whole family, by God, our entire legacy, the goddamned future of our name! You could ruin us. So, tell me, what is it you know, and more importantly, what are the two of you up to?' Gregory downs the brandy, and slams his glass down, getting up to refill it. 'I assumed you were clueless as to Mila's secret past, just a stupid boy infatuated by another pretty girl, but this... this is a whole new fucking level.'

Fabien winces at his father's language, and at the sound of the glass hitting the wooden desk top hard a second time.

'Dad.'

'Don't *Dad* me.' Gregory has not finished, but Fabien cannot wait a moment longer.

He interrupts. 'No, Dad, listen. You're getting this from Chloe, I presume? The girl loves to stir up trouble, as you well know. She's talking nonsense. She's jealous and silly and bored. She loves drama, and she hates Mila.'

'And why would she hate Mila? Why would a young woman from a decent background be jealous of a refugee girl with no future except quite possibly the inside of a jail? Hmm? Because of you? Really, Fabien, your ego never ceases to astound me.'

'No, not just that. Because she's beautiful, self-assured, clever.' Gregory takes a breath to speak, but Fabien is too quick, changes tack. 'Never mind that. Chloe's got it wrong. Mila is using a different name – that's where the mix-up started, this much is true, but it is her sister's name. Her sister was killed by her own husband. She already had the paperwork to come here, and Mila fled for her own safety. She was afraid, Dad, that's all. She looks enough like her sister to use the passport and she saw her chance to escape. And yes, she was in a small lobby group who opposed government policies, but they weren't terrorists! A few of them just got done for minor affray, a bit of jostling on demos, that sort of thing. Chloe's making it into something it isn't. I swear, you've got this all out of proportion.'

Gregory is leaning back in his chair, calmer than before. 'Well, that's the first I've heard of using a different name. It just gets better doesn't it, son?'

Fabien kicks himself for giving his stubborn old father more ammunition. He wishes he could have talked to Mila first, got his argument straight. She's so good at thinking things through logically, making sense of the world. But with Chloe hellbent on making trouble for Mila, Fabien didn't think he could afford to wait.

'And what about that awful group she's connected with here, through some anarchistic troublemakers back home?'

'I don't know. Chloe mentioned something about that. I assumed she was putting two and two together and getting five.'

'She has evidence. On The Facebook,' Gregory says, 'she showed me.'

'On *The* Facebook? Jesus. Mila isn't even *on* Facebook; she's understandably keeping a low profile. Look, Dad, Chloe is unhinged. Earlier, she suggested we should bump you off to fix my problems. You're going to listen to her over your own son?'

'She was obviously joking, albeit in poor taste, I give you that. I always thought the girl was below par in the intellect stakes, but it doesn't change a thing. Mila must be reported and deported. She isn't our problem; we have enough of our own with you. Speaking of which—'

'Now stop right there!' Fabien stands.

'Sit down, Fabien.'

Fabien retakes his seat. 'I must go on. I have a solution. Leave this situation alone, let Mila stay here a while, until we can figure out how to help her. The name thing is just paperwork! Her sister was killed, for God's sake, and her brother-in-law is dangerous and powerful. He has the children. She is looking for someone who might be able to help prove what he did, so she can make a case, and ensure the safety of her little niece and nephew.'

'Her little niece and nephew? She faked an identity to get into the country using the tragedy of war as cover, she lied to everyone, exploited our charity, then evidence appears on The Facebook proving who she really is – a terrorist! Then suddenly she feeds you this, frankly, far-fetched sob story. I mean, Fabien, if her sister had been murdered surely she would have gone to the police? I knew you had a soft spot for a good-looking woman, but I didn't have you down as the village idiot. Thank God Chloe came to me.'

'I believe her! I know her! She doesn't want to be here, or to stay for a second longer than she has to. More's the pity. Please, see sense, Father. I, I—'

'Love her?'

'Yes.'

'This is all very moving,' Gregory starts.

'I haven't finished. I agree to your terms. I will file for bankruptcy. I will take full responsibility for my actions. I will exonerate all my investors, and in time, they will come around. I will come home, fold my business, and fall under your tutelage. I will take my role as future Lord of Farlington seriously. All I ask is you give Mila some time. That you back me on this. I know I haven't always done the right thing, but I know this *is* the right thing to do.'

'Yet again, Fabien, you are ruled by your emotions rather than your head. Which is what always gets you into these messes in the first place.'

'No, not this time,' he protests.

'I'm sorry, but you're too late. Your week was up today. I've drawn up the paperwork. The estate will go to Elodie. You will make your own way, as you always have, and have always insisted you wanted to. You have your wish. I give up, I wash my hands.'

'And Mother? What's her view?'

'Your mother understands the gist. We will speak properly when she returns home in the morning. I'm convinced she will see sense.'

'And if she doesn't?'

Gregory shuffles papers on his desk. He doesn't need to say that Lydia cannot stop him, or that eventually she will forgive him as she always does, so long as her husband turns a blind eye to the odd handout.

'I am due to speak to the Wilsons tomorrow – as a courtesy, I should add – Mila's fate is already decided.' Gregory gets up and gestures for Fabien to stand and take his leave. 'Really, Fabien, it's fine to have a bit of fun with girls like Mila from the backwaters of society, a bloody *immigrant* of all things, but quite another to throw your life away for a lying, cheating, left-wing rebel. She just isn't worth it.'

A sheet of red distorts Fabien's vision as he grabs his father by the arms and throws him backward to the floor.

CHAPTER TWENTY-FOUR

Chloe is scrolling through her various social media feeds while tucked up under her duvet. It isn't that she doesn't like Mila. She's indifferent. But Chloe doesn't really see why Mila should be her parents' problem. They've barely mentioned her and Geoff's break-up, and spend more time asking her about what she plans to do next than giving her the space and time she needs to sit with her pain, and reflect on her feelings. Mila's pain and feelings, on the other hand, are top priority.

Also, Mila is clearly a liar. There's no way her parents would have had an activist in the house. Back when she was a teenager, Chloe wasn't even allowed to go to London that time for a political protest. She'd been furious. Afterwards, everyone went to a nightclub, and even though they didn't get in, they bought cheap alcopops and drank them as they wandered through the streets, taking in the sights. That's how Petra ended up going to prom with Bertie, who had promised he would take Chloe. It's no wonder she ran off with Geoff; she has been stifled her whole life.

Chloe searches online for Mila Kiss. She finds Nikolai again, his post looking for his "old friend", casually mentioning the group they both belonged to back home, which Chloe knows now, when written in full and translated into English, roughly means "Social Justice". They are always called things like that, she thinks. Making out they stand for the common good, when in reality they just go about destroying hard-earned property and dragging everyone down to the lowest common denominator. She was brought up to believe that if you worked hard, you deserved nice things. Not uniform equality through mediocrity. One day she'll find her calling, though it definitely wasn't in the pool sales and maintenance department she'd almost been sacked from twice in Australia, that was for sure.

Beneath Nikolai's appeal is a comment from A.J. – Lottie had heard of him – adding that The Full Circle offered their support and backing, and couldn't wait to meet her. Definitely all looks like a very dodgy little get together.

Nikolai's post has hundreds of likes and a few comments as he'd briefly been an internet sensation when he took to the stage impromptu at the anti-war march. *"Hope you find your friend, lovely Nikolai. Love and peace." "I'm sure you'll find her. I hope you and your group are surviving. Peace forever, man."* Lots of idiotic drivel suggesting the authors had not bothered to look up the group, and revealing that they didn't know much about them.

Lottie says the group is sort of on the periphery. Nobody takes them seriously enough to ban them, or arrest them, or even argue with them, as all they do is "spout shit slogans and wave banners". Nobody knows what they stand for, really, but a couple of anti-liberal writers had called them domestic terrorists once, and they'd PR'd the hell out of it, desperate to be noticed. If they hadn't, they'd still be unheard of, Lottie had told her. But as it is, a small portion of students and drifters cling on to the idea that they are revolutionaries in waiting.

Still no response from Mila on the post.

Because Mila isn't on Facebook, or any other social media channels. Because she's either a freak or she has something to hide.

So, she won't have seen this. Lottie wanted to tell Mila about Nikolai, but Chloe had managed to keep her quiet, for now. Which means she won't see any responses, either.

Chloe smiles as she logs out of Facebook, and starts to create a new profile.

'Who on earth could that be at this time?' Martin pauses the BBC drama, keen not to miss a critical revelation, as he gets up to answer the door.

'Search me,' replies Susannah.

Martin opens the front door and is surprised to see Fabien standing there, bedraggled and out of breath.

'Martin, hello. Um, I'm sorry to disturb you.'

'Come in, I hadn't realised it had started raining.'

Fabien looks puzzled, glances down at himself. 'Ah, yes, it's stopped now.'

'Did you run all the way up the hill? No wonder you're breathless. Where's the car?'

'Wouldn't start. Temperamental sometimes. I must look such a state. I came to see Mila.'

'At this time?'

'Um, yes. Sorry. I do apologise, Martin. Her phone is off, and, well, there's something I just needed to ask her, you see. When the car wouldn't start, rather than trying to fix it, I thought I'd walk over; some night air can do one the world of good. I got caught out in the downpour, so I ran the last bit.'

'What's going on? Fabien? Are you all right? You look terrible.' Chloe stands at the top of the staircase.

Susannah has suddenly appeared behind her husband. 'Fetch him a towel, Chloe, and knock on Mila's door.'

Chloe scowls, and flounces away. They hear her knock and call Mila's name, and then slam her own bedroom door shut.

Mila doesn't come.

Fabien, Martin, and Susannah stand awkwardly for a moment.

'So,' Martin says, 'how are things?'

'Martin, be sensitive, for goodness' sake,' his wife scolds.

'Oh no, that's all right. Been better, you know?'

'I'm sure it will all be ironed out, eh?' Martin says. 'Mila!' he shouts up the stairs, 'Fabien's here.'

'Have you had a falling out, dear?' asks Susannah.

'I'm not sure, actually.'

'Martin, go and tell her to come down. Whatever the issue, there's no excuse for rudeness. She's probably got her earphones in. Tea, Fabien?'

Martin returns to find Susannah watching the kettle boil, and Fabien seated at the table, nibbling at a biscuit he was too polite to refuse.

'She's not there,' he tells them.

'What?' Susannah swivels to face Martin.

'What?' Fabien drops the biscuit on the table, crumbs scattering onto the floor.

'Mila. She's gone.'

CHAPTER TWENTY-FIVE

The young constable manning the small station front desk in a town five miles from the village of Farlington awkwardly knocks on the door of the on-duty sergeant.

'What now, Atkins?'

'It's the Wilson family again, sir. The refugee girl still isn't home. She's been gone all night.'

'As you well know, it is not a missing person inquiry until 72 hours is up. She was last seen yesterday enjoying a family dinner. She's an adult, Atkins, which one day – when you become one too – you will come to understand entitles a person to leave their lodgings without explanation.'

PC Hoppy Atkins blushes, and wonders for the eighteenth time that week why DS Griffin Grant hates him so much. Atkins was top of his class. He works harder than any of the other new recruits.

'Anything else?'

Atkins is clever, and as there isn't much to do as he sits on the front desk, occasionally providing directions to passers-by, he has been giving the situation some thought since the Wilson family first called as his shift began late last night.

'Sir, with respect...'

'With *respect*? If you had respect, you would not still be letting the goddamned draught into my office.'

Atkins searches within himself, as he has been taught to do in his weekly meditation class, and finds some courage buried beneath a pile of anxiety. He says, 'I believe this warrants an exception, sir. The missing girl is Mila Kiss. She knows no one, her only friend was at the family home when they reported her missing. They have reason to believe she has been spooked into running away as a result of some local disagreement about whether she has the right to be here or not.'

'That village is always having some local disagreement, Atkins. It was only last week that stone-age farmer attacked a gaggle of journos with shit.'

'Of course, sir. However, the missing girl is a temporary refugee, without work or permanent residency as of yet. The family says she may have been upset as there was a paperwork error and they'd been to see the council. Then his Lordship called demanding a meeting about it all. If her paperwork is incorrect, and she has run away, and we don't try to find her before she gets too far, we could find ourselves being questioned later about why a refugee in our community's care, potentially with incorrect paperwork, and missing, is now outside of our ability to process her as per the correct procedures set forth by the Home Office.'

Detective Sergeant Grant finally looks up from his newspaper crossword, and sighs. 'Fine, Atkins, you can take this one. Go now, then toddle off home. Shift's over soon anyway.'

'Just one more thing,' Atkins says, knowing he shouldn't keep it to himself, although he wants to. This really could be a bigger case than Grant thinks it is. Atkins knows how important it is to look at the details, if you want to make detective some day.

'Yes, Columbo?'

'The one friend... It sounds like a romantic relationship, reading between the lines.'

'And?' Grant is losing the will to live.

'It's Fabien Knutsworth. The one being investigated over investments in arms for the very people Mila needed to escape from in the first place.' Atkins places the printouts of the tabloid articles he'd found online during his shift on the desk.

DS Grant looks at the headlines in front of him. 'Oh, for God's sake. We'll take my car.'

Fabien is still in last night's watermarked clothes when he is woken by his phone ringing. It is stuck to his cheek. He hadn't wanted to miss a call from Mila. He wanted to be ready to run to her.

'Ah, Martin, good morning.'

'Sorry to ring so early, Fabien. We couldn't sleep a wink. Mila's not home so we called the station again. This time they're coming. They're on their way. We thought, perhaps, you should be here too. If you don't mind?'

'God yes, of course, I'll come right away.'

'Good lad,' Martin replied, surprising both Fabien and himself with the softness in his tone. 'Did you get a chance to speak to your father when you got home? I'm seeing him later, but I'm beside myself and I tried to call last night, but it was late – of course he didn't answer.'

'Sorry Martin, not a peep from him last night, couldn't get an answer when I knocked and shouted. I tried.' Fabien had not tried. He had no intention of giving his father any more chances to hurt Mila. He had hoped to get to her before the police so much as opened a notebook. Usually, the nearby police treat village complaints as a teacher might treat a squabble amongst infants.

'And you've no idea precisely what information he'd come across regarding Mila's paperwork? It's just that the police will ask.'

'No, sorry, Martin. He only mentioned seeing you about Mila's status. Nothing more.'

He had stared hard at Chloe, who had narrowed her eyes in return when he had said the same to the Wilsons yesterday evening as they sat together, thinking the worst, and telling each other the best-case scenarios. He'd thrown her a quick smile as a last resort, as if to say, *we are the only ones who know; we are a team.* Chloe had said nothing, but had smiled back, looking inappropriately cheerful.

'I know it's barely reasonable at this ridiculous hour, Fabien, but perhaps you should bring your father to the house if he knows something that could help us find Mila. That's all we care about.'

'I'm not sure, Martin. He's been a little under the weather, he doesn't usually rise until much later. I doubt I'll be able to wake him. I...'

A more familiar exasperated tone, usually reserved by Martin for the likes of Fabien, returned. 'Just try, Fabien. For Mila.'

Fabien agrees, hangs up and strips, throwing on the first items he pulls from the wardrobe. Downstairs, he places his still-damp clothes in the machine tucked away in the utility, and then leaves quietly, disturbing no one.

'So, other than the fact that there were discrepancies in the administration surrounding Mila's placement, there have been no other issues since her arrival?' DS Grant asks the group around him. All of them are hunched, sitting too far forward in their chairs.

'No, she seemed happy. She was settling in. Fabien has been a darling, showing her around, taking her out, making her feel at home,' Susannah tells him.

'We've *all* tried to make Mila feel at home,' Chloe adds.

Ignoring her, Grant turns to Fabien. 'Did you argue, Mr Knutsworth?'

'No, Officer.'

'She didn't know about this?' Grant looks at Atkins, who retrieves the printouts from his jacket pocket, unfolding them meticulously.

'Do hurry, Atkins,' Grant snaps.

Atkins lays them out on the table, facing Fabien. The others shuffle closer and peer. Fabien straightens, and puts on the face he believes has the most authority when dealing with low-ranking jobsworths he has always been taught are beneath him. But before he can respond, Susannah grabs the papers, and refolds them.

'Really, Detective. We all know what Fabien and his family are going through; there's no need at such an upsetting time to confront the boy with such hurtful vitriol. The whole family, the whole village, in fact, is certain it will all be put straight.'

'Mrs Wilson,' Atkins says, to everyone's surprise as it is the first word he has uttered since entering the house twenty-five minutes ago. 'We do not mean to be insensitive, however, we are concerned that there could be a connection between Ms Kiss' decision to leave, taking all her things, and these... investigations into her romantic partner.'

Chloe laughs at Atkins' turn of phrase. Her mother takes a firm hold of her hand, and she swallows the laugh back down.

Atkins continues. 'That, combined with her fear of being

sent away, if the errors in the official documentation proved irreconcilable with the immigration procedures in place for the Homes for Refugee Programme, could mean she has reason not just to leave, but to stay hidden for the foreseeable.'

'What PC Atkins is trying to say,' Grant interrupts, 'is, do you think Mila was scared? Of what you might find out, perhaps, or of what her boyfriend was involved in? Or some sort of combination of the two?'

'Now, you look here!' shouts Fabien. 'Mila and I are in love, she knows I would protect her! I promised.'

'And yet,' Grant retorts, a smirk taking shape; he's always hated these privileged toffs, and has enjoyed the recent tabloid scandal around their own local blue blood, 'here we are.'

'Excuse me, officers, could we perhaps return to Mila, and how we might start a search?' Martin looks at his watch. 'I must leave to catch the London train in a few minutes.'

'Martin! You can't be thinking you'll still go at a time like this?'

'Darling, I don't see there's much we can do once we have briefed the police. I still fully suspect that she won't have gone far. After all, where would she go? I'm sure these fine officers won't take long to track her down, with all their CCTV and tactics, Right DS Grant?'

'Well, um,' Atkins begins trying to think if they have any working CCTV around here, before a fierce and short *"Ahem!"* from Grant persuades him to close his mouth and return his gaze to the notes on his screen.

'First, we will establish the facts in the lead-up, which will help us consider Mila's likely next movements,' Grant ticks off his index finger, and moves on to his middle finger. 'Next, we will–'

Fabien jumps out of his seat as his phone rings loudly. 'I must get this; it could be Mila!'

It isn't Mila.

'Mother?'

Fabien listens for a moment; the room is silent. His face goes white, and he falls back into his chair, whispering into the phone, 'I'm coming now,' before it falls from his hand.

His eyes close, as he quietly says to the assembled company, 'My father is dead.'

CHAPTER TWENTY-SIX

DS Grant and PC Atkins scramble to follow Fabien, who upon being released from the back seat of the panda sprinted straight up the steps calling for his mother, his sister, and even his father.

Grant shouts, breathless as he jogs up the steps, asking everyone to calm down and step away. Though at this point he isn't sure what or who he is protecting. Lord Knutsworth was old and probably indulged in fine wines, port, and brandy. The odd cigar, even. Grant is betting on a heart attack. He will be in bed, no doubt, wearing a smoking jacket. A quick pulse check, then call it in. He'd have to finish interviewing the Wilsons after that, but Atkins can write it up and file it. Grant is planning to go home, make a sausage butty, then climb straight into bed. His wife Sandra will already have left for work, and he looked forward to a few hours' peace and quiet.

'Oh my! You were quick. I only called the station two minutes ago,' Lady Knutsworth says.

'We were in the area. Atkins, call the station, tell them there's no need to dispatch further officers, but make sure a doctor is on the way.'

'Yes, sir.

'Madam, can you tell me what happened, and take me to your husband?'

Lydia falls to her knees and starts to howl.

'Madam, you're soaking wet,' Atkins says, the first to notice.

They help Lydia to her feet, and seat her in a large ornate chair in the hallway. A young woman appears from nowhere with a cup of tea. She is with a scruffy man with dirt under his fingernails, who places a scratchy looking blanket over her shoulders.

'Elodie! Where's Elodie?' Lady Knutsworth cries.

'Mummy!' Elodie runs towards them. Behind her Fabien walks so slowly he is almost still. His face is frozen, a caricature of shock – his jaw low, his mouth the shape of an "O".

Elodie is dripping wet. So is Fabien.

'Where is Lord Knutsworth?' Grant demands.

'Fetch more blankets!' Atkins instructs the man who had brought the first. 'They're all freezing. Quick. And hot tea!'

'Lady Knutsworth,' Grant bends down to eye level, 'we are here to help you. Where is your husband?'

Lydia looked at him. 'He's dead. He's been murdered!'

'Where is he, madam?'

Fabien reaches his mother's side, and puts an arm around his shivering sister. 'He's by the side of the pool.'

'So let me get this straight...' Detective Inspector Cora Payne had arrived with her team, 'your second act, after asking your CID to stand down from a potential murder investigation, was to allow the whole family into a crime scene, to wrangle with the body, and ultimately remove it from the pool?'

'Ma'am, I–'

'And this is before you managed to discover the location of the body yourself. Even though you drove the third contaminating member of the family here, and watched him run off in a direction where we can only assume he believed his father to be.'

'It was me,' Atkins pipes up.

'Nonsense, PC...'

'Atkins, ma'am. I'm new. Based at–'

'PC Atkins, you called the station because you were ordered to. DS Grant, what on earth possessed you?'

'We assumed it was a natural death, ma'am.'

'Assumed? And what does *assume* do?'

Atkins raises his arm halfway as he says, 'It makes an ass out of you and me.'

DI Payne looks at Atkins, takes in his skinny frame, bad haircut, and cheap spectacles, and discovers she likes this odd, straight-forward being.

'Quite, PC Atkins, quite.'

The pool room has been cordoned off, and Lord Knutsworth's body taken away in an ambulance. Grant has been informed that Lady Knutsworth returned home early from a visit to her sister's, and discovered her husband's body, face down in the pool. After trying but failing to drag him out, she called for help. First came the housekeeper, who was nearest, then the gardener who was outside, and finally Elodie who was at the bottom of the drive in the gatehouse, and already running up to the house having heard her mother's screams. Eventually, Fabien succeeded in retrieving his father, and concluded he was very much dead.

'Something doesn't add up,' mutters Atkins in a world of his own, nervously twiddling his thumbs, as they wait to be dismissed.

DS Grant elbows him hard.

DI Payne turns to them both. 'PC Atkins, thank you for your attempt at service, you are now dismissed. You too, Grant. You'll need to write your statements immediately. Leave nothing out, particularly the part where you allowed an already compromised body to be tampered with by three individuals whilst you were both on the scene organising blankets and tea.'

Griffin Grant is finally in bed, sated by a sausage butty, satisfied he has ticked the boxes for the MISPER investigation into Mila Kiss and convinced that the old lord probably fell into the pool drunk, as you do. He'd almost been able to hear the cogs turning in Hoppy's little head as he tried to connect the dots, but Grant had quickly put a stop to that nonsense.

Mila Kiss. Her boyfriend's a dick, her village isn't as inclusive as it likes to think it is, and the poor girl was probably going to be deported back to hell on earth over an administrative error. He looks at the framed photograph on the dresser against the wall – his wife Sandra and their adopted daughter, Taylor. She's a wild thing, had always felt like an outsider, unwanted. She'd just needed love, and they had tried their best. She's twenty-five now, same as Mila Kiss, finding her way in the world.

No wonder Mila ran off. Good luck to her. Sometimes it was better not to interfere.

Cora Payne would interfere. Oh, she had always meddled, played by the book, no stone uncovered. She was the type who would throw the book at the murderess wife for finally snapping and beating her abusive husband to death with a rolling pin. That's how you make Detective Inspector by thirty-three. His way wasn't so thorough, or so meticulous, but it was human.

And that's how you end up still being Detective Sergeant at a neighbourhood station a handful of years before retirement, looking after dipsticks like Hoppy Atkins, whilst your old charges like Cora talk down to you in front of the witnesses, on your own turf.

Still, Atkins would share the rap. They won't get rid of him over something like this, they'll just keep him out of the way, even more than they do already.

DI Cora Payne just has her knickers in a twist because whatever happened to Lord Knutsworth there is going to be press interest, especially given the current mess his son is in, and press interest means the Chief will be breathing down Cora's neck. He may not be the only one getting a dressing down this week, once the story breaks. Which it will.

DS Griffin Grant may not be a trailblazer, or particularly popular, but he is – *usually* – a safe pair of hands. Besides, they're hardly queueing up to run Hipton Town Station. Eleven two-horse villages, and two towns made up of about three streets each. Hardly fast paced, but mercifully quiet.

Grant suspects Atkins imagines he'll find a way to more a more cosmopolitan post soon, though this hiccup may delay his plans.

His mobile rings. Think of the devil. 'What do you want, Atkins? I was just nodding off. Finished our statements?'

'Sorry, sir. Yes, sir.'

'Well. What do you want?'

'It doesn't make sense, sir. Why did Lady Knutsworth tell the operator on 999 that her husband had been murdered? Why assume that, when he could have fallen in, drowned, or had a heart attack? And how did Fabien know where to find him? He didn't stop to ask. Also, according to my notes from earlier regarding Miss Kiss, Mr Wilson had been invited to meet Lord

Knutsworth later today, to discuss information he had about Mila's status, identity, and paperwork. Paperwork she may have been afraid could have her deported.' Grant closes his eyes, but not for peace and sleep as he had hoped, but to process the words and images conjured by Atkins' summary. 'A man's dead, sir, and it would seem there is a motive to want him so.'

CHAPTER TWENTY-SEVEN

Chloe had not reckoned on the strength of Fabien's feelings for Mila. Irritating as that is, at least she is finally gone, unlikely to return, and Lord Gregory is dead, paving the way for Fabien's bright future. As much as Chloe desperately wanted to spill the beans to the police about what she had seen on Facebook, Fabien talked her out of it. He probably hoped he could find Mila before they did.

Earlier that night, when the police were still fobbing them off on the phone, Fabien had eventually left the frantic atmosphere of the Wilsons' kitchen. Soon afterwards, Chloe had quietly left her home, and followed in Fabien's footsteps.

She had jogged to catch up with him, and he had been really quite rude when she called to him.

'What now?' he had barked.

Hurt, Chloe had told him she was just worried about him, and ushered him away from the row of cottages behind them, curtains twitching as usual. They were right outside Councillor Beard's front door, and Jenny, Lottie's mum, was a notorious gossip. The last thing she needed was her parents on her back, like she was fifteen again. Sometimes she regretted coming home at all.

Fabien must have seen the disappointment in her eyes, or more likely, suddenly twigged he needed her on side if Mila's connections were to stay hidden, because he had softened.

'I don't know much, you know? I've told you everything,' Chloe had promised, agreeing to stay quiet, for now.

'I think she'll get in touch when she's ready,' he had told her. 'But raking up gossip on Facebook can't possibly do any good, and if she saw it, she might be afraid to come home altogether.'

Damn right, Chloe had thought. Why on earth would she want to alert anyone to Mila's possible *"connections"* and lead the search party straight to her? The last thing Chloe wanted was for Mila to come back to Farlington.

No, she had thought to herself, best to support Fabien and help him forget all about Mila. This would be something they'd laugh about one day, or better still, completely forget.

Then there was the discovery of the dear dead Lord Knutsworth. You couldn't make it up. Now Fabien would be far too distracted to try and track down Mila's dodgy mates anyway.

Chloe had been looking forward to playing games with Mila, and seeing what she could uncover about the sneaky siren's hidden past, but now, looking at the messages she had sent to Nikolai from her fake Mila account on Facebook, she reconsiders her options. Best to let this line of inquiry go. She deletes the account.

'Anything come in yet?' A.J. asks Nikolai.

Nikolai shakes his head, sadly. He had been so touched that Mila had seen their message and replied. Her response had sounded so grateful for their understanding. She had said she wanted to talk more, to see how they could help one another. Then nothing.

They are sitting in A.J.'s flat. Rain is making a banner for the march they are attending this weekend. Benj is sleeping off a hangover in A.J. and Rain's bed. Apparently, Pops and Bananas are at work, which is news to Nikolai, who hadn't realised any of A.J.'s crew of amateur revolutionaries had day jobs.

Pops works on the front desk in a Travel Lodge, and most unexpectedly, Bananas works in advertising as a *creative*, which sounds very corporate and fancy, and not at all in keeping with Bananas' self-assessment as a *"revolutionary for the modern age with anarchistic tendencies, without being so reductionist as to lose respect for the finer pillars of society, such as equality, and the welfare state."*

A.J. and Rain are on benefits, but as they eloquently point out, they are giving something back by doing so much to improve the world with their hard work protesting against a vast array of social sins.

Benj is always stoned, and Nikolai doesn't like to pry. The boy looks miserable enough as it is, without having to defend his life choices to an old man.

Monty has gone to stay with his dad in Corfu, where they own an enormous villa overlooking the sea. It turns out Monty's impression of an impoverished rake is just a front.

Nikolai likes the gang. Sure, they aren't making much money, but they are passionate. They are going to change the world. Right now, that is what the world needs, rather than people like his snooty son, head in his computers all day long, counting money all night, no doubt.

Nikolai goes over to A.J.'s place a few times a week, while Peter is at work. He always gets home before his son arrives back after office hours, and they are muddling along, although he is still in the dog house for inviting his rebel friends in that one time.

Since then, Nikolai has been keeping his associates out of sight, and is coming to enjoy making his way across town. He walks there, and catches a bus back. Keeping fit at his age is important. He hardly hears from anyone back home, although he has Facebook now. He fears the worst. Old people don't fare well when war rages. They can't access doctors, or grocery stores. That's about ninety percent of his old life. That and cards at the local café-come-bar.

'Let's check again,' says Rain, and she points to the laptop. 'You can log in from here, Nikky.'

Nikolai likes it when Rain calls him Nikky. She is a pretty girl, but her head is in the clouds. She comes and goes, it seems, at all hours. A.J. dotes on her and never asks questions. He's a feminist, apparently. Nikolai worries about the boy.

The laptop lights up and whirrs to life as Rain types in a password and opens up Facebook. Nikolai logs in. The last message is still his response to dear Mila, urging her to provide a telephone number, to visit him, even. That his new friends want to change the world, and will help her.

'Click on her profile,' A.J. tells him, appearing over his shoulder. 'Let's see if she's added anything since last time. Could be a hidden message about what she's doing, and where she is.'

Nikolai does, but nothing happens.

A.J. squats next to Nikolai's chair and takes the mouse. He tries. Nothing.

'Her name is greyed out on the message, see?'

Squinting, Nikolai does see.

Rain comes over, and looks over both men's shoulders. 'She's deleted her profile. She's disappeared.'

CHAPTER TWENTY-EIGHT

Lord Gregory Knutsworth lies peacefully in a drawer waiting to be dissected, and for the truth about his untimely death to be discovered. His wife is being comforted by his daughter in the gatehouse, while crime scene investigators comb the sprawling house. His son is in an interview room. Behind the wall, looking at a screen, watching Fabien fidget, his eyes red, is DI Payne.

DS Grant and PC Atkins sit opposite the young man. DI Cora Payne holds her breath, waiting for the hapless duo to mess it up. Atkins has made some solid points already, his insights his own, his boss surly, throwing daggers with his eyes as Atkins piped up.

As Senior Investigating Officer, Payne does not relish the thought of this small-town team in the middle of something that has the potential to be blown up in the media and then in their faces. Dead aristocracy, missing refugee girls with something to hide, all right in the centre of a financial-slash-weapons scandal involving the already over-photographed and reported-on prodigal son.

But they are understaffed, there is no real evidence to suggest any link between Fabien's case and the other two potential crimes, and so the Chief wants it all quickly wrapped up and put to bed. Old man dies, young woman decides to move away. The money case is well out of their small-town jurisdiction. Resources are scarce.

Atkins seems to see something Grant doesn't. But then Grant has always been a lazy officer, keen to look the other way. She despises that sort of lack of conscientiousness. They owe more to the people who pay their wages.

Cora Payne's instincts tell her there isn't a link between the cases, and her instincts are more often than not spot on. But, what if the funny little man with his obsessive note-taking and unsolicited meditation tips is right? It's their duty to investigate, and she can't ignore the timing of Mila's disappearance, nor her apparent reasons for doing so. She doesn't have a choice of team; this isn't school netball. Atkins and Grant will have to do the grunt work. She will make the decisions. They are to do nothing without her express permission. They are to be, above all, sensitive, and careful. They are dealing with some powerful people here, and some highly contentious issues.

She watches as DS Grant turns on the machine, and announces those present. 'Please say your name for the tape.'

Fabien Knutsworth does as he is asked, without looking up.

'And you do not wish to have legal representation present?'

At that, Fabien looks up. 'Why? We're here to talk about Mila. Has something happened to her? What do you know?'

Smart, thinks DI Cora Payne. The young man looks genuinely bewildered, boyish, even.

'We haven't heard from Mila, but we hope you can shed some more light on that, given recent developments. We are interested in what happened to your father.'

Fabien looks blankly back at the two officers. 'I thought this was about Mila. My father's death has nothing to do with that. It was an accident, surely?'

'Was it?' Grant asks.

'I thought so. There was no one else there. No forced entry.'

Grant makes a *hmm* sound, and clicks his pen. Atkins is furiously making notes on his screen, and Fabien raises his eyebrows at the officers before him.

'Fabien, your father requested a meeting to discuss Mila's refugee status, and whether she had a right to be here in this country, with her hosts Mr and Mrs Wilson. He believed her paperwork was not in order. He had told Mr Wilson he had new, *"pertinent"* information.' Fabien returns his gaze to the cigarette burn on the cheap old desk between them. 'We are trying to ascertain if your father's death was naturally caused, or an accident. Or if perhaps someone had reason to want to end his life by force.'

'I beg your pardon?'

'Why did your mother assume Lord Knutsworth was murdered?' Atkins interjects.

Cora Payne straightens. Did young Hoppy Atkins have a strategy, or was he just curious, not considering how to drip feed their insights?

'Your mother's 999 call. She told the operator she believed her husband had been murdered when she found him in the pool. Why go straight to murder, not, say, drowning?'

Now DS Grant is fidgeting. Where is Hoppy going with this?

'I'm afraid asking anyone to decipher my mother's thought processes would be quite unreasonable, but as you do, my suggestion is this. He was fully clothed. It didn't look natural. Besides, he doesn't like to swim, usually. The pool is my mother's really, and mine and Elodie's. I think she must have been in shock. I think we all still are. My mother is dramatic at the best of times.'

Fabien suddenly appears to be more together. Grant doesn't

like it. They want him on the back foot. To slip up and tell them something, anything. From his perspective, if it does turn out to be foul play, then hopefully they can nail this on Fabien and the poor girl can get a clean break. They would soon forget her. Men like Fabien always think they can get away with whatever they want.

'You seem very calm,' Grant comments.

'I am trying, in difficult circumstances,' Fabien replies, knowing his cool exterior does him no favours, and yet unable to unlearn the buttoned-up dignity he has been tutored in since he was a boy.

'Strange though, isn't it?' muses Atkins, who seems to be enjoying himself now, building in confidence, and sitting up straighter. He taps his stylus, knowingly, then refers back to his notes, which are vast, and so it takes a few seconds to scroll.

Grant clears his throat. Payne is ready to knock on the door, and call an end to this charade. She *knew* they would bugger it up.

'Your mother told us about the inheritance,' Atkins says quietly.

In the control room still, Payne turns back to the screen. Grant swallows the words he has started to form in his throat, ready to silence his junior officer.

'She told the 999 operator it was murder, something she repeated to us at the scene, and then when asked why she had returned at such an early hour when she wasn't due back until later that morning, she told us she came back because she was worried about you. She believed her husband wouldn't wait to tell you his decision to cut you off, and to pursue the issues around Mila, despite her pleading with him to talk with her on her return first. She made it very clear, Fabien, that she was worried about how you might react, and what you might do.'

'I think I would like to call my lawyer now.'

'Yes, that's a good idea,' says Atkins, 'because it rather sounds like your mother has stitched you right up.'

Payne lets out a laugh. The clever little sod is playing at divide and conquer.

Payne, Grant and Atkins are just pulling on their jackets, and emptying their lockers, patting Atkins on the back. Whether his theory is right or wrong, his strategy is solid. The family has secrets, and this is a sure-fire way to uncover them. Whatever the post-mortem results, everyone on the case agrees something doesn't add up.

'Ma'am!' A young face appears around the doorway, 'Someone's out front to see you.'

'Take a message, Helen,' Payne tells the young officer on front desk duty for the evening. 'I'm buying these two reprobates a pint tonight.'

Griffin Grant smiles and shrugs; what can you do, surrounded by overly keen youth, but go with the flow? Hoppy Atkins may not be a full shilling half the time, but his brain works differently, and Grant thinks Payne needs someone like him to tear a few pages out of the book every now and again.

'Sorry, ma'am, I did tell her that, but she was quite insistent. She says she has information about the whereabouts of Mila Kiss.'

The three police officers put down their things and follow PC Helen Phillips. She smiles apologetically at Hoppy. They'd trained together, and although they hadn't talked much, they sympathised with each other quietly. Both awkward, both top of the class, neither well-liked. Hoppy is smitten.

'DI Payne,' Cora says to the girl. She hasn't seen her before. 'And this is DS Grant, and PC Atkins.'

'My name is Lottie Beard, and I should have come earlier. I think I know where Mila is.'

And with that, she bursts into tears.

Lottie hasn't planned to get anyone in trouble, certainly not to say anything about seeing Chloe and Fabien beneath her bedroom window in Rose Cottage the night of the possible murder, but PC Atkins is a conversational wizard. She gets all confused and ends up spilling all the jumbled thoughts in her young mind, in no particular order.

'Right then,' says Grant.

'Right then,' says Atkins.

'Well, well, well,' says Payne, 'we had better speak to Chloe again. We'll find out who Mila's Facebook friends are, and that should lead us straight to her. In the meantime, I'd like to know what young Chloe and Fabien were doing together late at night, halfway between their respective homes outside Rose Cottage, on the night of Lord Knutsworth's death.'

CHAPTER TWENTY-NINE

Mila disembarks the train at Manchester Victoria station. She has only her rucksack containing the items she arrived with a few weeks ago. She wears the same jeans and hoodie, clumpy boots grounding her. The slip of paper Nikolai gave her is in her pocket.

The phone lies discarded in a bin. She briefly turned it on, saw Fabien's messages. The last text had read:

> He knows your real name; please get in touch and let me help.

Fabien has betrayed her and now she will have them after her. She must find Xristina before it is too late: for her, and for the children.

Her hair is dirty and she is cold, because whilst the summer days and early evenings in Lancashire have been surprisingly warm, when the darkness comes, the chill descends, and the minutes go very slowly.

Mila stayed the night in an old fisherman's hut Fabien had pointed out as he relayed his family's history and talked of the beauty of his home village. At dawn, she had taken the direct footpath over the fields back to the village railway station, too early even for dog walkers, avoiding the main paths and roads, passing no houses until she emerged from the alleyway by the church, and watched for the train arriving, hidden around the corner, not wanting to spend a moment more than necessary on the platform where she might be seen.

She had bought her ticket from the rusty old machine in the corner. One or two early birds were commuting, but she didn't recognise them. Given that she was recent village news, she kept her head down all the same. They didn't look up from their phones. They wouldn't be looking for her yet, Mila had thought. They wouldn't even know she was gone until later that morning.

From the map of multi-coloured lines representing the rail services in the small village station, she had worked out that to get to Alderley Edge she would need to change at Manchester. Now she is here, she realises that the train to Nikolai's son's house departs from Manchester Piccadilly, which is actually across the city and not accurately represented by the connecting lines on the train station wall back in Farlington. There are trams, but they are confusing, and the train station is full of people jostling and swearing and drinking from paper cups.

Mila decides to walk. She checks the map of the city, makes a mental note and closes her eyes. The image of the mess of streets dances on her inner lids. She buys a coffee and borrows a pen. She uses the napkin she takes from the counter to draw her route to the station.

Even with the map, the busy city centre is an attack on all her senses. Her own city never overwhelmed her; it was a blanket, her family and friends and familiar cafés and bars its beating heart, its air, and its soul. There are smells of grease emitting from little burgundy trailers offering fried sausages and bacon. Buskers are already playing their hearts out. A woman with a pram almost runs her over. A cyclist on a pedestrian shop-lined street does the same. Men in doorways sleep on cardboard in tattered sleeping bags marred with dirt. Their early rising friends drink lager from cans and put out their hands as she passes, not bothering to ask for change. No point.

She pulls her hood lower, and walks a little faster.

Men and women in expensive looking shoes overtake her, talking into their phones, or tutting about the speed of the person in front of them. All around her, people vape fruity flavours of toxic smoke, making her cough.

Mila needs to know exactly where she is going when she alights at Alderley Edge. She needs to be somewhere safe. She stops suddenly, and a body bumps into hers. 'For fuck's sake,' it says as it brushes past, not looking back.

She scans the street, walking slowly now as she does so. She sees police heading towards her. She lowers her head once more. They walk straight past. Looking up, she spots it almost immediately: an internet café. Thank goodness they still exist in cities, though why, Mila does not know as surely she is the only person in the whole city without a smartphone attached to the end of her arm.

The computer whirrs as she types in the address, and finally a map and directions appear. Nikolai's son's house is, if the satellite pictures are to be believed, a modern mansion on the edge of town surrounded by green fields. Apparently this disappointing, geeky son of old Nikolai's hasn't done so badly for himself after all.

'Bloody hell, sir, this isn't bad for a war refugee. I'm sure on that video clip of the protest his trousers were tied with string.'

'It belongs to his son. Mr Peter...' DS Griffin Grant flips open his pad, 'Peter Popov.'

'As in Peter Popov, the tech prodigy college kid?' PC Hoppy Atkins has frozen, hand ready to press the intercom bell at the huge wrought iron gates, flanked by imposing red brick pillars, each topped with a stone statue of a small bird.

'Um...'

'He invented AnswerApp when he was still in university. He was in every magazine when he sold it for several million pounds a few years later.'

'Every magazine?'

'Well, the ones about technology.'

'Never heard of AnswerApp. Guess it flopped, did it?'

'It was an unprecedented success among early adopters.'

'Are you an early adopter, Hoppy?'

'I like to think so, sir. My brother keeps me up to date; he's a computer genius too, apparently.'

'Then what?'

'He moved to Silicon Valley, doesn't even come home for Christmas. Breaks Mother's heart.'

'I mean, then what with Popov's app.'

'Oh. Nothing – the app was sold, taken down and rebuilt bigger by whoever bought it, and Peter Popov disappeared from mainstream public life. I think I heard he invests in start-ups now. He keeps a low profile, but the few snippets I've read online suggest he's a bit of a Robin Hood of the tech community. Invests in tech that changes the world, but takes no public credit, and moves on. You think it's him?' Hoppy Atkins has the crazed look of a teenage girl about to meet her favourite singer from a boyband.

'Not a particularly common name, and with a house like this, guess it probably is your man.' Grant sighs, and presses the buzzer. 'Atkins, did you just do a little skip?'

'Yes?' says a polite disembodied voice, through the speaker on the gate.

'DS Grant and PC Atkins. Could we come in?'

The gate opens without another word.

Nikolai is hunched in his chair, his eyes low, his mouth sullen.

'Papa, how could you? I told you those people were trouble. I begged you not to bring it to my door.'

'They're my friends. They just want to find Mila.'

'You're sure you haven't seen her?' Grant gently prompts.

'She didn't come.' The old man looks like he may cry.

'So,' Atkins says, scrolling through the endless notes he has made in the last thirty minutes while sipping expensive smelling coffee in Peter's pristine kitchen, 'you met Mila on the plane by chance, but did not swap details.' Nikolai nods and swallows, just a little half lie. After all, she didn't give him hers. 'You then hoped to make contact, and your new friends helped you write a message on Facebook. You believed she might have been involved in CC back in your home country, because, as you say, *"She seemed the type."* What do you mean by that?'

'Ah, she's young, feisty, they're all part of little offshoot groups like that. Harmless. Young, political, it's natural.' No chance of mentioning the news article back home; the poor girl is clearly in enough trouble.

'And you mentioned it in the message because...?'

'I'm an ancient old man. I thought if she knew I was interested in the same things, and had young friends also interested in the same things, she would be more likely to reach out.'

'Why were you so keen for her to reach out, Mr Popov? Did

you think she was in trouble? Did she say something to you to suggest that she was?'

'No, no, no, I just think we need to stick together. She has no one from home to talk to. She needs to be with her own kin.'

'Right,' interjects Grant, 'so, you simply want to help a young girl, who is alone. You send out a post on Facebook with her name, and it seems she stumbles across it, and responds.'

'Then nothing. Account deleted, just like that.'

'We have reason to believe her so-called friends from the village she was staying in may have written that message, in a bid to find out more about her. They've admitted as much. Mila, according to them, doesn't use any form of social media. They thought it strange, especially what with the talk of her paperwork not being accurate, that a young woman would want to be so invisible on the channels they all seemingly cannot live without.'

'Hold on,' Peter says, in his polished, clipped accent, not a trace of home, or even of Cheshire, 'you're here to question my father about a missing girl because she corresponded with him on Facebook, except she didn't, and so there is no reason to suspect she would be here at all?'

'As far as we can tell, Nikolai is the only person Mila knows in the UK outside of Farlington. Given that Mr Popov was actively looking for her, we needed to follow up. She disappeared the night a member of our community died, just before he had a chance to share new information he had about Ms Kiss' identity.'

'You want to question her about a murder?' Peter asks with despair, mainly aimed at his troublesome father and his ridiculous friends, who have embroiled their household in some kind of village farce.

'We aren't ruling anything out until after the post-mortem. But she knew the family. So–'

'Frankly, Detective, this is absurd,' Peter interrupts. 'You don't seem to have a single crime on your books, and yet you are in my home upsetting an old, displaced man, on the basis that he was on the same evacuation flight as a girl your community has harassed out of the village, with most likely no real basis other than bureaucracy and bigotry.'

Nikolai nods furiously. 'Yes, quite right. Poor girl. It's very hard for me,' he sniffs dramatically and blows his nose into a crumpled hanky from his pocket.

'We are very sorry for the loss of your community member, and sad to hear a young woman has been forced to flee for the second time in weeks, although this time due to administration failures rather than bombs. We hope very much that both matters may be resolved satisfactorily. May I see you out?'

Grant stands, and Atkins follows. 'Please,' he addresses Nikolai, 'if she does contact you, let us know. You may think you're protecting her, but if she is running from something, we are in a better position to help her.'

'Of course.' Peter shakes his head in his father's direction, as Nikolia looks like he might want to add something.

'If we find her, we can get to the bottom of this so-called mix-up, and she may be able to help us with our other investigations.'

'I'll be in touch if we hear from her,' Peter says, taking DS Grant's card, and walking towards the entrance hall.

Nikolai looks around the vast empty kitchen. Where are you, Mila Kiss?

He hears voices down the hall, his son's irate, the gruff older fella's pompous, and what seems to be some odd high-pitched questions from the younger one.

Getting up slowly, knees creaking, Nikolai wanders over to the French doors and stares out onto the manicured garden. He opens the doors and steps out into the cooling air, taking a deep breath and exhaling slowly as his heartbeat starts to slow.

'Nikolai,' says a voice.

He turns and walks along the side of the house, peering around the corner as he hears the front gates clunk shut and the roar of an engine starting in the distance.

And there she is: Mila Kiss.

CHAPTER THIRTY

'It was Fabien. He told me to lie,' says Chloe, arms folded across the desk in the shabby interview room, facing Atkins and Grant.

The police officers say nothing, and wait patiently.

Chloe continues, 'Everyone suspected Mila was up to no good. She wasn't who she was supposed to be. She was secretive. I was just looking out for my family, my community. I just searched online. That's not a crime.'

'Though posing as another person might be, in the right circumstances.'

Chloe glares at Grant. 'I wasn't *posing*, I was *investigating*. I was trying to find out who she was, and if I just asked her, I knew she'd lie. She might even have run.'

'She *has* run,' points out Atkins.

'Well, yes, because clearly I was on to something.'

'So, you told Lord Knutsworth, who then contacted the Wilsons. You told him she was connected to terrorist groups at home and in the UK. If that's what you believed, why didn't you tell your own parents at this point?'

'They wouldn't have listened to me. They don't take me seriously.'

'So, nothing to do with the fact that Lord Knutsworth might have influence over his son's relationship with Mila? I believe you have a history with Fabien?'

'Oh, for God's sake! I expect Lottie told you that, and now you think I'm jealous of Mila too? I wish I'd never come back to this small-minded little hole.'

'Why didn't you tell us about the Facebook interaction? Perhaps we could have helped.'

'I told you! Fabien told me to keep quiet. He didn't think she'd come home if it all got out.'

'And you were as keen for her return as Fabien, I suppose.' Grant raises an eyebrow at the young woman, pouting and angry before him. She has been seen running home on the night of the lord's death, after a whispered rendezvous with Fabien in a dark corner of the village, beneath Lottie's window. She has lied.

It's possible she and Fabien decided to get rid of Lord Knutsworth. That was one of the lines he and Atkins were pursuing: Fabien to secure his inheritance, and Chloe to secure Fabien. Once Mila had run, the coast was clear for Chloe – she could have her parents and Fabien all to herself, and Lord Knutsworth would no longer be a problem.

But Grant doesn't think Chloe is guilty of anything more than being a total, utter, brat.

'It's Fabien you should be talking to,' she replies, examining her nails, an air of feigned nonchalance. 'And if this really is an *"informal chat"* I'd like to go home now.'

Fabien looks up as the door to his interview room opens. Harrop, the family solicitor, rises and introduces himself.

'Sorry to keep you waiting, Mr Knutsworth,' says DS Grant.

'Lord,' corrects Harrop.

'Excuse me?' Grant says.

Atkins jumps in to help clarify. 'As Lord Gregory Knutsworth has sadly passed away, his son is now the Lord of Farlington, namely Lord Knutsworth, which means he should be addressed in speech with his title. Now, sir, it would have been a courtesy to refer to him as lord prior to his father's death in speech as the heir apparent, though you would have suffixed this with his Christian name rather than his surname.' Atkins stops reading the Wikipedia article, and looks up from his beloved Android tablet.

'Thank you, Atkins, that will do,' Grant begins again. 'Lord Knutsworth...'

'Fabien is fine, Detective Sergeant, we are all friends here,' Fabien says.

Grant swallows his irritation, and takes a breath. 'Fabien, there has been a development. Atkins?' he instructs.

Atkins clears his throat. 'Your father had bruising to his arms and back, as well as a small cut on the back of his head. It appears that these injuries were caused *prior* to him falling into the pool. The water damage has not made life easy, Lord Knutsworth. We still await the full post-mortem results to establish the cause of death.'

'Fabien, please.'

'Fabien, perhaps you are experiencing shock; it's a lot to take in.'

'No, PC Atkins. I am sad, I am grieving, but I am no longer shocked that my father died. I found him in the pool, and never once suspected it was murder.'

'Do you have any thoughts about how your father may have sustained injuries the day of his death?'

'No,' Fabien says.

'I don't believe it is Lord Knutsworth's job to speculate on such things. My dear late client could have sustained those injuries in any number of ways, given his country pursuits,' Harrop says.

'He rides... *rode* most afternoons,' Fabien informs them. Grant thinks he spots the beginnings of a smug smirk, but it vanishes before he can fully register it.

'Time of death is to be confirmed, but our timeline suggests it was between seven and ten pm. You were seen by staff entering the study at around 6.45pm.'

'I left my father in good health.'

'Did you argue about your inheritance? Or Mila, perhaps?' Fabien narrows his eyes. 'We know that you were well aware that Chloe Wilson had information that you believed could hurt Mila, otherwise why ask her to keep quiet? And I suspect you knew that your father was also privy to this information, and due to pass it on to the Wilsons.'

'We had words, but that is all, officers.'

'And then you went to the Wilsons.'

'Yes, and Mila was gone.'

'You were wet.'

'Sorry?'

'Mr Wilson recalls you were soaking wet when you arrived.'

'It was raining.'

'You hadn't been in the pool area at all that day?'

'DS Grant,' interjects Harrop, 'may I politely suggest you reign in your young PC? I can see where he is going, but it really makes very little sense. Surely you don't mean to insinuate that Lord Knutsworth was wet from being in the pool but didn't think to change before leaving the house?'

'Atkins, let's move on from this,' Grant tells his junior, 'though we would have liked to see those clothes, Mr Harrop, Lord Knutsworth. It's a shame you washed them, and it then turned out that you – being a washing novice – shrunk them, and disposed of them. Why didn't you leave them for Anna?'

'I'm not in the habit of making any more work for the house staff than I have to,' Fabien tells him. 'We are not all the same, despite your quite obvious prejudice.'

'Could you tell us about your movements that morning?' Atkins continues.

'I was woken early by the telephone, summoned to meet with the two of you at Low Beck Barn. I was there by eight. While I was there, my mother called me in a dreadful state, and you drove me back to the house.'

'Mr Wilson says he asked you to wake your father and bring him along. He believed he might be able to help. You said you would try to wake him, but you didn't. Couldn't have done. If you had, you would have discovered him to be dead. Why did you lie?'

'My father had issues with Mila, as you well know. He had... unevolved beliefs about immigration at the best of times. I didn't think, despite Mr Wilson's insistence, that he would be any help at all, and I felt he would in fact only upset the family further. He was mixed up, mainly due to Chloe's nonsense, again, which I'm sure you're well aware of.'

'Nonsense?'

'I believe so, yes.'

'So, you didn't fail to try to wake your father because you already knew he was dead?'

'No, no.' Fabien shakes his head.

'Be careful,' Harrop tells him. 'My client is grieving, and has not been charged with any crime, because you have no evidence at all to suggest it was anything other than a natural death. He is here to assist, not to be slandered.'

'Was he usually in the pool room at night, your father?'

'Occasionally.'

'And you have no idea how he sustained a cut to the head and bruising. He didn't mention it when you saw him?'

'Um, no.' Fabien looks slightly less sure of himself, for the first time during the interview.

'We wonder why he might have been swimming, fully clothed, at bedtime,' states Atkins, swiping away at something on his screen, using his stylus to make yet another note.

'I can't explain his bruising. He's clumsy, he rides, he rambles through the woods on the estate regularly, dodging branches. I doubt he meant to swim at all, PC Atkins, though he did sometimes sit beneath the tropical plants, and read a paper. He and Elodie talked there and played Scrabble at the little table occasionally. She used to love it in there as a girl, and he would always let her win.' Fabien smiles at the memory. 'He wasn't usually found wandering around the pool at night alone, as far as I've ever known, but people break habits; perhaps he couldn't sleep.'

'On account of your fight?' interjects Grant.

'Disagreement, Detective. Words, that's all. But yes, he may have felt unsettled, guilty, anxious about my mother's opinion on the matter. Who knows what he was thinking?'

'How did you know to run straight to the pool room when we arrived? Odd choice.'

'I shouted as I entered the hall, and my mother ran towards me from that direction – dripping wet – where she had found him. Have you spoken to her yet?'

'It's outrageous. The grieving widow, in a cell! I won't say a word until my lawyer arrives. And where's that tea I was promised?' Lady Knutsworth is red-eyed and tight lipped.

'You aren't being formally questioned, and this is an

interview room, not a cell,' DS Grant informs the woman fidgeting and sighing across the table from him. He adds, for good measure, 'Lady Knutsworth,' and to his own annoyance bows his head a little.

Atkin nods in satisfaction at his boss' correct terminology. He had explained in great detail that the dowager retained her title and should still be referred to as lady in speech as a courtesy, unless she chose to remarry. Atkins loves to learn, and finds being absolutely correct the most satisfying way to be in life.

'We can wait until your solicitor arrives, but I believe he's just on a call to his office. Really, Lady Knutsworth, we just want to clear up a few things so that we can leave you in peace.'

'Fine.'

'You returned earlier than planned, from visiting your sister. What time exactly?'

'I don't remember. I couldn't sleep with worry about Gregory's ongoing arguments with Fabien over his business, his girlfriend, the estate. It was all such a mess, and Gregory was so very upset when I spoke to him earlier in the day. I was tossing and turning. I got up, the dawn was not yet broken. I drove home.'

'And none of the staff, or your daughter, were present when you arrived home?'

'The staff live in converted housing around the back. Elodie sleeps like the dead,' she replies, and then crumples. 'Oh, my darling Gregory is dead!'

Atkins passes her a tissue, which she takes, dabs her eyes, and quickly recomposes herself.

'And you went straight to the pool?'

'Of course not! I went to my husband's bedroom. He wasn't there, so I wandered round the house. Sometimes he sits in the pool room to read. I found him there.' Lady Knutsworth starts to cry.

'What do *you* think happened, Lady Knutsworth?'

'When I saw him there, clothed, face down in the pool, I thought our worst nightmares had come true. Intruders, and my darling husband, trying to fight them off.'

'In the pool room? Do you keep many valuables in there?'

'No, but it is at the back of the house, and one could perhaps smash the glass walls to get in without disturbing the rest of the house. I often thought how vulnerable I felt when swimming alone there at night.'

'No windows or glass doors were broken when you found him.'

'No, now I see I panicked, jumped to silly conclusions. He must have slipped and drowned. Though I don't know how he could have drowned. He was no Olympic medallist, but he could swim. For heaven's sake, why didn't my dear Gregory just stand up and get out? He was fit as a fiddle.'

Atkins and Grant share a look. They have been wondering the same thing.

CHAPTER THIRTY-ONE

Mila sips her peppermint tea as Peter looks at the images on the kitchen table. The lid of the tin box lies open.

'I thought my sister was weak,' Mila, formally Sofia, explains. 'I didn't blame her. She had only wanted a normal life. Janos was a bully, powerful and adored. I thought she couldn't fight him, that she was stuck. Then all this time, it turns out she had a plan. Plans much greater than mine. She told me only days earlier, showed me where she hid the tin. She knew the risks she was taking. I had no choice but to finish it for her. It's what she wanted, if the worst happened.'

The photocopied images are of Janos, some more grainy than others, meeting with the enemy.

'He was a spy, Mila? Sorry, Sofia,' Peter says.

'Stick with Mila for now; that's who I am now. It's safer, it's Sofia they are looking for. But yes, according to the letter his ex-wife Xristina sent to my sister, he has been for decades, his whole *distinguished* military career.' Mila takes the letter from the tin box, and pushes it towards Peter, who starts to read.

'Wow,' Peter says, allowing Nikolai to take the letter from him as he finishes, 'this is bigger than your bully Janos, this is widespread corruption. Big business, international connections. Pockets lined, wars started, innocent dead, and for a few to become rich and powerful. It makes me sick.'

'My sister was coming here, to find Xristina, to help put the case together. To make a safe life. At first, she just told me she was coming as a refugee, then she told me Xristina had been in touch. She said important papers were hidden beneath the loose floorboard, beneath the chair. But she didn't tell me everything. She was protecting me, making sure I didn't know anything when she left me behind, to keep me safe. I thought I was the brave one, that it was me who would protect *her*.'

'She was your big sister,' Nikolai gently tells her. 'She didn't want to burden you with all this.' Nikolai gestures to the papers all over the table. The copies of evidence collected by Xristina, and her son Anton, who's Janos' son too.

'I have to finish what she started. Janos killed her rather than letting her and the children leave.'

'Your nephew and niece?' Peter asks.

'Konstantine and Karlie. They're so lovely, so young,' Mila sniffs, eyes watering. 'Innocent. I can't leave them with him. He must have known she had something, somehow. He will have guessed I have it now. He's behind the witch hunt.'

'We must help Mila, Peter.' Nikolai is distraught. 'We must hide her, send all of this to the police anonymously, the papers. A.J. can help, I'm sure.'

'No, Papa. A.J. cannot help. But I can. I think we need to find this Xristina; she has all the originals, and more evidence too, if her letter is accurate. She and her boy Anton are the key.'

'You'll help me? You believe me?' Mila's voice is small, surprised, it breaks on the last word. She's got so used to being alone.

Nikolai looks at his son, eyes wide, mouth open. Peter does

not engage in risky behaviour. Peter doesn't help runaway women accused of murders. Nikolai does not understand.

'Close your mouth, Papa; do not look so surprised. I know you think me a coward, but this is what I do. I mine for information. For people who want to uncover truths, and put right the wrongs of the powerful. This is what I do with my head in my computer all day. I invest in start-ups to keep nosey parkers at bay. The rest of the time I work in intelligence gathering.'

'For the government?'

'No, not really.'

'It's risky?'

'It is. This situation could be very dangerous. We don't yet know where the connections begin and end, and who is involved. It could be limited to the sides involved in the war, or there could be powerful investors across the world. If so, it is possible the police or UK politicians or journalists could try and shut this down, twist it around, and get rid of Xristina and Mila before they have a chance to expose the lies and betrayals at the centre of all of this.' Nikolai feels a rare surge of pride for his son, so overwhelming it makes him dizzy. 'Mila,' Peter's voice softens, 'I do believe you, and I'll help you because it is the right thing to do, for you – to clear your name, for your niece and nephew, for your sister's memory. But most of all, for our country – our values, our whole upside-down messed-up world. Crooks like Janos have been slowly chipping away at its very fabric for decades. This runs deep and has been orchestrated from on high. I've been monitoring traitors and their cronies and money men over the years for different clients across multiple countries and wars and scandals – good people, usually, trying to expose the bad ones – as I say, mining for information. It's partly why, Papa, I prefer not to have young social media mad small-time revolutionaries connected to my personal or business addresses.'

Nikolai colours. 'A.J. is a good boy.'

'Perhaps, Papa. But we need to be under the radar, not living, breathing TikTok memes.' Nikolai doesn't know what TikTok is, and decides not to ask. 'I need to know who may know you're here, Mila, any trace you could have left. The police have already visited once; we may need somewhere else for you to stay, for now.'

Fabien knows she took her sister's name, and he must have told Lord Knutsworth, who was going to tell Mr Wilson, except it turns out he died before he did. From the little the police had said, at least Fabien hadn't disclosed her other secrets to them – yet.

Peter hard-deletes Nikolai's account and messages, but has no doubt the police will check in again. 'They will find the article about the murder with your photograph next to it eventually,' he explains. 'You looked at it, right? On the iPad they lent you?'

Mila nods, sadly. She had thought she was being so careful.

'We do need to think about where you can stay,' Peter says, almost to himself, lost in thought.

'I know!' Nikolai announces. 'And Peter, you may be cleverer than me, and richer than me, and know all about secret conspiracies and plots, which, really you could have shared a little of – it's been tedious living here with you – but that aside *for now,*' Nikolai throws a stern, paternal look at his only son, 'you can hear your old man out. Don't say a word until I've finished. A.J. has–'

'For Christ's sake, Papa!'

'What did I just say? Shush,' Nikolai demands. For once, his son obeys. 'A.J. has a friend. Rich boy, got his own penthouse in the city. Goes by Monty. He doesn't do much, he just likes hanging around the flat pretending he's a normal twenty-something, rather than heir to some household brand I've never heard of. Rain says it gives him a sense of freedom. Done a bit in banking, but Rain reckons he's a creative soul at heart. He smokes an awful lot of weed, so I'm not sure if she's getting the two confused.'

'What do *you* know about weed?'

'Never mind that. His flat is empty. He gave A.J. the key to water his plants.'

'Doesn't he have a concierge to do that?'

'Not these plants, Peter. They're special ones. He only trusts A.J. to do it.'

Peter sighs and Mila laughs despite herself.

'And just for the record, Mila, you didn't kill the old lord, thinking he'd expose you?'

Mila smiles. 'I didn't kill anyone, Peter... but I will get my revenge.'

CHAPTER THIRTY-TWO

'Have you lost your minds?' DI Cora Payne barks before Atkins has closed the office door behind him.

Grant takes a seat. 'You wanted to see us, ma'am?'

'Damn right I do,' she says. 'Atkins, stop loitering, and sit down, please. I take it the post-mortem results are still not back?'

Grant looks at Atkins, who is making a meal of getting seated next to him, smoothing down his trousers and almost dropping his stylus as he gets ready to take whatever notes are necessary.

'No ma'am,' Atkins begins, placing his device in front of him and swiping, tapping, studying the screen intently.

'Put that bloody thing down!' Payne tells him. She closes her eyes, takes a breath, demonstrating the effort required to retain her composure in their presence. 'And have you chased up on the PM? I mean, I know water damage complicates matters, but this is getting ridiculous. In fact, I'll phone them myself.' Payne lifts the receiver, her eyebrows raising too, as PC Atkins goes to speak. Pausing before hitting the numbers, she waits, eyes narrow.

'I did tell Dr Mukherjee it was very urgent and must be prioritised.'

Grant snorts, wondering how the senior pathologist, deeply intelligent and fiercely protective of his domain and processes, might have reacted to a demand from young Hoppy.

'I then chased yesterday, though not today. I was about to, actually, just after I'd—'

'After you'd what, Atkins? After you'd harassed the victim's family playing Poirot, looking for murder and intrigue in the village when we've almost certainly got a natural death on our hands, and all we need is a bit of paper to prove it, but instead I have a strongly worded letter of complaint for Mr Harrop, the solicitor, claiming bias and prejudice and the potential for a claim due to the trauma the Knutsworth family has experienced at the hands of,' Cora Payne pauses as she pulls a typed letter towards her, and reads, 'a shockingly inept force with a complete disregard for protocol and victim support procedures.'

'Are all suspects to be given feedback forms going forward, ma'am? Or just the rich, powerful ones with the ear of the big brass?' Grant asks.

DI Payne suddenly seems very still and the air very cold. Only her eyes move to stonily stare at her irksome detective sergeant.

'I mean,' Grant goes on, seemingly unaware of the building danger, whilst next to him, Atkins gulps for air and wrings his fingers, 'Fabien has motive, clear as day, he had means, and he had opportunity. He'd argued with his father, he had little time to protect his girlfriend's secrets, but most of all, the greedy oaf needed to stop his father from removing him as heir. His mother rushed back in fear of the consequences of her husband disinheriting him. It adds up.'

'Careful, Detective, I'm aware of the facts. Ever heard of the word circumstantial? Also, you seem to have forgotten all about your MISPER case – has either of you made any progress with regards to finding Mila Kiss at all?'

'You can hardly blame the girl for wanting to get away, she was hounded out!'

'Nonsense, Grant. She was looked after, and has bolted for no reason at all, unless of course you look a little closer at her motive, means and opportunity, but that doesn't seem to fit your narrative. This inverted snobbery is exactly the bias Harrop is talking about. And as much as that dreadful little sycophant makes my skin crawl, he has a point: Fabien didn't murder his father in the swimming pool and then stroll to the Wilsons in his wet clothes. It was raining. It isn't beyond possibility that there is foul play, but we have no real evidence of that, and if it *is* foul play, then why aren't we looking at Mila, the girl who disappeared on the night of your alleged murder?'

'Mila doesn't have motive, for Christ's sake. The only secrets that bloody Chloe uncovered were totally insignificant – the apparent terrorist organisation is a perfectly legal lobby group. Mila wouldn't kill to keep that quiet. You know that, Cora!'

'DI Payne or ma'am, if you please, Detective. And perhaps she is hiding something more. By your reasoning, that secret alone wouldn't be enough reason to run, either.'

'DI Payne,' Grant says behind gritted teeth, silently adding, *in the backside,* 'Mila Kiss has lost everything. She is in a strange country where not all have endeavoured to make her feel welcome, while her host's daughter snoops and gossips, and the village conspires to "prove" her paperwork isn't in order. She's terrified of being sent home, but she isn't going to murder for it. She's just hiding, trying to avoid being thrown into a war zone or a no-man's land of bureaucracy and immigration centres.'

'You've a soft spot for that girl, and it could be clouding your judgement.'

'Rubbish,' says Grant, shaking his head, and thinking back to all the times his daughter Taylor had run away from home.

'And what about Lady Knutsworth? Did she have motive and means and opportunity, when she was away visiting her sister in Skipton and weighs about six stone? Why were you harassing the widow, answer me that?'

'We were harassing Lady Knutsworth because–' Atkin starts to say.

'Interviewing, Atkins!'

'Sorry, sir. We were *interviewing* Lady Knutsworth, ma'am, to get her to provide insight as to Fabien's state of mind.'

'I've heard enough.' DI Payne holds up her hand. Grant visualises her as a traffic cop, and smirks. 'What are you smirking at, Grant?' she demands, and then raises her hand once more. 'On second thoughts, don't answer that. Just chase up the PM, and leave the family alone until we have the results – they're not going anywhere. And get to work on finding Mila Kiss.'

'She's innocent,' Grant tells his boss as he stands. 'If we find her, I just hope this bloody system doesn't let her down.'

'Just do what I ask, please.'

'Yes ma'am,' Grant and Atkins say together. Atkins feels part of a team and stands taller as he moves towards Payne's office door. Grant feels exhausted, and just as irritated with his idiot junior as he is with his jumped-up senior.

Atkins pulls the door open, and is confronted with Helen's face inches away from his own, her hand a fist, ready to knock. He jumps back into Grant, who stumbles and swears.

'Yes, PC Phillips?' says Payne.

'We have managed to finally retrieve the search history from the iPad Mila had been using at the Wilsons' house. She'd done a pretty good job of deleting it, mind. The tech guys got there in the end,' Helen spoke in breathy punctuated sentences, blinking nervously, hopping between her feet, like a child in need of a bathroom break.

'And?' Payne prompts.

'Ma'am, she's been looking at a news site from back home. One story in particular, she searches for and finds several times a day.'

'Which is?' Even Atkins is impatient now, despite Helen's dewy skin looking particularly delightful today. Her fieldmouse hair is neat and professional, just lovely.

'A woman with a different name, different coloured hair, but very much the same woman, very much Mila Kiss...'

'Spit it out, Helen, for goodness' sake!' Grant snaps.

'The woman, who looks like Mila Kiss, who the facial recognition program confirms is *our* Mila Kiss, is known in her homeland by the name Sofia Kiss. According to the articles, she is wanted for the murder of her sister: the real Mila Kiss.'

'Still so sure she's innocent, DS Grant?'

CHAPTER THIRTY-THREE

Elodie has called a house meeting in the gatehouse. She has bought lemon slices from the village shop, and dusted off her teapot to avoid any unnecessary words with her mother. She imagines Lydia will, even in her grief, expect tea to be served in the correct fashion.

Fabien sits on the old armchair, torn on the rests, chipped at the feet. Lady Knutsworth perches on the edge of the sofa, pulling the crochet throw from underneath her and discarding it, like the pea in the princess' bed.

'Mummy,' Elodie, who sits on the upright old dining table chair between her remaining close family members, takes her mother's hand, 'I miss him too, we all do.'

Lydia wipes a tear and blows her nose into a floral handkerchief. 'I know, darling.' She places her other hand on top of her daughter's and squeezes. She doesn't catch Fabien's eye.

Fabien stares at the floor, brushing dog hairs from his trouser leg. He notices crumbs on the floor, and the chewed, frayed edge of an antique chair. Evidence of Offal, who is allowed to run wild throughout the gatehouse and all over the furniture, as well as around their land. Elodie always was a softie when it came to dogs.

'Does Anna not clean in here?' he can't help but ask.

'I can manage, I told her not too,' Elodie replies, irritated, but focussed on her peace-making task. 'Listen, Fabien, Mummy was terribly upset when the police started to question her. Of course she wasn't implying you had anything to do with Daddy's tragic death. We all know nobody here could have ever intentionally hurt him.'

'Evidently the police don't agree,' Fabien says. 'How dare they question us in such a manner when they have no reason to? I'm not sure Harrop's letter is enough, we should–'

'Rip them to shreds! Ensure they never work in public office again. Sue them for every penny the little bast–' Lady Knutsworth is starting to get red in the face. She stands and paces to settle her heart rate, idly brushing her hands down the heavy, velvet curtains that are faded with age, inspecting them for dust.

'Mummy, we will seek retribution for the pain they have caused our family. But look here, we are letting them get underneath our skin. Causing rifts when we should be united. We must support one another, and honour Daddy's memory. It is what he would have wanted,' Elodie says.

'I didn't expect my own child to turn on me at such a time. I'm quite heartbroken, dear.' Lydia continues to only address Elodie, as if Fabien isn't less than two feet away in the small living quarters of the gatehouse, crowded with unfinished canvases.

'I think, when Fabien suggested you might be cross with Daddy about his plans to change his will, he only meant to explain why Daddy couldn't sleep and you were home early. I'm sure Fabien, in his own thoughtless, cavalier style,' Elodie risked a subtle glare in her brother's direction, 'was actually trying to demonstrate how the whole awful business made sense just as it was, and they ought to do the right thing and stop digging where there is no dirt, and leave us to organise a proper send-off. Right, Fabien?'

Fabien looks up. 'Right. Yes, indeed. Sorry again, Mother.'

Elodie glances at her mother, who stares resolutely ahead, unblinking. 'Mummy?'

'Yes, Fabien, Elodie is quite correct,' she eventually says, straightening her back, and raising her chin haughtily. 'I was in deep shock and grief, and continue to be.' Lydia retakes her seat, and notices the rug crumpled at her feet. She pulls the tattered antique fabric to straighten it, covering the edges of the ancient priest hole. 'I do so love a priest hole, especially here. Demonstrates the loyalty and morality this family has always exhibited.'

Realising that is the best they will get, the siblings share a rare smile. Elodie takes Fabien's hand. 'So we are agreed. No more in-fighting. Say no more, they will just try and twist it and make a mockery of our family and our way of life. They are prejudiced against us, and can't see beyond their own noses.'

'Well said,' Fabien tells his sister. 'Mr Harrop is coming to the house later to talk through Daddy's wishes and will, and how best to handle my, um, my other business.'

'When your father said he'd drawn up the papers I was livid, darling, I won't lie. But no sign of them, so as usual the silly old goat was simply pushing buttons. I'm sure he never intended to go through with it, Fabien. He was just angry. Teaching you a lesson. You know how he could be? Determined to do the right thing as a father.'

'Yes, Mother, I'm sure you're right.'

'He was such a good father,' Lydia adds, wistfully. 'More tea?' She offers to pour, her version of an olive branch and a very sturdy one at that. Her children nod, their faces suddenly more relaxed, brows no longer furrowed, lips loosened, though mouths still downturned and sad.

Fabien stands and takes a couple of paces, glancing at the canvases his sister has started and left half done. True to character, he thinks, though he concedes that they are not bad at all. One, by the window, has a sheet over it, and he casually lifts it.

'Is this Anna?' he asks, stepping back, treading on Offal's tail, who yelps, and jumps onto Elodie's lap. But he needn't have asked. This painting is almost complete. It's striking, and immediately one can see the care and attention to detail that's gone into it. He had never thought of their housekeeper as beautiful before.

Elodie jumps up and recovers it. 'It's not finished. You shouldn't pry.'

'Is that really appropriate?' Lydia starts to ask, suddenly concerned about her bohemian free-thinking daughter's relationship with the staff. 'It looked a little risqué from here.'

A commotion stops the conversation short. Beeping and shouting. There is a knock on the door.

'Danny, what's going on?' Elodie says as she opens the door to the gardener.

'They've been ringing the main house intercom. Anna told them to bugger off. Doesn't look like they're planning on going anywhere. The press is back.'

Having decamped to the main house where the intercom was off the hook, as well as the phone, at least Lydia, Fabien, and Elodie could no longer hear or see the reporters harassing their gates, which at least were tall and spiky, not to mention alarmed.

The police had told them they could do nothing to help –

after all, the large gates made it impossible for the journalists to commit the crime of trespass.

'They're refusing to help on purpose,' Lydia says, as Anna quietly dusts the high corners and cornices with her extendable feather duster. 'They want us to feel cornered. Honestly, it's as if we have something to hide!'

'Don't upset yourself, Mother.' Fabien pats her arm. 'This isn't malice, just their typical incompetence.'

'Shall I text Harry, Lady Knutsworth?'

Lydia turns around, and her children look up – Fabien from his phone, and Elodie from her book. 'I didn't realise you were there, Anna!' Lydia says. 'Who's Harry?'

Fabien and Elodie notice a look cross Anna's eyes, a flicker of hurt. 'Harry Postlewaithe, the farmer?'

'The farmer who rents all our land, Mother,' Fabien adds, and winks at Anna, but she doesn't return the friendly look, the one that says "Silly old Lady Knutsworth, losing her marbles". Fabien feels embarrassed, like he's done something wrong, but he isn't sure what.

'He managed to get rid of the press last time,' Anna explains, her voice quiet.

'Of course, of course. Gregory dealt with everything to do with tenants and land, you see. I'm really feeling very off colour. Please do, Anna. I need to go and lie down.' Lydia Knutsworth gets up, and leaves the room, feeling bad about forgetting Harry's name. 'You know, dear,' she says to Anna as she reaches the door where her housekeeper stands, 'I am very fond of you. I do appreciate what you do. You must be grieving too, please take some time to yourself if you need it.'

Anna nods and smiles, and follows her ladyship from the room, turning the other way to go back to her quarters. She wonders how long it would take Lady Knutsworth to forget her name if she wasn't always there right in front of her nose, and just how invisible a person could be in a house like this.

'What's with the portrait of Anna?' Fabien asks his sister, now that they are alone.

'It's nothing.'

'Come off it, little sister, clearly it isn't *"nothing"*.'

'Which bit are you worried most about Fabien, Mr I'm-so-woke-when-it-suits-me? The fact she's staff, or the fact that we're—'

'Anna?' Fabien interrupts as the housekeeper runs back into the room, breathless.

'The police are here again.'

CHAPTER THIRTY-FOUR

Fabien, Elodie and Anna are sitting together in the drawing room. The police are gone, the curtains are drawn.

'I don't believe it,' Anna says quietly.

'But, Anna, what do we really know about her?' Elodie says, her hand on her knee. Fabien notices, but no longer cares. He didn't really care before, as he'd started to see the signs. His sister may think the whole family lives in a different century, but she's wrong.

'Anna's right. It isn't true.'

'And you know for sure how?'

'She told me.'

'What? When? You know where she is, and you didn't say anything?'

'No, I don't, and she didn't tell me *that*. She told me that her real name wasn't Mila, that she used her sister's papers. She said her sister was murdered by her husband. He must be setting her up.'

'A bit far-fetched, Fabes. And if she's innocent, why run?'

'She's scared. She was looking for someone – a friend of her sister's. She must think there's evidence somewhere. Her sister had kids, and she thought the only way to keep them safe was to prove what her sister's husband did,' Fabien tells her.

'Fabien's right. She was scared. There's no chance she would have done something like this,' Anna says.

'I didn't realise you were so close,' Elodie says, accusingly.

'We're not, but we texted sometimes. I felt sorry for her. I know what it's like to feel like an outsider looking in. I know the hell my mother went through. I wanted to help.'

'She asked for my help. Then she ran. Because she thought I'd betrayed her, though how she could think that...' Fabien shakes his head, and closes his eyes.

'It's easy to think the worst when everyone lets you down,' Anna tells him.

'Seriously? You both think she's innocent, and had nothing to do with Daddy's death? You're absolutely sure this woman who is wanted for murder in her country, who is pretending to be her dead sister, and who did a runner on the day our father died, just before he was about to tell the Wilsons she wasn't who she said she was, is the victim?'

'Yes,' Fabien and Anna both say, with force.

'Elodie,' Anna adds, 'she didn't hurt your father. She wasn't here. I know that, because I was in the main house until late, and then we were both in the gatehouse all evening. We would have seen someone come in.'

Fabien interjects. 'But now the police think she did, and they're ramping up their efforts to find her. She will be sent home, and handed over on a false charge. And sis, they seem to suspect that she didn't act alone – that I know more than I'm letting on.'

'To be fair, you did, as it turns out,' Elodie reminds him. 'So what are you going to do?' she asks, softening, seeing her brother and Anna united in their absolute belief in Mila's innocence. She wishes she could be as sure. She knows her brother, stupid and selfish as he is, and he couldn't be such a bad judge of character, could he? And Anna, well, Elodie suspects a little bias, but she's always had the best instincts.

Fabien looks at his sister and housekeeper. 'I'm going to have to find her first.' He had been hoping she would get in touch when she was ready. The police had said the Facebook connections had been a dead-end, but it was all they had to go on.

Fabien types away on his screen, clicks send.

Chloe replies quickly.

> It's all been deleted. I deleted Mila's profile, and Nikolai, the guy who did the post looking for her, has disappeared too.

Fabien tries again.

> Do you remember anything about the author of the post?

> He's from the same city. He went viral for a bit back at the Manchester protest. Why? The police already checked – they told us. She isn't there, time you just realised she's on the run and she could be dangerous. You shouldn't get involved. You need to look after yourself. Do you want to get a drink, and talk about it? I'm here for you, sweetie.

But Fabien is involved, more so in his heart than he has ever been before. He opens up a new tab and starts searching for *"Nikolai war protest viral"*.

He has to find her, and he has to start somewhere. He's going to start with the old man called Nikolai.

CHAPTER THIRTY-FIVE

Mrs Wilson is feeling faint.

'So, you see, Mr and Mrs Wilson, Miss Wilson,' PC Atkins says, 'we just wanted to offer the courtesy of letting you know. We understand you were very fond of Mila Kiss, previously known as Sofia Kiss.'

'Oh Martin, what have we done? I told you something was up as soon as we got back from the airport. Why did you stop me from reporting it? We've been harbouring a murderer!'

'I did report it.'

'We can't be sure she is responsible for the death of her sister, she is only wanted for questioning,' says Atkins.

'Oh, dear God, what will everyone think of us? They'll think we're involved. What will Lydia think? And with Fabien mixed up in it. Oh, I think I need a brandy. How could she lie to our faces? After all we did...'

'We don't know the details at present, Mrs Wilson. Only that it would appear there is an accusation against Ms Kiss. The best thing we can do is locate her, and try to get to the bottom of it.'

'Hmph,' Chloe interjects, folding her arms, 'I don't expect an apology, though clearly you could all at least acknowledge I saw it first. My investigations were absolutely justified.'

Atkins glances at his notes, and opens his mouth. He takes a breath, as he plans to explain that taking the law into one's own hands and impersonating another through digital profiles is never at all justified, but Martin stands suddenly, and raises his hand.

'Enough, Chloe.' Chloe looks around at the room, but eyes avoid her own; support is lacking. 'You've done and said enough at all the wrong times, and not come clean at the right time. If you'd mentioned your little bit of online detective work when Mila first disappeared, maybe the police would have found her. In the end it was down to that silly child Lottie to show the moral stamina you are quite clearly lacking.'

Chloe is aghast, but not finished. 'Dad! We were trying to protect Mila. Fabien said—'

'I've heard quite enough about Fabien. Officer,' Martin's tone changes as he turns to Atkins, who is rising to stand with him, 'thank you for the courtesy. We are at a loss as to what has gone on. Mila seemed a very nice young lady, and I'm shocked at these allegations; we all are. If we hear anything, we will be in touch. Won't we, Susannah? Chloe?'

'Of course, of course,' Susannah is now white. The refugee programme has a lot to answer for. She thinks she won't engage with this sort of charitable act again, and instead will stick to bring and buy sales.

'Chloe?' Martin looks sternly at his daughter.

'Sure, whatever,' she says as she gets up, not picking up the cushions she knocks to the floor in her haste to return to the sanctuary of her room.

Chloe's phone beeps. Fabien again, still obsessing about that damned crazy, possibly murdering bitch. Make that *almost certainly* murdering bitch.

She responds in a supportive tone. He'll come around; Chloe is certain of it. In the meantime, she supposes she ought to be a friend, indeed.

CHAPTER THIRTY-SIX

'So, he pushed you right under a bus, then, didn't he?' A.J. takes a drag of his joint while leaning against Monty's penthouse balcony, admiring the dots of cars below.

'Pretty much,' Mila replies.

'He'll get his comeuppance. Karma, that is.'

'I don't believe in karma, not since my sister was killed. Nothing's fair. Even the people I thought I could trust here have let me down.'

'Not us, we won't let you down. Peter sounds pretty smart, right? Doesn't like me, though.'

'He thinks he can find Xristina. I just hope my sister was right about her, and that she has enough evidence to finish him for good. They think I'm a killer. If I ever saw him again I think I could be.'

'Why do you think your fella – Fabien, right? – Why did he do that? Give you away?'

'To get his father to change his mind about the inheritance and his business? To some people, money matters more than anything else. Maybe getting rid of me was his best bargaining chip – after all, it's clearly what the Knutsworths wanted. I despised him when I left. I think I still do. But I should have known better; those types are all the same. Still, it was Chloe who led them to Nikolai, and you who put my name on social media.'

'Shit, I'm sorry Mila.'

Mila sighs, unable to offer A.J. reassurance, despite feeling sorry for the boy, maybe even liking him, though she is amazed at his carelessness. He hadn't thought about the possible consequences of broadcasting the contentious political activism of a war refugee – even if she *wasn't* here with a stolen identity – and he should have done.

'Here, have a drag.' A.J. offers the joint to Mila.

'I don't think so. I need a clear head.'

Mila and A.J. fall into silence. A.J. continues to lean precariously from the balcony, and Mila stares at the walls around her. They are dotted with obscure and varied art that suggests a collector who knows they should like art, but hasn't worked out which art they actually like.

A.J. had been more than happy to meet them here with the key. Monty isn't due back for weeks, and they decided it was best to keep it from him for now.

Having settled Mila in, Peter had made the surprising decision to summon Nikolai home with him, 'In case the police return, we need everything to look normal,' and for A.J. to stay with Mila, 'because they may well go looking for him too, and he can't be trusted not to let the cat out of the proverbial bag,' and then had spent another ten minutes explaining the phrase to his father. Nikolai's English was quite brilliant by now, but his son's adoption of local proverbs and dialect continued to flummox him.

A.J. had been insulted at the lack of belief in his integrity, but silently repositioned himself as Mila's valiant bodyguard, and a central part of a secret mission to break open an international conspiracy theory by the powerful elite in order to right the wrongs of the flawed capitalist system, solve a murder, and save an innocent war refugee from vengeful murder by treacherous associates of her dead brother-in-law. It was very exciting. He had kept quiet, and happily settled in with Mila.

'I'll need your phone, A.J.,' Peter had instructed. 'We'll be back later.'

A.J. had protested, insisted he wouldn't post anything on Twitter or TikTok or even Facebook. To no avail. In his narrative, he'd gone dark, and this was much more exhilarating than any of his marches, or banner making, to date. He wished he could tell Rain – she'd wonder where he was, but he realised this was the price he must pay to serve his purpose in the revolution.

'Maybe your boyfriend didn't tell his dad,' A.J. says now, watching a seagull soar, and wondering if there is a landfill nearby.

'Hmm?' Mila replies, distracted, lost in her own world.

'Fabien. If Chloe found the Facebook stuff, maybe it was her who told the lord bloke.'

'Maybe.' Mila isn't convinced. All Chloe had to go on was the stupid Facebook message; it sounded like Lord Knutsworth knew a lot more than that. 'It just doesn't make sense – the panic and the calls and the texts. He must have said something.'

'Then we conclude that Fabien and Chloe are *both* horrible snakes,' A.J. laughs as he walks back in from the balcony, and sits by Mila on the large leather white sofa. 'I'm sorry, though, Mila.'

'For what?'

'For what I wrote on Facebook. For mentioning CC. At the time I just thought it would be fun to meet you. I thought our groups were going places. Maybe, one day. But this, well, it...' A.J. shrugs.

'It puts our political activity into perspective?'

'Right.'

There's a knock. Morse code for safe.

Precisely thirty seconds pass; everyone is silent. The song of the door sensor sounds as Mila opens it, and Peter and Nikolai walk through the entrance hall, into the open plan living area.

'We've found something!' Nikolai announces with glee.

'What?' A.J. and Mila ask together.

'Not what, who. We have found Xristina.' Peter removes a sheet of paper from his inside jacket pocket and smiles. 'She goes by Xristina Knight, her paternal grandmother's maiden name. We have an address.'

Mila runs to Peter and jumps into his arms. Nikolai looks on happily.

CHAPTER THIRTY-SEVEN

Fabien's embossed leather Purdey holdall is packed and in the boot of his beautiful, but unreliable car. He has Nikolai's full name, and one of the online articles mentions that he is residing in Cheshire with his son. After that, it didn't take long to make a list of the handful of addresses registered to a Mr Popov.

Fabien calls his (ex) business partner again. Still no answer. He disappeared as soon as the shit hit the fan. Fabien has known him since boarding school. He railed against their privilege, rebelled against the rules, and had always been convinced he was going to revolutionise the system.

Fabien got a grad role in banking straight after university, while his trusty friend spent his time networking in politics, high up, and in the shadier corners. By the time they had their own capital, setting up their own ethical fund was the most obvious plan in the world to Fabien. Fabien would look after the money, and his partner would look after the networks and the ethics. Except he didn't, did he?

And now he is AWOL.

Fabien is furious, mainly with himself. He has begun the process of agreeing reimbursements to his misled investors, which are likely to have to be paid from his own family pot. He knows it will leave the family short of cash. His father had exaggerated about having to sell the estate to make up the money, although it may have to work a little harder to pay its way going forward.

Mr Harrop's team is desperately looking for alternatives to save the family fund. But money aside, he thinks that other than the ongoing trading standards investigation, the issue will quietly disappear. Fabien won't bank again. His father has got him home, trapped in titles and land and obligation, just like he always wanted. Heaven forbid Fabien would find his own passion. That wasn't the upper-class way, not for eldest sons at any rate.

No wonder sometimes it was hard to stand Elodie, barely aware of the extent of her comparative freedom. Not seeing his chains.

He feels fresh guilt at the memory of burning the papers his father used to threaten him. It rises up then down, in waves. He shouldn't have lied, but in the end, now his father is dead, he finally has Fabien exactly where he wanted him, before he lost his temper over Mila and tried to cut him off. His mother is right; Father would have come around. Burning the papers just means less fuss, less admin, fewer legal fees. It means Fabien is head of the house, where his mother wants him, where he belongs. He plans to make some changes, to use that house for good. No more will the privileged few rattle around, lonely and separate and disconnected. Mila will love him for it.

First, he needs to find her, and explain he didn't give her secrets away to condemn her – he had only been trying to convince his father that Mila needed their help. He will tell her he is winding down his company; he's clean and free of that. Explain he was guilty of believing in his partner. Fuck it, he'll admit he's guilty too. Maybe he was greedy: for his own earned money, for success in his own right. But he isn't a weapons investor; well, not on purpose. He isn't a bad man. He loves her. He will find a way to help her out of this mess. He thinks she'll like his plan for Farlington Hall. He hopes she'll want to be part of it.

For once, Fabien is going to be one of life's finishers. He won't get distracted, or drunk, or take a holiday to the Riviera when he should be managing his affairs. He will find out what really happened, and he will move heaven and earth to sort out whatever confusion remains over Mila's family and the crazy accusations against her. Whether she wants his help or not.

'Ah Anna, thank you,' Fabien says, as the housekeeper runs down the stairs with his umbrella.

'Just in case, sir.'

'Yes, better to be prepared. And Anna, please don't keep calling me sir.' Fabien puts his phone back in his jacket pocket and starts to open the driver's side door, but Anna takes a step forward, with hesitation.

'What is it, Anna?'

Anna, he notices, is holding a sheet of paper. On closer inspection it looks to be a page cut out from the paper. She hands it to him.

'It's Mila,' she says, 'they've put her picture in the paper. It's going to be all over town, all over the country – she won't be safe now.'

Fabien takes the page from Anna and as he reads, his pulse races, but his breathing seems to stop. Has Mila seen this yet? She must be so afraid. He will not, he reminds himself, falter.

'She couldn't have done it,' Anna tells him again. 'You know that. We know her.'

Fabien nods.

'You will help her, won't you? You'll keep her safe?'

'I'm going to try, Anna.'

CHAPTER THIRTY-EIGHT

'It's all very odd,' Payne says to Grant and Atkins, as they study the post-mortem and accompanying GP records, which have finally arrived, 'husband and wife not talking about a serious heart condition? She said he was fit as a fiddle. A wife not being the one to nag him to take whatever he takes?'

'You sound borderline sexist, Payne,' Grant jibes.

'Actually,' Atkins says, 'they have separate rooms, quite some distance apart. They don't share a bathroom, let alone a bathroom cabinet. The housekeeper – Ms Anna Kowaski – fulfils all the prescriptions, looks after the whole family, and so Lady Knutsworth has never needed to worry about the finer details of the household – medications, etcetera. In fact, it would seem, from basic information gathering amongst the staff, that she didn't even have to look after the children all that much; they had nannies for that, who stayed until they were both adults.'

'Serious cardiac episode estimated around 9pm. Records show a prescription for beta-blockers, which he may or may not have taken as prescribed, alongside some mild sleeping tablets. That's that, then. Case closed. Write it up.' DI Payne gives a sigh of relief, happy to wave goodbye to Tweedledum and Tweedledee and stop reminding them every five minutes that they are basic fact collecting, not interrogating hardened criminals. 'I know there were a number of oddities around the case, not helped by the sudden disappearance of Mila Kiss, but this is why I told you to be sensitive. It was always more likely to be the most obvious answer than a conspiracy.'

'Occam's razor,' says Atkins. Payne frowns. 'The simplest explanation is more likely to be correct than any other,' he adds.

'You surprise me,' Payne tells him.

'It's a well-known philosophical theory, ma'am.'

'I know what Occam's razor is, Atkins, it just seems unlikely you would prefer your answers so streamlined.'

'Oh.'

Payne stands, an invitation to her officers to leave her office for good. They take the hint, and make for the door.

'But what about the bruises?' asks Atkins, turning just as his hand grips the door handle, and Grant loudly sighs behind him.

'Accidental. Stories from the family add up.'

'Why was he in the pool room?'

'Irrelevant. It is his home. He can be in any room he pleases.' Payne closes the folder with unnecessary show.

'And Mila Kiss suddenly disappearing?'

'Never you mind. That's with the Home Office now.'

CHAPTER THIRTY-NINE

As far as the Chief, and by extension DI Payne and DS Grant were concerned, Lord Knutsworth had been unable to sleep, went to the pool room to relax, had a heart attack, and slipped into the pool. The final tox report showed beta-blockers and sleeping pills in his system.

Knowing the lord had taken beta blockers and a sleeping pill, Hoppy had pushed for additional tests. Had the drugs interacted? Could the sleeping pills suddenly have kicked in when he fell into the pool, hindering his ability to save himself? Unlikely, Helen had told him as they whispered over the water machine, afraid to draw attention to their ongoing interest in the case; the shock would have countered the effect of a single mild sleeping tablet, surely. Hoppy just felt that there was still a missing piece of the puzzle. Grant said he thought too much. The lab said get in the queue. Payne removed him from it almost as soon as he did.

Hoppy is still struggling to grasp the notion that a man would go to the pool because his sleeping pills were not working. Wouldn't a normal person lie in bed and count sheep?

That, Hoppy concludes over and over as he writes and rereads his notes, is very strange behaviour.

Hipton Station had to inform the police searching for Mila back in her home country that Mila was in the UK, last time they checked, but they had accidentally lost sight of her. They in turn had insisted the team in Lancashire put out her image.

The investigation into Lord Knutsworth's death was to be wrapped up, Mila's case was out of Hipton's jurisdiction. The Home Office politely refused Hoppy's enthusiastic offer of help to find Mila, which Grant seemed delighted about.

And there was to be an internal investigation, Payne had explained, before slamming the door in their faces. All in all, Hoppy accepted things were not going well for any of them. What he couldn't accept was that he was in the middle of a domino-effect of quite unbelievable coincidences, or that there was nothing more he could do to solve this most puzzling case. Or cases.

Anyone would think Grant didn't want to find Mila, or to know precisely what happened to Lord Knutsworth that night, Hoppy kept thinking to himself. Heart attack may be the cause of death, but the full picture wasn't clear yet, and in Hoppy's view the details were critical before filing. After all, this record would remain in perpetuity.

Fabien's brush with the fraud team had been brief, it seemed. Apparently, a settlement was being discussed with the investors, though he'd heard the tabloids were back shouting questions about warmongering money and dead lords.

Hoppy was sure Lady Knutsworth was acting suspiciously, but Grant said she was just mad as a box of frogs. 'They all are, that lot,' he told his eager junior. 'Put it to bed, there will be other cases, real ones, in your career. This is just a perfect storm of a blow in from the war in the wrong place at the wrong time, a greedy toff, and an unfortunate heart attack.'

'But what about the accusations against Mila?'

'Never mind that, son,' Grant had said with uncharacteristic kindness, 'nothing we know or can do there. Other things to focus on now.'

'Lord Knutsworth will know where Mila is, sir, if we could just speak to him,' he had said.

'Forbidden. Besides, the Knutsworths have closed ranks. Typical of that lot.'

PC Hoppy Atkins is on paperwork duty, filing the case away. He's been told to keep his head down. He is doing what he is told, but the cogs in his downward facing head are whirring. He just knows that they are missing something, and he intends to find it.

CHAPTER FORTY

The lift is broken, so Mila and Peter take the concrete stairs all the way to the seventh floor. The graffiti on the walls informs them that they should leave due to over-reliance on self-pleasure. They take no notice.

They knock on the door and a woman in her forties with grown-out bleached hair pulled back in a scrunchie answers, the chain still on.

'Xristina?'

'Who are you?'

'I'm Mila's sister.'

'You! I saw what you did! It was on the news! How could you – your own sister – hadn't she been through enough?' Xristina shouts, pushing the door shut.

Mila jams her foot in the gap just in time. 'No, you know that isn't true. It was Janos. Please. Why else would I have come?'

Xristina's eyes narrow as she seems to peer into Mila's soul. Her expression is steely.

'Please, Xristina, he has the children. He set me up. You know he's capable of it.' Mila removes her foot, helpless now, as she waits for Xristina to decide what to do next. She knows she can't force Xristina to believe her, or to help.

Xristina's expression remains firm, and the door closes. Then they hear the chain slide, and the door is fully opened for them.

Mila and Peter sit together on a two-seater black leather sofa as Xristina weeps and uses a handkerchief to quietly blow her nose, as Mila tells her everything that has happened. Mila sips her room temperature water. Xristina is on a matching chair at a jaunty angle, and between them sits a glass coffee table, covered in dust and today's newspaper supplements. Xristina reads the broadsheets, and the main paper is open to a double page spread on the war. In the far corner, covered in books in Mila's native language, is a chair with a high back, head support, and straps hanging loose at its sides.

'I was going to tell her how to find me, once we were sure she was safely away from Janos. Now it's too late. I should have found a way to bring her here sooner.'

'It isn't your fault, it's his.'

'Anton, my youngest, was keeping watch.' Xristina looks up with fear in her eyes, 'I haven't heard from him in so long. Oh God, Anton.'

'We'd have heard if a British citizen had been killed,' Peter says calmly.

'Peter's right,' Mila tells Xristina, who smiles wanly, and nods.

Mila takes her tin box from her bag and opens it up. Xristina clears a space on the table, and they spread out the photos of Janos caught in the act of betrayal against his country.

'Your letter to my sister said you had more evidence.'

'Yes, these photos would not be enough. Enough, though, I hoped, to convince her to flee.'

'She did, but he found her before she got too far. She had

booked her tickets, been assigned a host family. She planned to find you – to do whatever it took to help bring Janos down.'

'Come,' Xristina rises, and they follow her back into the narrow hallway, and through another door into a bedroom. The single bed is stripped, not even a pillow in sight, and the walls are covered in clippings, photos, sheets of printed numbers, and connecting arrows.

'Some I collected before I left the bastard. I started following him when I thought he was cheating. Before he started hitting me, before it all got a lot worse. The children were small then. Happy, even. I did my best. But he wasn't cheating, or not on me, anyway. The first time I asked him about it,' she smiles ruefully, 'I didn't know how dangerous he was. That's the first time he broke my nose.'

'Oh Xristina,' Mila starts.

'No, it was a long time ago, and I know your sister suffered too, I'm so sorry. I wish I'd been able to do more, before he got his claws in, before he did the terrible things he did.'

She goes to a tiny desk by the small window on the back wall. The blind is down, although it is just midday. She brings over papers, and hands them to Mila, who scans them, Peter reading over her shoulder.

'I hired a private investigator to look into his bank accounts. I told him I was gathering information for child support. I remember him looking around this place, looking at my boys, and thinking, *"You need it, love"*. 'Course, I couldn't file for it, because he'd find me then. My parents live here. Dad's from Gorton, brought Mum home when we grew up. They've helped where they could.'

'My sister knew you had family here. Janos would still rage about his children being snatched and sent to Manchester, after a drink or two.'

'Yeah, but I changed our surname, and I go by Chrissie now.

I picked up the local accent, so did the boys. Anton goes by Ant. Janos threatened me, "If you take my children, I'll find you," fists pummelling, over and over. But he soon forgot, with his drink, and his fighting, and his secrets. And then with your sister, and his new children. I don't think he really tried to find me in the end. I was lucky in that respect.'

'But you found this,' Peter says, looking up from the sheets of paper.

'My PI did. Don't ask me how. He gave me a discount, too. Said it was awful. Noticed my scar, but it was the boys he felt most sorry for, I think. He said he had two of his own.'

The records were bank statements, showing large sums being deposited.

'Come, sit back down, we'll talk more.'

They followed Xristina back into the living room and retook their places, sinking into the sofa, springs creaking. Mila's eyes darted to the strange chair, then flicked down again to the statements.

'It was well hidden, but not well enough. He started dipping into it. He needed to start buying stuff outside of the country, in case it was all seized. He might have been in bed with the enemy, but I expect he didn't trust them any more than they probably trusted him. That's how we found it, a trail of payments in his name, your sister's name, even the children's names.'

'My sister's name is tied up with all this criminal activity?'

'Your name, now,' Peter reminds Mila.

'Not just criminal; treacherous. War crimes. He's been working for foreign spies his whole damn career, he isn't just a pawn for the enemy making a quick buck. He *is* the enemy. And he's well protected. These people, they're not waving enemy flags – they're hidden in every country behind big desks, in fancy suits. They're money men, not soldiers. Then Janos started moving the money around. Buying property, making investments here, other places. I knew I needed to warn her, but I couldn't risk him finding my letters, my information, so I sent things with no return address. I wanted her to get away, but I knew how long it took me, what it took...' Xristina tails off. 'I knew if I ever made a case, she would be in trouble too. I hoped by then she'd have left him, perhaps it would be clear then that she too had been scammed.'

'There's so much evidence, Xristina,' says Mila.

'But not enough. We can't trace the people paying him yet, so we can't link the payments to the photos to show that he is taking payment from the enemy, undermining his own country's defence.'

'And he has the children,' Mila reminds everyone. 'That's the only thing that really matters to me right now. Saving Karlie and Konstantine from that monster.'

'Xristina, you said Anton was looking out for them. Do you have any idea where he is now?' Peter asks gently.

'I don't know, he just stopped calling. Anton went over there to fight. Fight who? I asked him, them or your father? He wouldn't listen. I told him I had it under control, that we'd get him. He couldn't leave it alone. He wanted to protect the children. That, I could understand. He didn't want what happened to John to happen to them.'

'John?' asks Peter.

'My other son, Anton's big brother. Xristina glances over at the big, high-backed chair with the straps hanging at its side, by the neck, by the middle, at its feet.

'What happened to him?' Peter says quietly. Mila is too afraid to speak, to even open her mouth for fear of the screams that might escape and give her away: all the horror buried within.

'His father beat him so badly, he suffered terrible brain

damage. That's when I escaped. I'd been living in the hospital by his side. We lied about what happened, but the doctors were suspicious, so Janos disappeared for a while. We took our chance. John lived in that chair. I cannot throw it away. He died five months ago yesterday, a month after Anton left to fight. He'd been helping collect evidence, delivering it to your sister, and sending it back to me. After John died, he changed. He couldn't come back for the funeral, and it destroyed him. I became afraid of what he might be capable of. He was consumed by rage against his father.'

Mila gets up and crouches by Xristina's chair. They embrace, bent and crumpled, holding tight. Both thinking, how many lives have been ruined by one man?

'When did you last speak to Anton?' asks Peter.

Xristina closes her eyes, then after a few moments she gets up and looks at a calendar hanging on the back of the living room door, and turns back a page. 'June 22nd. I always marked his calls, just in case.'

'Then nothing?' asks Mila, and Xristina nods. 'That's the day Janos killed my sister and took the children.'

CHAPTER FORTY-ONE

PC Atkins is still on desk duty, typing up reports, answering the phone, making watery instant coffee with milk past its best. However, Hoppy Atkins, in his downtime, has been doing some excellent detective work.

Fabien is taking a trip, he has filled his car with petrol, and called in to see Chloe for some reason. Surprising, as he didn't think they were currently on speaking terms.

Lydia and Elodie are visiting Lydia's sister.

Out of uniform, Anna doesn't recognise the young police officer through the video intercom.

'Good afternoon, Ms Kowaski,' he says, 'May I come in please?'

'Just passing, you say?' Anna asks, as she acquiesces to the young officer's request to step inside, and offers him a chair in the kitchen, explaining she is midway through cleaning out the storage cupboards.

'Yes, and now the investigation is concluded, I thought I'd pay a social visit, see how the family is doing.'

'But as I said, they're not here.'

'Yes, what bad luck,' he says.

'Yes,' Anna's voice is muffled, from the inside of what Hoppy presumes is the spices cupboard, given the array of perhaps a hundred orange topped jars on the table before him.

'And how are you?'

'What?'

'I said,' Hoppy enunciates, voice just below a full-on yell, 'how are you?'

Anna stops scrubbing, and reverses herself out of the cupboard. 'I'm okay, PC Atkins,' she tells him, looking a bit perturbed.

'Everything okay here, then? With the family?'

'Well, no, they're very upset. Lady Knutsworth offered me some time off, but I couldn't, not when they need me. Elodie said I should, but...'

'You feel you can't?'

'I feel I *shouldn't*. PC Atkins, when you live and work side by side the relationship can be complicated. But I respect this family, and I take pride in my work.'

'Will you be going to the funeral? I understand arrangements are being made now it's all cleared up.'

'Was it *ever* unclear, PC Atkins, or were you just jumping to crazy conclusions without evidence? And no, I expect I'll be busy preparing for the wake.'

'Call me Hoppy, Anna. I'm off duty, remember.'

'Hoppy, then.'

'It must be very difficult for you, Anna,' Hoppy returns to the matter at hand, remembering his open questions and empathy training.

Anna takes the seat perpendicular to Hoppy. 'Yes, I've lived and worked here for years, since I was just seventeen, when my mother passed away. It's been an awful time for everyone.'

'You are like family. I expect you know them all very well indeed. You must have noticed the late lord's views were not always progressive. He wasn't fond of Mila, was he? I imagine that can't have been easy.'

'You after some dirt, Hoppy? Thought this was just a social.'

'No, no, just making small talk.'

'You're not very good at it, Hoppy, if you don't mind me saying,' Anna says with a smile.

'Not at all.' Hoppy clears his throat.

'You're not happy with the police conclusion that the case should be closed, are you, PC Atkins?' she prompts, eyebrow raised. 'I mean, Hoppy. You think someone in the family did something wrong, don't you? Or Mila?'

'I believe the investigation has been fully carried out with the utmost of care and the conclusions by my superiors are entirely satisfactory,' Hoppy delivers unconvincingly. 'But what do you think, Anna? Are you satisfied? I only ask as a friend.'

'Friend? Would you like some tea then, friend?'

Anna is teasing him, Hoppy knows this, but tea in the kitchen with Anna is what brought him here. It isn't going too badly after all, if she can just shed some light on the family. Hoppy remembers something a school teacher once told him: if you want to get someone to open up, you must first reveal something of yourself. It builds trust.

'I live in the same town I grew up in, just on the Yorkshire border, not too far away to commute,' Atkins takes a sip of tea. When Anna says nothing, and waits for an explanation to this unnecessary and impromptu nugget, he adds, 'My father left a long time ago, but my mother and I muddle along happily together. My brother left to live in Silicon Valley. He is a computer scientist; he's a nerd.'

'Your brother's the nerdy one?' Anna laughs, and drinks her own tea. 'Well, as we are friends now, I am from Poland originally, which I think you already know given your oh-so-subtle remarks. My mother brought me over here when I was twelve. It was just the two of us too, so we have something in common. She worked hard, taught me to do the same. I planned to train to be a teacher. But no matter how hard my mother tried; they wouldn't accept us on the estate we lived in. They were bullies. It was different then, people know better now. Or so I thought.'

'What do you mean?'

'They hounded her, you know? My mum. In the end, I think they drove her to an early death.'

'Suicide?'

'Cancer.'

'I'm so sorry.'

'Mila came, and I thought the whole village was supportive – you'd *think* they were from the endless self-congratulations on the Facebook page, in the WhatsApp chat, and in the pub. Everyone was so nice to begin with. She was dating Lord Fabien! I was so happy the world had changed. Then, they started to hound her. They made her afraid. They always see the worst in anyone just the slightest bit different. So quick to believe gossip from liars and people full to the brim with prejudice.'

'The late Lord Knutsworth was about to reveal that Mila wasn't who she said she was . He was about to cut Fabien off. Seems the whole village could talk of nothing else when we did our door to doors. I know you know all this.'

'That Chloe has a lot to answer for, if you ask me,' Anna mutters, mainly to herself. 'And dragging poor Lottie into it, she's a good girl.'

'You think it's connected? Mila's involvement with Fabien, the threat of what she's hiding coming to light, being deported – worse, arrested, I take it you saw the pieces about the murder investigation?'

'I saw she was wanted for questioning. Doesn't mean anything.'

'Her sudden disappearance?' Hoppy continues, filing the mention of Chloe for later, along with Anna's conviction of Mila's innocence. Though it's no great revelation that Anna isn't a fan of Chloe.

'You think Mila's a killer? On the run for murder, then bumped off a lord who also happens to be her boyfriend's father? A lord, who apparently wasn't even murdered? You don't think all this gossip is just village drama, and a chance to blame the refugee? Perhaps you're just as bad as the rest of them. Maybe you should listen to your boss more. DS Grant seems to get it. I'm sorry PC Atkins, but I feel I know Mila a little, and I just can't see her hurting anyone.'

'Please, Anna, call me Hoppy, and I'm not suggesting that at all. I'm just making sure we aren't missing something. I just like to be thorough. I didn't mean to upset you.'

'Hoppy, as this is just a social visit, why don't we wrap it up, hey? I need to get on.'

Anna marches ahead of Hoppy to the front door while he jogs to keep up. She holds the door open, and says, 'You know, if you want to play detective in your spare time, maybe you should forget about the lord, who sadly passed but had a heart condition and a clumsy gait, and instead figure out how you can help an innocent girl who is fast becoming a scapegoat for all the ills around her. If you all did your jobs, then Fabien wouldn't need to do it for you.'

'You know where Fabien is? It's just we couldn't reach him with the news of the PM.' Hoppy lodges his cheap size nines in the door, to buy himself a few more seconds.

'I do not, though I am sure Lady Knutsworth will have passed on the news that his father died of natural causes and his family will no longer be the victims of a dogged police campaign against them.' Anna slams the door as Hoppy jumps backwards to save his foot, almost toppling down the stone steps, but catching his balance just in time.

He knocks again, and surprisingly Anna opens it. 'What now, Hoppy?'

'Um, just thought I'd say, as this was a friendly social visit, no need to mention it to anyone.'

'Oh, for crying out loud!' The door is slammed again, and the sound of heavy iron bolts being drawn punctuate the finality of the goodbye.

CHAPTER FORTY-TWO

Fabien pulls over and parks on the side of the wide, tree-lined road in Alderley Edge. Large, red brick houses fronted with pillars and painted facades hide behind high metal railings and vulgar statues. These are the homes of footballers and new money CEOs; proud owners of everything money can buy, bereft of taste.

Mr Harrop has just dialled off speakerphone with instructions for Fabien to read the email and get over the finish line. The email explains in no uncertain terms that it is Fabien's signature as CEO, no one else's, on the paperwork. Unless they can track his slippery partner down, Fabien will take the rap. The losses from reimbursing investors are Fabien's own in their entirety, and therefore those of his family and household. Nothing he didn't already know. He can't even file for bankruptcy, for fear of losing Farlington Hall and leaving his family homeless. He wonders if he should have let it go to Elodie after all; at least it would have been safe then.

Butterflies inside him try to stir up a panic. Not now, he tells them.

The investigation is unlikely to prove criminal fraud. Mr

Harrop is making a case for negligence of duty instead. Basically, Fabien must suck it up, admit to not knowing what he was doing, that he hadn't meant to invest his ethical funds in arms, and with everyone paid off, Fabien can then move on.

You could invest in a screw company, Fabien my boy, and it would turn out those screws held fighter jets together. We can draw a close to this matter, no real damage done.

That's what the email says. No damage done. His project dead, his career over, and his name mud. He had wanted to make a difference. He believed that you could change capitalism for the better. Money could be made without the injustice the left raged about. It was his compromise to the world: let my family be, stop hating us, and I will work hard to show you wealth doesn't have to be bad. His father had never understood. Hadn't bought it for a moment. He told his only son that he was greedy, obsessed with money when he should be paving the way for a life of duty. His family, title, and land were everything.

Fabien quickly types out the email before he can change his mind, and hits send. For once, he will take responsibility, do what his father told him it would take to make him proud. His phone rings again. His mother this time, Elodie the three previous ones. He ignores them, and another text comes through.

> Call me back this instant. We cannot discuss
> this on a text message. Mummy x

Fabien puts the phone back in his pocket. Whatever tree the police are no doubt barking up now, he must locate Mila before he is dragged back into the mess at home. And if he or Mila are suspects in his father's death, he can't risk alerting anyone to their whereabouts, assuming he ever finds her. Sitting in his car, outside the last house on the street, he thinks that if this were a movie, Mila would answer the door, and jump straight into his arms.

He rings the intercom bell, and looks at the stone likenesses of two nightingales, one either side of the wrought iron gates. Manicured gardens are visible beyond.

Fabien waits. No answer. He rings again. And again. Still nothing.

He goes back to sit in the car. He slides back in his seat as best as his large frame allows in the tiny space. Maybe his mother is right, and he should get something more practical and less showy. Perhaps he will start to drive the old Defender. Live in wax jackets, and simply mutate into his father.

The sun starts to dip, and still there's no sign of anyone returning to the house. It might not even be the right house. He's sure it is, something must go right at some point, probability demands it.

Fabien turns on the engine and puts the heaters on. They blow noisily and emit a strange, dusty smell. He turns them off, and gets out of the car. Walks to the boot, opens it with the key, and starts to search for a jumper from his holdall.

'Fabien?' a female voice says.

He turns to see a familiar face. 'Chloe?'

Chloe gets back into the driver's seat of her mother's car, and Fabien gets in and sits in the passenger seat, staring ahead.

'Let me get this right. You stole your mother's car so you could stalk me?'

'I *borrowed* my mother's car so I could follow you. You are trying to track down a murderer, alone. I came to protect you.'

'You were going to step in and bring down a murderer for me, Chloe?'

'I could have called the police if she tried anything. You should be grateful. What the hell are you playing at, anyway?'

'What am I playing at?' Fabien scoffs, sighs, disbelief in the air.

'You should be grateful. I was right about Mila, wasn't I? She isn't who she said, and she's wanted for murder.'

'She was hiding from the man who killed her sister. There's no way she did it. She wouldn't have. She is the most courageous, moral woman I know.'

Chloe folds her arms, beginning to wonder why she bothers trying to help people at all. 'And it isn't brave and moral to help a friend, blinded by lust?'

Fabien decides not to answer. He knows it is futile.

'Is this where she's staying then?'

'You need to go home, Chloe; your parents will be worried.'

'I'm not a child, Fabien. I lived on the other side of the world until recently, don't you remember?'

'Yeah, I remember, and look how that worked out.'

'What's that supposed to mean? Your life is hardly all perfectly put together now, is it?'

They sit in uncomfortable angry silence, as the sky starts to darken.

Fabien turns to Chloe. 'If this is where Mila is staying, I don't think you should be here when she shows up. I need a chance to explain myself, and to find out what's going on. She's not going to talk if you're here.'

'You sure she wants to talk to you? After all, didn't she run away from you without a goodbye?'

'She probably thinks I betrayed her. I need to tell her I didn't.'

'You mean you need to tell her I did? Well, I'm not sorry; if she's got nothing to hide, she should show up and fess up.'

'Fess up?' Fabien smiles, despite himself. 'Which one are you, Scott or Bailey?'

'Fuck off, Fabien.'

'Look, it's getting late. Go home.'

'I'm not leaving you here, even if you are an ungrateful, blinkered fool. Where are you planning to stay, anyway?'

Fabien doesn't answer.

'Here?' Chloe laughs, her head swings back, she hoots. 'You really are ever the optimist, aren't you?'

'Fine. Let's go and find a hotel. We can get something to eat. In the morning, you go home, and I'll come back here to see if anything has changed. If you're really worried about me, which to be honest I think is unnecessary given we're in the middle classes' answer to Fort Knox with private CCTV probably blinking out of every bush, then I promise I'll ring you when I find her. And in return, you promise to keep your bloody mouth shut, while I figure things out.'

Chloe goes to protest, but Fabien raises his palm. 'I mean it Chloe, if you want to show you care about me, we do this my way.'

CHAPTER FORTY-THREE

It is half past two on a Friday afternoon when the final CSI reports are handed in from the now-closed Knutsworth case. The full lab reports were added to the file the day before, with nothing of note, the technician explained in the covering email, to add or point out. All in line with the initial findings.

PC Atkins' job is to make sure all the various bits of paper, emails, evidence, and final reports are filed properly. For most junior officers, this is a tedious job to be done quickly and with little care. After all, you have to trust the others did their jobs properly in the first place.

Hoppy Atkins isn't like other junior officers, and relishes the task. This is his chance to go over everything one more time with a fine toothcomb, legitimately and in uniform. Every time a door swings open, or a senior officer's voice starts to bellow from a hallway somewhere in the building, he freezes, sure that Anna Kowaski has made a complaint and he is in imminent danger of losing his job.

To Hoppy's disappointment, everything so far seems to be in order in the files.

Still, he reads every report, renames the files properly where required, and saves them in an intuitive and logical taxonomy within a secure folder on the system.

'Are you still doing that?' Grant complains more than once. 'I've other tasks for you, PC Atkins, so get a bloody move on.'

It is after 6pm and Hoppy is doing the final proofread, his eyes strained, the bright white lights flickering overhead. Colleagues shout their goodbyes, tell him to meet them later at The Bay Horse for a pint.

It is as he calls back that he'll be there in an hour that he spots it.

Lord Knutsworth's health records show that he was prescribed his heart medication on a monthly rolling script, which was delivered to his home. The sleeping pills were ordered as and when he needed them, and collected from the surgery. The officer had only taken a screen shot and saved the last page of the record, which showed the previous few months. His six-monthly check up with his cardiologist, a trip to the GP for a suspected hernia, the monthly dispatch of his heart meds, and three repeat scripts for his sleeping pills. One back in March. The next, the week before he was found dead, and the final, the morning after.

Grant is suitably unimpressed to be dragged out of the pub by a breathless Atkins, but now that the boy has found the discrepancy, he is going to have to let the bloody nuisance underling look into it.

Which is what he explains to DI Payne on the phone, who is very irritated to have been disturbed on her first date in over a year.

'You know, they probably just typed in the wrong day, Hoppy lad? And regardless, it doesn't change the cause of death, or a perfectly innocent tox report,' Grant tells him, as they stand outside the pub, shivering in the wind, Atkins convinced that the conversation must be held as privately as possible.

'Yes, I know, sir. Still think something is fishy, sir. Permission to go to the GP surgery tomorrow?' PC Atkins says it so formally and enthusiastically that Grant half expects a salute.

'Permission granted,' he replies, downing the dregs of his pint and marching back to the warm embrace of the stale smelling boozer.

Just another few weeks, he tells himself, then retirement awaits. No more bollockings, no more paperwork, no more stern superiors like Payne, with a stick up her arse, and no more blabbering idiots like Hoppy Atkins who, despite all the evidence to the contrary, believes he is some sort of policing savant.

CHAPTER FORTY-FOUR

'If you can tell me what the problem is, I'm sure I can help you.'

'It's official police business,' PC Atkins explains again to the receptionist at the surgery.

'Yes.' The receptionist is unflappable. She has sat behind this desk for over twenty years protecting the doctor from unnecessary consultations, and wasn't about to the let the side down now, police matter or otherwise.

'If you could just let Doctor Walton know I'm here?'

'Doctor Walton doesn't work on Mondays, PC Atkins.'

'But you said he was busy with a patient...'

'I said all the doctors who are in today have a full schedule, PC Atkins. Kindly please don't mince my words.'

'Um,' Hoppy had hoped his uniform would give him authority, but people seemed to see right through it. Some kids at the bus stop had thrown a paper cup at his head the other day, then pretended to be whistling into the sky when he had turned around to tell them off. When he took out his tablet to make a note of their names and give them a bit of a scare, they'd glowered at him and asked him what model it was. Hoppy had put it away and decided to leave the discipline to their unfortunate parents.

'PC Atkins, I'm sure you're a busy man, and I know I'm a busy woman. Why don't you just tell me what you need to know. I keep extremely thorough records. There's nothing I can't lay my fingers on in under forty-four seconds.'

'That's rather specific.'

'Mike timed me.'

'Mike?'

'My staff member. At my level you need assistance, officer, you'll understand one day. Besides, with my experience, it would be a travesty not to pass my knowledge to the next generation.'

'Right.'

'Mike!' the receptionist calls behind her, and a young boy with a crumpled shirt and an acne-pocked face appears.

'Yes, Aunty?'

'Mrs Worthington!' she hisses, but as Mike goes to correct himself, she speaks loudly. 'Please take over desk duties, while I assist the young police officer with his investigation. Follow me, PC Atkins.' Mrs Worthington hauls herself out of the large padded office chair on wheels and disappears from view. A door opens to the side of the reception hatch, and Atkins is beckoned through.

'Prescription records?' Mrs Worthington says, 'Well, why didn't you say?' The large woman stands and strides one and a half steps to the filing cabinet, which takes up a third of her office which, Hoppy thinks, might more typically be called a store cupboard. 'I process all prescriptions, and repeat prescriptions need not even go through the doctors, so long as they are still valid. Usually with this sort of thing, they can keep refilling them for six months, maybe a year, sometimes longer, without a check-in.'

'Isn't that a little worrying?' Atkins muses aloud.

'PC Atkins, I don't believe policing school will have trained you in the art of secondary care and the nuances of its administration so let me assure you, everything is monitored in the precise way it ought to be with the exact requirements of safety checks in place. If one was to revisit every patient on lifelong medication every time they refilled, the NHS would be on its knees. People would be dying in corridors! Patients would wait months for urgent heart surgery.'

'But, isn't that–'

'I'm sure you think you could do a better job, young man, but let me tell you...' Mrs Worthington has pulled out some records, and is checking them. She retakes her seat, her meaty index finger, adorned with gold rings slightly too tight and in need of a polish, traces the record first, and Atkins' printed record second, eyes beadily flicking between the two. She pushes her glasses up her nose, a last-ditch attempt to see things differently.

PC Atkins waits. He is impatient, but he can see the agitation rising in the woman before him. Her calm, controlled exterior is giving way to something unpredictable. Her face is screwed up, and her breathing is quick. Although they are in a surgery, given that he hasn't seen a doctor since he arrived, and Mrs Worthington's efforts to blockade the consulting rooms, he is afraid that if she suddenly has a heart attack, it will transpire there are no doctors here at all. While he waits, he tries to remember his first aid training; when that fails, he silently repeats a meditation mantra.

'I filled this one here,' she points to the record of the sleeping pill prescription dispatched a few days before Lord Knutsworth's death. 'As usual, Anna called to order it, and then collected it.'

'And this one?'

Mrs Worthington shakes her head, 'That wasn't me.'

'It was me, I filled it,' a voice says.

Atkins and Mrs Worthington turn to the door.

'Mike, what are you doing back here? Reception must never be unattended!'

'You filled it? Despite the fact the same prescription had been filled only days before? Isn't there a protocol for that?'

'Of course he didn't, and yes there is a protocol!' Mrs Worthington's face is red. 'I always check the last date of refill, and if there are any alarm bells we have certain questions to ask. Mike isn't allowed to refill prescriptions without my supervision. He's still in training.'

'I did. You had been called away. Lady Elodie was in tears on the telephone, you were comforting her, and it seemed to be taking ages. I didn't want to interrupt; I know we have to treat them with respect, like you said, not like the regular patients.'

'I said no such–'

'You'd shown me how to do it, so when she came and asked for the prescription, I... I was only trying to help. She said Anna had misplaced it, was afraid she would be in trouble, and could I do them a good deed, as a friend? She said maybe we could go out some time. So I did, then I filled out the record like you showed me and gave her the meds in one of the little paper bags. I thought I was doing it all right.'

'You didn't ask the questions! You didn't follow the protocol.'

'I'm so sorry, Aunty, she very persuasive. She always has been.'

'Who? Who came and persuaded you to fill the prescription, Mike?' Atkins demands.

'Lottie Beard. We went to school together.'

CHAPTER FORTY-FIVE

Mila doesn't believe in coincidences. The jury is out on karma. Maybe justice will be done after all, but it is by no means certain. Serendipity is another matter. Meeting Nikolai on the plane turned out to be a lifeline. Those kind eyes, that cheeky smile. And now, walking with Peter, who has the same kind eyes, who has the means and the technology to help her, she knows she was meant to follow this path.

The path underfoot is paved, and the streetlights dim. Gardens are untended and shops boarded up. It took only thirty minutes to drive here, but Xristina's neighbourhood, Levenshulme, is a million miles from Peter's world. Despite the darkness, her sunglasses remain on. Her hood is, as always, pulled up. Mila has become accustomed to hiding. She doesn't stand out; hoods casting shadows over faces seem to be the norm in this part of town.

'What now?'

'I'll do some digging on these statements. We just need to work out who is behind them. These business names will be fronts in front of more fronts, the true payers buried under a complicated paper trail designed to be an impenetrable maze.

Inevitably, many of the companies will have existed for just long enough to move money and seal deals, only to be closed without a trace. Named MDs and CEOs vanished.'

'I can go through everything too, help to organise the chaos. It used to be a strong point.'

'It still is, no doubt. Finding Anton would help; I think he must know something and that's why he's lying low.'

'Maybe, or maybe Janos hurt him too. If he was there, watching... if Janos found out...'

Peter cannot answer. He does not know.

'We can't rely on Anton turning up, so we need to deal in the facts and photos we have. It might take some time. There will be some dead ends. I can't make promises right now, Mila. I'm sorry.'

'You don't need to make promises to me, Peter. I trust you.'

'If we can prove Janos was up to his neck in corruption and treasonous acts, then it hugely compromises his accusations about you. It also becomes a more complex case; one in which you may serve them better as a witness to his character and activities than as a suspect. And with Xristina coming forward about his history of domestic violence, they'd be crazy not to think it was him who killed your sister. God knows if this will play out as it should, but we can only try.'

They get into Peter's Tesla, and although Mila has sat in the passenger seat several times, she is still amazed at how ludicrous the dash is. 'Still feels like a spacecraft to me.'

Peter smiles. They drive to his place first. He wants to pick up a change of clothes, then they will go back to their luxury penthouse "Hideout HQ" as A.J. has named it, and get to work.

Mila feels terrible that Peter has been so uprooted and inconvenienced. That he has put himself on the line for a family he doesn't know. But he patiently reassures her every time she protests. He is doing it for his country. He's always investing in risk. Time, money, whatever. He's doing it because it's the right thing to do. Besides, he tells her, he can keep on top of his own work wherever, and having her there to check facts speeds everything up. It's not a problem, he repeats again as they move across the Cheshire border. But he does need fresh socks.

As Peter slows on the twenty mile an hour wide, tree-lined street he calls home, serendipity strikes again.

'That's Fabien's car.' It is impossible to miss. There are only a handful still in existence, fewer still on the road. 'Up ahead.'

'Fuck.' It is the first time Mila has heard Peter swear, or sound the least bit frazzled. He stops, the car silent as ever, and expertly starts to turn, lights off.

'Jesus, that's Susannah's car, too.'

'Susannah?'

'Mrs Wilson, my host. Chloe's mum.'

In the distance, illuminated by a strong moon and well-designed yet subtle street lighting, Fabien steps out of the passenger side of the car. Mila strains to see what is happening.

Fabien unlocks and climbs into his own car. His engine revs several times, not unusually, and then it is alive, lights on. The car behind him does the same, but the Mini Countryman comes to life first time. It isn't Mrs Wilson in the driver's seat; lit by the inner glow of the car, ever so briefly, Mila can tell it is Chloe turning to check her mirrors before pulling away.

They are in it together, and they've found her.

'The audacity!' Nikolai is pacing the living space. 'Turning up in his swish car, he didn't even try to hide. The arrogance!' Nikolai hates Fabien. Nikolai loves Mila with all his heart.

'I don't understand, what do they want from me now?'

'They could be helping the police,' A.J. looks up from his

doodle, his fifteenth attempt to create a *"Hideout HQ"* logo. It isn't that he doesn't understand when the others tell him they won't be branding or marketing their secret location, ever, it's just that banner making has become a bit of a compulsion in recent years. Something to show for his work. 'Fabien was in a load of crap, right? Chloe did all that Facebook imposter shit.' A.J. takes a drag of his joint, and Peter stomps over to the balcony with a dramatic intake of breath. 'They might have shaken them down, you know? Scared them into co-operating. Given them the address, told them to flush you out.'

'Seriously?' Peter says, 'Shaken down, flushed out?'

A.J. scowls at Peter's mockery. 'I'm only trying to help.'

'And he has a point,' Mila places her hand protectively on A.J.'s shoulder. He's young and passionate, and wants to make a difference. Like she was at his age. Still is, really. 'That logo is great,' she tells A.J., 'have you thought of going to art college?'

A.J. turns crimson, but can't help but grin with pleasure.

Peter sighs. 'You're right, I'm sorry. It's just getting more surreal by the minute. I think I should go home. If they *are* helping the police, I should expect another visit. If Papa and I are there alone, they have no reason to return for a while. Mila, I'll be back in the morning. Okay?'

After they've said their goodnights, Mila makes tea for her and A.J., who sneaks another beer from Monty's well-stocked fridge and lets the tea go cold.

The intercom rings.

They ignore it. There is only one knock they answer to these days, in this place. Mila and A.J. are silent, and do not move. They barely breathe.

It goes again. And again. And again.

'Should we just see who it is? You know, on the video thingy?' A.J. asks. 'It's been, like, ten minutes. What if it's an emergency?'

'No, it's two-way, they'll see us. They're not here for us. The real resident isn't here. No one should be. Best we leave it.'

A small gust of wind blows the balcony drapes inward, and the door knocks against the garden chair on the balcony deck with a clang of metal frame against metal frame.

'Shit. We left the door open. They'll know we're in.'

'Come on, I know you're in there! Let me in now!' bellows a familiar voice from below.

Mila's heart leaps into her chest.

A.J. switches the lights off.

'What did you do that for?' Mila likes A.J., but she suspects he might be a bit of an idiot.

'Come out, you cowardly bastard, and I might not fucking tear your head off!'

'Oh, crap.' Years of scuffling in low-key protests has not prepared A.J. for threats of such sinister violence.

'For God's sake, you're drunk!' says a woman. 'I never should have brought you here.'

'He's ruined my life!' the man shouts, pleadingly, and now Mila comes to think of it, with a bit of a slur.

'Let's go back to the hotel. Get in.'

Mila uses the shield of darkness to creep towards the balcony, and tries to strain her neck to see who is having this strange altercation below.

'You can't tell me what to do! You shouldn't even be here! This is my mess. This is my life. Why are you even here? Come on, I know you're in there!' He aims his shouts to the open balcony above.

'I'm here because you downed half the mini-bar, and I couldn't stop you from coming, so driving you was the only way to keep you safe,' the female voice hisses. 'Someone has to protect you from yourself, you know.' The woman sounds fed up.

Mila risks shuffling forward, gently pushes the door wider so she can get her head closer to the railings and get a better look at the warring couple.

She glances at A.J. He is curled into a ball on the floor. Mila manages to move her head into an awkward position where she can make out the owner of the shouting voice beneath her. Her suspicions are confirmed. She jumps back.

'A.J., get up. Now! They're not after Monty, they're after me.'

'What?'

'It's Fabien and Chloe. They must have followed us.'

'What the hell? Why is he threatening to kill us?'

'I don't know, A.J., but we are about to find out.'

CHAPTER FORTY-SIX

A.J. opens the door to reveal Peter and Nikolai, their arms stretched around folders and papers, juggling a bag for life that's bursting at the seams. A.J. spots a Monster Munch pickled onion six-pack. He may be nearing twenty, but those crisps are not just for kids.

'We made some progress, but some of these names are completely untraceable so far,' Peter begins as they follow A.J. down the hall.

'We got some snacks, it's going to be another long day,' adds Nikolai, trying to sound less excited than he is by the prospect of another day of sleuthing.

'Where's Mila?' Peter asks. 'Ah, there you are.' Peter notes that Mila is sitting on a dining table chair the wrong way round, with her legs either side, her elbows propped on the top of its back as she looks straight ahead. She is facing them as they enter, the sofas and living area behind her, the window outside of her line of sight. 'Why are you staring at the wall, Mila?' he asks.

There's a crash as Nikolai's grocery bag drops to the floor, and a jar of stuffed olives smashes, oil going everywhere.

Peter turns. He sees what has startled his father. 'What in the world is going on? Who is this?'

Peter, Nikolai, A.J., and Mila face the two additional visitors in Monty's apartment. Their hands are tied behind their backs. They appear to be fastened to the stylish tall grey radiator behind them. Their ankles, too, are tied, with what could be socks. Their feet are bare.

'Peter, Nikolai, this is Lord Fabien Knutsworth and Chloe Wilson.'

'How do you do?' Fabien quips.

Chloe nods, as if meeting a passing acquaintance in the street.

'Can you untie us now, please?' Fabien looks at Mila.

'You promised, Mila, you said when the others get here,' Chloe whines.

'She said you can try your story with them, actually,' A.J. informs his prisoners, 'and then we can decide if you can be trusted.' A.J. has quickly adapted to his role as captor. He hasn't felt real power before.

'Anyone would think we were the ones wanted for murder and pretending to be our dead sister.'

'Enough, Chloe!' Fabien's head is pounding from the hangover, and he's wondering if this is all a terrible dream. He almost misses his dusty old existence, his uninspired and formulaic promise of a future path trodden by generations before. At least that didn't involve being wrestled to the floor by the love of his life and tied up with his own socks by some spotty teenager. 'But, Mila, you must believe me, I didn't come here looking for you. Well, I *did* look for you, but when I didn't find you, I came here instead.'

'Why did you come here?' Peter asks, regaining his composure.

'I was looking for my business partner, Hugo Montgomery. He's shafted me and done a runner.'

'Monty's in business with the evil lord?' Nikolai is aghast. They'd all seemed such nice boys.

'Evil lord?' Fabien splutters. 'What the hell–'

'To be fair, you have done some wicked things,' Peter tells him, shooting a disapproving look, but still deeply uncomfortable with the hostage situation.

'I think I can explain,' says Fabien.

An hour later, Fabien and Chloe are still bound, as they tell their unbelievable tale. Chloe begrudgingly admits it was she who told Lord Knutsworth that Mila was a terrorist, driving his urgency to have her paperwork examined. Though it was Fabien who made things ten times worse by revealing the fake name part of Mila's story when confronted by his father, who Fabien thought knew more than he did.

'I pleaded with him to leave it be, Mila. I offered him everything for a chance to fix it. Please believe me,' he tells her.

'Why should we? Who is to say you're not in it together, and just saying all this so we release you and then you can run off to the police and get Mila into more trouble?' Nikolai folds his arms triumphantly. He prefers to keep Fabien cast as villain, and Peter as Mila's hero, with a little help from his old papa.

'True or otherwise, they can't leave now,' Peter says.

'What?' shouts Chloe. 'This is outrageous! We haven't done anything.'

'That isn't true. If you were seen at my house, you have compromised me, my father, and made it even harder for us to help Mila.'

'I'm sorry, Mila,' Fabien says, eyes now to the floor. His shoulders slump further. 'My father died. They think you did it, Mila, and that's why you ran.'

All eyes turn to Mila. 'I didn't kill him. I didn't even know he was dead until the police told Nikolai and Peter. I'm sorry he's dead,' Chloe snorts and Fabien glares at her. Mila ignores Chloe, 'but I left for very different reasons.'

'I know,' Fabien tells her.

'You don't know all of it.'

'Big surprise, Mila has more fucking secrets,' Chloe spits.

'Shut up, Chloe,' Fabien says. 'The police don't have a cause of death yet. They're suspicious. We all think it was an accident; we found him in the pool. It has to be an accident. We will know for sure soon. But there's more.' Fabien nods towards his pocket. 'The paper clipping, take it.'

Mila bends and pulls the crinkled cutting from Fabien's pocket. She unfolds it. Silently, she passes it to Peter. They look at the article revealing Mila's real name, and saying that she is wanted for questioning over a murder.

'We knew they'd find this sooner or later,' Peter says, 'but for now, Mila is in more danger than ever. And you may have led them straight to us.' He paces. 'Nobody is leaving until we finish what we started. Or we never will.'

'I'm sorry about your father, Fabien,' Mila replies. 'Truly, I am. But Peter is right; we all need to stay here for now. There's a lot we need to work out, and until we do, we can't risk anyone tracking us down. We only get one chance to do this.'

'Okay,' Fabien says, 'thank you.'

'Thank you?' Chloe screeches. 'For what? For kidnapping us and holding us hostage? For lying to our entire village, and taking advantage of my parents' good nature? Don't you think they'll wonder where we are? They'll look for me, you know. They'll look for him too,' she nods in Fabien's direction, 'He's the bloody Lord of Farlington!'

'Chloe,' Mila says gently, 'I know you don't like me. But you don't really know much about me, or why I'm here.' She starts to untie Chloe's binds. 'I think if you did, you would understand. I believe you were only trying to do what was right for your family, the same as me. I think we have more in common than you think.'

'Wait!' A.J. says, at the same time as Nikolai. 'What about his claims about Monty? He could be lying!'

'Check online on Companies House. It's no secret.'

'Why on earth was he hanging out with a group of rebel kids in a squat?'

'Hey–' starts A.J.

Fabien smiles drily. 'He always hung out with younger kids, people who looked up to him, had low expectations, they came and went. He was pretty damaged by his upbringing, to be honest, and I didn't really give that enough weight when I brought him on board. It's no surprise to me that he'd be dealing low level drugs to low level rebels.'

'Just wait a min–' A.J. tries to interject.

'He's right,' Peter says, speaking over A.J. as he looks up from his phone, 'Hugo Montgomery – of this address – is Fabien's business partner.'

'Small world,' muses Nikolai.

'Still, no need to be rude,' A.J. mutters to himself.

'It's time we all showed some trust, told the whole truth. Maybe we can help each other.' Mila kneels down to the floor, and resumes untying the socks from around Chloe's feet. She notices the coral nail polish on her toes, and thinks how nice it must be to have time to do something so pointless and pretty. 'You will promise to stay here and help, Chloe. I think we might be able to get justice for an innocent family, and expose a really bad man. A killer, a traitor, a man who hurts women.'

As the ties are loosened and Chloe and Fabien shake their limbs free, Peter holds out his hands. 'Phones, please. Switch them off and hand them over.'

'Monty's in Greece, you know?' Nikolai says, not really paying attention, still baffled by the revelation that his friend Monty is connected with the posh twit trying to steal Mila's heart, which should belong to Peter. 'He went on holiday. Lovely man, genuine I thought,' he adds, looking at Fabien pointedly. 'I'm sure he hasn't run off, probably just a dodgy signal out on the coast.'

'He isn't in Greece, though his parents are. They haven't seen him, don't want to either, from the short shrift they gave me when I tried to get their help. Reckon they'd rather he disappeared until it's all blown over. Once I've taken responsibility, paid everyone back out of my own pocket, then maybe he'll show.'

'Can't you get the money off the people you bought all the weapons and stuff from?' Chloe asks, standing and stretching, as the others jump back as if she might lash out. She rolls her eyes, and takes a dining chair, arms raised in surrender.

'I didn't buy weapons! Bloody Monty did. I just, well, I signed for them, I guess.'

Nikolai tuts, Peter sighs, and Mila shakes her head.

'I trusted him. He was so passionately anti-war, so ethical, so left-wing, he brought me good idea after good idea. The profits soared, the investors loved us. I guess I stopped looking at the details. They weren't all named *Bombs Are Us*. Then they just disappeared. They have the money, but when you follow it, they've folded, CEOs vanished, anyone my solicitor manages to track down blames the war for companies folding, people missing, hiding, moving money around, and is so junior or loosely connected by paperwork that they just stop answering the phone, emails bounce back, and we are ghosted yet again. My investors are suing me personally, basically. Mostly, they don't even need the money, they just want to cut ties with the business.'

'Boo hoo,' says Nikolai.

'Papa!'

Fabien, now released, gets up and stretches. He takes a step towards Mila, and gently says, 'Can we talk?'

'Later, another day, maybe. For now, we have work to do, and maybe you can help.'

CHAPTER FORTY-SEVEN

'Have you got hold of Fabien yet?' Anna asks, trying not to move her mouth too much.

'No,' replies Elodie, squinting at her canvas, 'absolute donkey isn't picking up. Mother was having a fit and almost called Harrop as he told her that's where he was going. I persuaded her not to. In the end I've had to text him the PM results, but no reply. For all I know, he's tracked Mila down and they're on the run for no reason whatsoever, thinking they're a modern-day Bonnie and Clyde without the actual crime.'

'Tell that to everyone else, seems Mila's been found guilty by the mob.'

'I don't believe she did any of it any more than you do, but why run?'

'I wish I knew. I wish Fabien would call, let us help him, and Mila.'

'Oh, as if! His hubris is on another level. Carries the burden for us all, he'd have us believe. Father always told me, I was lucky to be born female, and escape the trappings of the patriarchy and all the rules entwined within it, which I really don't think he meant to be funny. Hold still, my sweet; I'm just finishing your chin.'

Offal is curled at Elodie's feet, snoring softly. She carefully applies her tiny brush, the hairs coated in a glorious colour from her palette, peach tinged with a colour she would describe as light itself. She brushes against the likeness of Anna before her. She wants it to be her best work. She doesn't plan to sell it. It will hang here in her gatehouse.

Elodie crinkles her nose and cocks her head to one side. She pulls the brush away and smiles, looking over the canvas, shyly, at Anna's semi-naked form. The man's shirt is half undone, a breast a little exposed, thighs curving out from its hem. She knows Anna inside out, but when she paints any subject: fruit, animal, model, friend, or lover, she feels like a voyeur, capturing something they don't know she sees. Something that doesn't belong to her.

'Happy with it? May I speak, milady?' Anna sticks her tongue out. They both laugh, breaking the spell, and Elodie places her brush into the little jar of water on her little artist's table, made from a vintage stool.

'Not yet.' Elodie studies the canvas, then allows her eyes to flit to study Anna. She sighs.

'I'm so sorry, Elle.' Anna moves over from the window where she has been leaning, posing whilst wistfully staring out, as instructed.

Elodie moves towards her, allows herself to be embraced. Her hands touch the soft skin beneath the loose-fitting shirt on Anna's back, cold from the breeze blowing through the open window.

'Poor Lord Knutsworth, poor Fabien, and poor Lady Knutsworth. But my heart breaks for you. I shouldn't be here, carrying on like nothing has changed.'

'Fabien will be fine, we all will be. It was his heart

condition. You have nothing to be sorry for, and you're the only one I want here.'

Offal lets out a little growl as he dreams.

'Apart from you, of course, my little baby,' Elodie coos down at the dog. His tail wags involuntarily as he wins the imaginary dream stand-off he must have been having.

Anna opens her mouth to say something else, but Elodie stops the words with her lips.

Susannah Wilson puts down the phone, and calls to her husband.

'Yes, dear?' Martin appears in the doorway with a tea towel, midway through drying up the last of the pans from tonight's dinner.

The house still smells of roast chicken and with Chloe away, and no further visits from the police, it feels like life is returning to normal. Of course, Martin worries for Mila, but he can't help but think that DS Grant may have had a point, when he'd quietly suggested one might be able to understand why some people prefer to disappear. He hopes she is okay. He feels guilty for hoping that he can have his predictable old life back. Perhaps boring Geoff wasn't such a bad match for his daughter after all.

'That was Lydia.'

Martin's smile drops, as he thinks to himself, what now?

'They have set a date for the funeral, now that the case is closed. She's terribly frail. I said I'll help. Elodie has locked herself away in her studio, and apparently Fabien is in London. Honestly, you'd think they'd rally around a little more.'

'Hmmm.' Martin wonders how much rallying Chloe would do if he dropped dead, then feels bad for doing his daughter a disservice. He knows she is a kind girl really, wracked with insecurities. Probably their fault for spoiling her.

'I'm going to call the florist first thing tomorrow, and the caterers.'

'What about Anna? Won't she help?'

'Well, you'd think,' Susannah says, 'but Lydia says she's been awfully quiet and absent of mind since poor Gregory died, and she's been told to take a little time off to grieve, which seems terribly inconsiderate. After all, she's staff, not family.'

'Right.'

'Lydia, such a compassionate soul, thinks perhaps his death has brought back memories of Anna's mother's death. Lydia said they were like parents to her. Anna was very fond of the lord; she saw to his every whim.' Martin raises an eyebrow. 'For goodness' sake, Martin, get your mind out of the gutter! The Knutsworths aren't into that sort of thing. Their marriage was rock solid, like ours is.'

'No, of course.'

'The upshot is, Lydia is determined that things go to plan. After all, the press will be there, invited or not, and they've been on the wrong end of that stick for a few months now. She desires dignity.'

'Don't we all.'

'Anna is still to do the work, but I shall direct and supervise whenever Lydia finds it too much.'

'You couldn't be more suited, darling.'

'Martin, are you being sarcastic?'

'Of course not... but Lydia just phoned you to ask you to help manage her housekeeper?'

'Not exactly. I phoned the house as I still hadn't heard about the funeral, and it has been quite some time. Lydia wouldn't dream of imposing on such a good friend. After all, I'm not her staff!' Susannah lets out an odd high-pitched giggle, 'I offered. Insisted. It's the least I can do. As her friend.'

The phone shrills loudly next to Susannah.

'Hello Jenny,' she says, mouthing pointlessly to Martin, "*It's Jenny*".

Martin turns to leave the room, and hears his wife say, 'No, she isn't here. Chloe's away staying with friends. She took the car actually, without asking – just left a note saying she'd had to rush off somewhere. They're all so inconsiderate, so I know how you feel. I gave her a piece of my mind when I spoke to her. Apparently, there was some drama with a friend from university in Manchester – a girlfriend meeting called urgently, etcetera, etcetera. She's keeping us posted around her return, but it really isn't on...'

Susannah's voice fades, as Martin hangs the tea towel on the hook and clicks on the kettle, which whirrs into life, steam almost immediately emitting from the spout.

'Martin,' Susannah says, as she walks into the kitchen, 'Lottie hasn't come home, and her phone is off. Jenny's going out of her mind. We need to phone Chloe, in case she's with her. She wondered if she'd gone along after on the train; you know how she worships Chloe. You call from your mobile; she'll ignore me after I told her off about taking my car. She knows I need it most days.'

'This place has gone mad,' Martin says, retrieving his phone from his jeans pocket, finding his daughter in favourites, and tapping call. '... It's switched off.'

CHAPTER FORTY-EIGHT

The doorbell chimes at Rose Cottage, Jenny and Keith Beard's pretty roadside dwelling. Jenny stops wringing her hands, and looks at her husband expectantly.

'See, dear, what did I tell you? That will be them now,' he says, using his authoritative councillor tone to mask the fear.

Bad things don't happen in nice places like Farlington. Except, lately, that isn't true at all. To avoid rising panic, Keith has been working on his lecture, which he will bestow on his daughter when it turns out she's followed that dreadful Chloe to some party. He will ground her until she is twenty-one.

He only called the police because Jenny insisted. A rather curt woman on the end of the phone had told him that as she was sixteen, she wasn't automatically considered high-risk; it was quite common for older teenagers to be late home, and that perhaps he might like to give it at least until the end of the day. Councillor Beard had insisted they send someone immediately, and hung up before they could refuse.

Both Jenny and Keith stride down the hallway to greet the humble policeman.

'And about time, too!' Keith greets the young officer and

swings the door wide open, gesturing elaborately for him to enter, mock welcoming.

'Sorry?'

'PC Atkins, isn't it? I expect your colleague has filled you in, but we are happy to go over it one more time. Important to be thorough, don't you think?'

'Um, yes. But–'

'Through here, PC Atkins,' Jenny leads the way to the living room and gestures to the chesterfield armchair in the corner, but Hoppy Atkins remains standing.

'I'm here about Lottie.'

'Yes.'

'I'd like to speak with her.'

'So would we, so what do you propose? Have you found her?' Keith looks at his wife quizzically, shrugging his shoulders, palms up, thinking perhaps the young officer is a bit dim.

'You've lost her?' Hoppy Atkins' phone starts to vibrate in his pocket, 'Sorry', he says taking it out, 'It's my DS, one moment.'

After less than one minute of indiscernible grunts quietly muttered into the phone, Hoppy returns to the living room, both sets of eyes boring into him, searching for meaning in this odd exchange.

'I see what has happened here. You spoke to PC Helen Phillips, who was on the desk earlier, to report your daughter missing. She recommended, perfectly in line with procedure, that you wait to see if she comes home a little later before we officially file a report. So, I didn't know she wasn't here. That, in fact, you believe her to be missing.'

'What are you talking about? You're here, so what's going on? Something terrible has happened; I just knew it. You've found her, haven't you?' Jenny's hysteria pierces her voice, and her husband puts an arm around her.

'Just tell us, now,' Keith swallows. His heartbeat is irregular, his stomach feels unusual.

'I'm terribly sorry to have worried you both. I have no information about Lottie's whereabouts, and no reason to suspect she has come to any harm at this time.'

'What–'

'DS Grant and I have recently come across new information into the investigation into Lord Knutsworth's death. Information that involves Lottie. I came to ask her about it. Perhaps if she was alerted to the fact she may be about to be questioned, she has absconded.'

'What's Lottie got to do with his death? We heard it was a heart attack, case closed. The funeral's a week on Tuesday.'

'You have no idea where she could have gone?'

'What is it you think she's done, officer? She's a good girl. If she's been associated with any wrongful acts, mark my words, Chloe will have put her up to it.'

'Did anyone call her, as far as you know? Or text her, shortly before she left?'

'She's surgically attached to her phone, she is constantly called and texted and TikTok'd, and God knows what else,' Keith tells him.

'She's very secretive about her messaging, they are at that age,' Jenny says, almost to herself.

'She's just a child. We're her parents; tell us what you think she's done. I'm sure it's nothing, and if she's frightened because you've got the wrong end of the stick, this will be on your head, Atkins.' Keith's emotions are having an epic battle, soaring through his veins, tightening his muscles. She isn't dead in a ditch. She's probably run off with Chloe, embroiled in some stupid stunt. It will all turn out to be a misunderstanding. He'll have to put one of those television appeals out reassuring her she's not in any trouble. He'll wear his new silk tie, the one she bought him for his birthday, and she'll know how much they love her, and come straight home.

'She's not in any trouble, is she?' Jenny asks.

'Right now, we just need to speak to her, to find out why she collected a prescription for Lord Knutsworth.'

Jenny starts to untense. A cautious smile on her lips, she exhales. 'She runs errands for Elodie, sometimes, walks Offal, that sort of thing. She was probably just doing a favour for the family. That's all.'

'You've managed to get all worked up about that? I expect that strange young lad always trying to impress her who works on reception got wind of your *"enquiries",* Keith mimes quotation marks with his index fingers, 'and told our Lottie she's in trouble, and now look what you've done. You better bloody find her, Atkins. You'll need to organise a press conference.'

'She has been very upset, since all the trouble with Mila, and then Lord Knutsworth. She's not been herself. My poor baby girl,' Jenny starts to cry.

Hoppy passes her a handkerchief, a spare he always keeps for bad news calls, one of his personal special touches he is proud of. It is good quality, and freshly ironed.

'She filled the prescription the morning he was found dead.'

Jenny stops mid blow, and Keith removes his arm from her shoulder. 'Excuse me?'

'We need to ascertain why she would fill a prescription for the sleeping pills he had received just days earlier, the ones we know he took on the night of his death, after his body had been found.'

'Somebody told her to. They must have.'

'Perhaps, Mr Beard, and my colleague is looking into that as we speak. But, you understand, it is important that we speak to Lottie too.'

CHAPTER FORTY-NINE

Anna is, as always, wracked with feelings of guilt. She is trying to catch up on her work, scrubbing furiously on hands and knees, making the pantry floor shine, despite it rarely being seen by anyone but her.

She hasn't been able to think straight since that night. Lord Knutsworth dead, Mila vanished, and everything suddenly an insurmountable mess. Secrets in shallow graves, itching to be discovered by the next passer-by looking in the right direction.

She must finish her week's worth of work, because she has a rare few days off, starting this evening. A surprise, Elodie told her. Anna has packed her bag and her passport. She still cannot believe Elodie loves her so much. If she knew the truth, that would all change. She owes her the truth. She keeps telling herself what she did was of no significance, but can she really be sure? After all, Hoppy seems pretty convinced something is amiss.

She shouldn't go. It can't go on. She isn't right for Elodie. She can't pay her way, and Elodie could lose her family over such a scandal. Bad enough to sleep with the help, but a woman, to boot? She is expected to marry well, to bear children. Tradition is everything here.

If she cares about Elodie as much as she tells herself she does, she will end it now. Free her from living with the woman who is a magnet for trouble and death and scandal.

Wallowing in self-pity is not how she was brought up, but Anna feels the heavy drag of responsibility in every breath. She could have done more for her mother. She should have gone to college and made more of herself. Could she have looked after this family better? One of them dead, Fabien a mess, and Elodie trapped in a relationship that can't possibly work in the long term. She wants to go back in time, be a better friend to Mila, offer her whatever help she needs. She worries every day about the girl who blew in and blew out, like leaves in a storm.

For many years, Anna believed she was worthy. She worked hard, built a life. It was a trouble free, simple life, until now. She tells herself she must be a fool, not to have seen how superficial her normal was. How easily it could all implode.

She buffs the floor and admires her work, then tips the dirty water away down the huge Belfast sink, and steps outside to retrieve the doormat and rugs that are airing on the line. She lays the rugs down on the dryish floor, and starts to ready herself to go to the gatehouse, to tell Elodie she can't possibly go. That she will leave, and allow Elodie to grieve in peace, rebuild her life away from her and the memories and pain seeing her face will always, inevitably, bring.

In the kitchen, she sits down, feeling dizzy.

Another voice joins the cacophony of conflicting demands in her head. Her mother this time. *"Be happy, just for a while, one more weekend, one trip. Don't ruin everything yet. What's done is done. You didn't mean to hurt anyone. You didn't hurt anyone, not really. You're a good girl, Anna. I could never be happy there, but you can. Do it for me. Elodie would be devastated, too. She needs you, just for a little longer, until she is strong again. Don't throw it all away for nothing. Don't make our sacrifices mean nothing."*

'It's not for nothing though, is it, Mum?'

Strolling back from the shop a little while later, Anna notices she feels less heavy. The sky is blue, and she watches the butterflies dance as she inhales the honeyed smell of the roadside buddlejas. She passes Mary, who waves at her, calling, 'Off to the rehearsals. We're doing Joseph this year, and the piano accompaniment is really quite lovely.'

Anna wishes her luck, and carries along her way, thinking how nice *almost* everyone is, and how sad she will be to leave, if that's what it comes to.

She tucks herself into the hedgerow on the narrow road as Harry carefully goes by in his big old tractor, trailing some machinery behind him that looks very unsafe. He raises a hand, and she returns the gesture.

As she passes the Old School House, she sees a notice with Lottie's image. She reads it and discovers the Beards' daughter is missing although it would appear not for long enough to warrant a grand scale search appeal. The sign urges her to come home. It says she isn't in trouble. It asks, if you see her, please persuade her to see sense. Poor Jenny, poor Keith, Anna thinks. Lottie is a lovely girl, though impressionable, a little silly. At her age she had been more mature. But Anna gets it; teenage girls will rebel. She won't have gone far.

She continues along to the outskirts of the village, where the road widens and the occasional traffic increases in speed, heading towards the estate. The ground walls already cast their shadow, although it's another ten minutes by foot. The birds are singing and the air feels fresh.

Anna keeps a steady pace, the familiar steps soothing. She carries a bag of peaches, and a bottle of wine for her and Elodie to share as they wait to leave for their flight that night. The peaches are a gift; Elodie's favourites. They'll be perfectly ripe when they come home from their trip. She'll tell her then. Or maybe she'll just disappear, like Mila. Like her mother, turned to dust.

This road sees few cars, so she is surprised to see the panda car fly past at the national speed limit.

She arrives at the estate, and inputs the code for the gates, then heads down the drive to the gatehouse.

Anna gently knocks to alert Elodie to her arrival, and then turns the large iron door knocker. It's locked. She takes out her key and lets herself in, calling Elodie's name.

Offal answers by charging up to her, tail wagging, barking his hello.

'Hello, cutie.' She scratches behind his ears, and he rolls over for a tummy tickle.

'Elle!' Anna calls again.

'Anna? Is that you? Anna, help me!' The voice is muffled, and distant.

'Elodie?'

'Anna, I'm in the priest hole!'

'Jesus Christ, what?' Anna throws back the rug covering the ancient priest hole and pulls it open.

A head pops up, a face streaked with tears. A girl, but not Elodie.

As she offers her a hand to climb out, she exclaims, 'Lottie! What were you doing down there?'

CHAPTER FIFTY

Elodie is saying nothing. She stares defiantly across the table at PC Atkins and DS Grant. DI Payne had nodded curtly as she passed her in the corridor, a different reception from when she was mopping up the incompetent handling of her father's death, when she was considered a victim rather than whatever they considered her to be now.

'You do know you're not under arrest, Miss Knutsworth?' Grant reminds her. 'We just need to follow up. Answer a few remaining questions.'

'No comment.'

'We are just trying to ascertain if you asked Lottie to go to the surgery and request they provide a repeat prescription for sleeping tablets for your father.'

Elodie remains silent.

'We can see no reason why Lottie would do that unless asked. Unless you think Lottie had any reason to want to replace tablets that had perhaps been used prematurely, or misplaced? Is there any reason Lottie would have had anything to do with Lord Knutsworth's medication supplies?'

'We know Chloe visited the house earlier that day. She and Lottie are close, aren't they?' Hoppy adds.

Elodie snorts, forgetting her stoicism. 'Chloe just uses her, like she uses everyone.'

'It's just odd that at the exact moment that Lottie was asking for pills that otherwise might have raised questions in the surgery, you had Mrs Worthington occupied on the telephone. One might think you were creating a distraction.'

'No comment.'

'We understand the scripts are usually collected by the housekeeper, Miss Anna Kowaski. Someone will be speaking to her shortly. Let's hope she can be more enlightening than you.'

'I'm happy to help, officers. I'm just waiting for legal advice. Given your handling to date of the tragic episode that killed my father, your inability to find a local refugee wanted for murder, and now your clumsy attempt to make a mystery out of a prescription mix-up by dragging a daughter in mourning to the station, when I'm supposed to be flying for a much-needed break tonight, you'll understand I simply want to ensure that the matter is managed correctly.'

'About that trip,' Hoppy says, 'I noticed the tickets on the table by the door. Honduras, very nice. Any reason you and your housekeeper only seem to have one-way tickets?'

CHAPTER FIFTY-ONE

Peter is returning confiscated phones to the group like a parent unsure if his offspring can be trusted. But with everyone fully filled in on what really happened to Mila's family, their responses were unmistakably genuine. Chloe had cried, with only a little added dramatic effect, and embraced Mila. 'I'm sorry,' she had whispered, 'I didn't know.'

Mila has insisted they have to build trust by trusting. Besides, the process of deciphering the paper trail Xristina and her PI have been collecting over the years is going to be arduous, and they all need access to the web. Xristina has joined them at Monty's place, and they are sitting around the large dining table covered in papers, as Fabien, Chloe, and A.J. switch on their devices. Immediately, two of the phones let out a series of angry beeps.

'Crap,' mutters Chloe, 'I'd better call my mum.'

'What the...?' Fabien stares at his phone.

'What is it? What's wrong? What's happened now?' Mila asks.

'It's good news! Finally!'

'Spit it out, boy!' demands Nikolai.

LISA NICHOLAS

'My father died of a heart attack!'

'Um, congratulations?' A.J. says.

'What the hell?' Xristina says, 'How is this good?'

'It means they know he wasn't murdered. By me, or by Mila. It is one less obstacle for us to clamber over when trying to get justice.'

'It means it is time to grieve properly, too,' Mila tells him, walking over to stand behind him, a hand on his shoulder.

Fabien places his hand on top of hers and closes his eyes. Suddenly, his father's death is raw and real, not part of a crazy nightmare. An old man, taken too soon in the age-old cliché of his damaged heart giving out.

Fabien wipes away a tear – no time for that right now – and calls his mother. He listens and apologises, and explains he will be home in time for the funeral. At that she starts to cry, and Fabien promises he will be back sooner if he can be. He feels terrible for not helping more. He doesn't know what Elodie is doing, though it would appear to be nothing.

'You should go now,' Mila tells him. 'They need you.'

'I'm needed here more. Let me help, just for a day or two. We might break it open. If not, I'll go.'

Everybody gives it everything they can, even Chloe, who finally realises what it feels like to be part of something, to help, and it feels good. But the work is arduous, and the long lists of leads to follow creates a maze of unfathomable data that even Peter's algorithms are finding a slog.

'It's bloody endless,' Fabien complains a few hours later. 'I never was great at online research.' Each name on the statement he searches for, follows the data, until inevitably he finds nothing.

'What if we can't find any connections?' A.J. asks, scrolling through the foreign news channels and social media pages suggested by Mila, looking for familiar names. A.J. is immensely experienced, and very efficient, in the quirks of social media and is relishing the role. He hasn't found anything they haven't already seen before, though.

'We will,' answers Peter, not looking up.

'Peter's right,' says Chloe.

'If we don't, we might have to just send what we have to the papers, the police. Hope they see something we don't,' Xristina adds, 'and maybe Anton will stay hidden forever.'

'And me,' Mila says quietly.

'I just wish I knew what has happened to him,' says Xristina, 'or what he might have done. I just don't know anymore. If he knows what Janos has done to his new family, with the death of his brother so raw, he will be full of rage. He already was.'

'We're going to solve this, Xristina. Anton is going to come home, and Karlie and Konstantine too. We have to believe it. Then I can go home, as well.'

Fabien looks at Mila.

'I'm not here to start a life in Farlington,' she says. 'Sorry, Fabien, I don't mean it like that, but I came here to find Xristina, and expose Janos. I came here to get justice for my sister, and rescue the children.'

Fabien nods, sadly, and goes back to his work. He can't blame her. Then he sees something, and freezes, looks a little closer. 'Wait a minute,' Fabien says, 'I know this name.'

'Really? It's a real name?' Peter says, not believing it.

'Halleluiah!" sings out Nikolai.

'We thought someone had to slip up somewhere, we hoped. Who is it?'

'It's one of Monty's companies; one he said we should invest in.'

'Another dead end.' Even Mila was starting to become despondent.

'What's the name?'

'Horton Fawcett Industries. Monty said they specialised in drones to make wars safer, get supplies in, but it turned out they were selling drones to deliver bombs to the enemy.' Fabien glances at Mila, who cannot look him in the eye.

Peter types, Fabien types, A.J. types, and all the searches lead to nothing more than search results taking them to similarly named companies.

'I remember them, because we put a large tranche of investments to them, not long before it all blew up. I should have seen something was up. Monty was on edge, bad tempered, insistent we get the deal done. I thought he was just finally feeling the pressure of proper employment, and that maybe he was doing too many drugs.'

'We need to find Monty,' Mila says. 'If Peter's software can't track these people down, we have no chance with a search engine. And if they're paying creeps like Janos, who knows how deeply they're involved. They're not just selling weaponry to the bastards; they're clearly actively involved in spying, in trying to change the course of the war. If Monty knows them, he must be terrified.'

Xristina's phone rings. 'I don't know this number,' she frowns into the screen and answers it anyway. She says nothing, but breathes heavily, swallows loudly, and at the end she whispers, 'I love you too.' She collapses into her chair.

Everyone looks at her.

'That was Anton. He's okay, thank God. He was calling from a burner. He said, "Don't say anything Mum, just listen." He had convinced Janos he was on his side; he's been with him this whole time, and that's why he couldn't risk being in touch with me. He started to gather even more evidence against him, but someone in their circle started to suspect, and now he has to lie low,' Xristina says, wiping away a tear, swallowing.

'And the children?' Mila asks quietly.

'Janos has them. But they're okay, for now. Janos is in with some dangerous people. But Anton will watch Karlie and Konstantine from a distance – I know he won't let anything happen to them. He's hiding out in a cabin in the woods where we used to camp when the children were little.' Xristina bursts into tears, and Mila sits on the arm of the chair and strokes her hair. 'He said he's going to go back for them. I just pray he doesn't do anything stupid.'

Mila says nothing. She knows what a huge risk Anton is taking, but if he can't get Karlie and Konstantine back, then at best they face a life of misery, their minds polluted with Janos' lies and hatred. Hands reach across the table, making a circle and squeezing gently. There's nothing to say, just work to do and faith to keep. They can't fail now, and time is shorter than ever. But a breakthrough feels heartbreakingly unlikely.

'He called on a burner phone?' A.J. asks quietly.

The group releases one another and turns to him.

'I just remembered; Monty has a burner. For his horticulture stuff.'

'And you're just telling us now?' Fabien is both incensed with rage at the idiotic youth, and absolutely delighted at the potential of this baffling information.

'Well, I wasn't thinking about it before you mentioned we need him to solve this whole thing two minutes ago. Didn't really pay attention to your beef with him.'

'It doesn't matter now,' Mila says, squeezing Fabien's arm. 'You have the number, A.J.? We need a strategy, and then we need to call him. We just have to hope he hasn't got rid of the phone already.'

CHAPTER FIFTY-TWO

Mila Kiss is standing at her makeshift whiteboard. They have stuck their printed sheets together, pinned onto what A.J. remembers Monty describing as a priceless piece of art, and which Fabien knows to be worth about a hundred grand. However, nobody is feeling very sympathetic to Monty right now, so they both decide to keep quiet.

Mila has gone into full professional lawyer mode, and to Fabien she looks more beautiful than ever as she furrows her brow, draws incomprehensible diagrams, and tries to help them keep up with the jargon. 'You understand that you were most likely to be found wholly liable for the claims against your business by the investors as CEO and sole signatory, which in corporate law is fine, except there is another avenue: the tort of deceit. Basically, your friend defrauded you intentionally, and so you can claim against him, separately, to recoup your losses in the business. It's a more complex case, because we have to prove that he misrepresented information on purpose – and that you acted on the basis of this fraud and manipulation.' The group nods along, obedient, brains whirring, feeling rusty and like they might need more fuel. 'Now, it seems that will be easier than I thought originally, because the company he persuaded you to invest in has been paying someone we believe to be a traitor and a spy. This is something we have evidence for. It's limited, I grant you, but as we take each piece of the puzzle, it starts to create a compelling whole.'

'I'm very pleased Fabien can get all his money back, but how does this help our cause? I mean *your* cause?' A.J. asks.

'Simple: leverage. This is what we use to get Monty home. We have a strong criminal case against him. There will likely be something that connects him to a company that his and Fabien's investors were used to fund, without their consent, who then turn out to be paying spies and supporting an invasion that has been universally condemned by the world. Not to mention the fact he has a marijuana farm in his spare room. If he comes home, and gives us Horton Fawcett, we can do a deal with him. It wouldn't be too hard to argue he too was duped.'

'He does sound like a bit of a nitwit. Easily duped,' Nikolai interjects, sampling another new insult he has recently discovered on an old British sitcom.

'He won't know we don't want the police involved yet, so we can tell him that our next move is to officially report him for fraud. And drug dealing. Monty won't want to hide forever, which he'd have to do if his name came out in all this.'

I can tell you,' adds Fabien, 'the thought of his father will scare him more than prison.'

Fabien's phone silently buzzes for the tenth time in as many minutes.

'Maybe you should get that?' Mila tells him.

'It's my mother. She's going to try and call me back to help with the funeral. I can't leave now.'

'Answer it,' Mila and Nikolai demand in unison.

'Family first,' Nikolai adds.

Fabien walks away as he greets his mother, stepping out

onto the balcony, into the fresh cold air not yet warmed by the sun slowly rising up into the sky. He pulls the door gently closed behind him.

When he returns, blinking, his mouth is opening and closing as he struggles to form a sentence.

'Was it about the funeral, Fabien?' Chloe asks.

'Yes,' he manages to reply quietly, 'and no. It might have to be postponed. They've taken Elodie in for questioning. Harrop's on his way to represent her. They think she's involved in something illegal around our father's death. It's impossible. And apparently it has something to do with Lottie who, as seems to be par for the course these days, has gone missing. It's all a bit of a mess. Mother is beside herself.'

'Go,' Mila instructs. 'We can manage.'

Fabien is perched on the hard plastic chair in reception. The police station is quiet and his polystyrene cup is still full of insipid beige liquid. He taps his foot. He glances around, but the doors remain shut. The top of PC Phillips' head is visible behind the front desk screen, as she concentrates on something he can't see due to the height of the counter.

PC Phillips has informed him that Elodie is with Atkins and Grant, and Harrop has arrived. They have prepared a statement, and are going through it now. They shouldn't be too much longer.

'And then I can take her home? It will have all been cleared up?' he asks.

'I couldn't say.'

Hoppy Atkins knows there is more to it than Elodie Knutsworth is giving them. Even Grant seems less keen than usual to find the path of least resistance.

'You asked Lottie to collect your father's prescription, because you had agreed to run the errand and then forgotten. You asked her before you knew of your father's death, but she didn't go the surgery until the day his body was found. You were supposed to be running the errand as a favour to your housekeeper, who had misplaced the original pills, and was upset about being in trouble. Rather than send her back to face up to questioning from the receptionist, you offered to sort it out.'

'Yes. I knew she was upset over nothing, but it was a simple kindness to offer, I thought.'

'But you didn't sort it; you sent Lottie. And you didn't see there being a problem with Lottie, a sixteen-year-old girl of no relationship to the patient the prescription is for, with no precedent of collecting his prescriptions, having any issues with the notoriously fierce Mrs Worthington?'

'I ran out of time. Everyone knows Lottie works for me–'

'But you *did* foresee such an issue arising,' Hoppy continues, 'as just at the moment that Lottie reached the desk, you telephoned Mrs Worthington and proceeded to keep her on the phone, distracted by your distress, as by then your father had been found dead and therefore the mission was defunct, yet you continued with your plan. You stayed on the phone until Lottie was safely back out of the door with the prescription. You knew she would be seen by Mrs Worthington's nephew, and I expect you imagined he would be more of a pushover.'

'You are full of speculation this afternoon, gentlemen,' Harrop says with a smirk. 'It may be surprising to you – after all, we know you suffer from a touch of reverse snobbery – to find that Elodie and Anna are good friends, and Elodie was trying to help her friend, but lost track of time, and to rectify her forgetfulness she asked Lottie, who often does small jobs for Elodie, to help out. And as for the notion there was a *"plan"*; that's utter nonsense. The phone call made to reception at that time is a coincidence, and I'm sure you won't fault a daughter for calling a doctor upon the sudden death of her father. We are simply faced with a series of unfortunate events.' Atkins snorts, and Grant shakes his head. He opens his mouth to argue. Harrop taps his palm on the desk loudly, and clears his throat, silencing the officers. 'I will give you that it is unfortunate that two of the three people in question were unable to fulfil a simple task of collecting a prescription and keeping it safe, but beyond this lapse in competence, the three women have done nothing wrong, and simply each tried to be helpful in their own way. I respect you are both doing your jobs, but really, the post-mortem was clear; Lord Knutsworth died of a cardiac event and slipped into the pool. The tox report didn't show an unreasonable amount of the sleeping pill medication in his system, but we do know he had a heart condition. We are all devasted, and your insistence on treating this tragedy as suspicious is doing untold damage to a grieving family. We will be taking further action against this constabulary at the appropriate point.'

'Three women, all trying to help one another, you say,' says Atkins, trying to sound breezier than he feels.

'Hmm,' Harrop is making notes, starting to close his notepad, readying himself to leave, his client beside him.

'So, where is the third?' Harrop looks up. 'The woman, Miss Charlotte – Lottie – Beard, who was sent to the surgery to collect a repeat prescription that had already been collected by the housekeeper, by your client, who for no reason we are yet to see was choosing Mrs Worthington to confide in–'

'It wasn't for no reason! I thought we needed to speak to the practice, to get the death certificate or something! To at least register what had happened. I was trying to be helpful to Mother, who was quite hysterical,' Elodie interrupts.

'As I previously mentioned, it was just a coincidence that Lottie was collecting the medication at that moment,' says Harrop, shushing Elodie with a look.

Atkins scowls. 'The woman who was sent to the surgery is missing.'

'Missing?' asks Harrop.

'Doesn't that strike you as odd, Elodie? Do you know where she is? If we find her, what will she tell us that you won't? And the other two women involved in the farce of prescription collection have two one-way tickets to Honduras, leaving first thing tomorrow.'

There is a knock on the interview room door, and PC Atkins gets up to answer it. He smiles warmly at Helen, feeling good about his interview, sure he is getting somewhere. He'll finally ask Helen for a drink this week, tell her all about it.

'A word?' she asks.

Outside, she says, 'We have Anna Kowaski on the phone. She's at the gatehouse with Lottie Beard. I think we need to get over there. She said she knows what happened the night Lord Knutsworth died, and she insists it has nothing to do with Elodie.'

CHAPTER FIFTY-THREE

'Drive fast!' Elodie commands her brother. 'And if this ridiculous car breaks down now, I swear I will torch it while you sleep.'

Her patience has almost expired, as she was kept waiting in the interview room for another twenty-five minutes once the two officers had swiftly exited following the interruption by PC Phillips. Eventually, Harrop had gone to investigate, and discovered that Elodie was free to go, although they expected they would need to continue another day.

Fabien puts his foot down and the old white Jag roars its engine. The tyres squeak as they sharply turn, pulling out of the police station car park. The second they're on the road, Elodie calls Anna. She answers after half a ring.

'Elodie, are you okay? What have you done? They've released you?'

'For now, they've had to it seems, as they have literally nothing. I told them it was all a misunderstanding. That duo of clowns hasn't a clue.'

'Lottie told me everything.'

'She shouldn't have. She *can't* have; she doesn't know everything.'

'I think I've worked it out, though, from what she does know. I know you. You saw, didn't you? What I did with the pills. Why didn't you tell me? I could have explained. You don't need to protect me. It's not what you think.'

'I know that *now*, but I couldn't tell you after what I did.'

'You couldn't tell me what you thought me capable of...'

'I didn't want to spoil things.'

'And you shouldn't have locked Lottie in the priest hole.'

'I didn't lock her in; it just doesn't open from the inside very easily!' Elodie exclaims, outrage lacing her voice. 'She came over, all hysterical. I suggested she hide there when the police arrived because she wasn't ready to talk to them. That boy, Mike? He dropped her in it.'

'Mike dropped her in it?'

'Look, Anna, I can explain. I just wanted to help her, to fix it.'

'You got us one-way tickets. Just us! Lottie would have been left behind to sort out her own problems.'

'She just had to say she was running an errand for me! It would have been fine. The girl is a half-wit, she really is.'

'Why help to hide her, then? Her parents must be worried sick.'

'I just wanted to give us a chance to get away for a while, before she mentioned my name.'

'To Honduras.'

'I hear it's lovely this time of year.'

'We weren't coming back, were we, Elodie? You wanted us to run. Why?'

'I hadn't thought that far ahead. But Lottie showed up saying the police were looking into discrepancies with the pills, that they'd find a way to blame you, or me, or both of us.'

'But it was a heart attack.'

'But he slipped and fell! I wondered, maybe the pills... maybe they'd think they were the cause.'

'You think I caused his heart attack?'

'No, no of course not! I don't know what I think, or what I thought. I just knew you weren't to blame, not really. Please, if the police show up, just stay quiet. Harrop is right behind us. We'll talk when I get there.'

'They're here now, Elodie. I can see the car through the intercom. Don't worry my darling girl, I know what I'm doing. You are innocent, like me, just trying to help. But it is my mess, not yours. I worry too, you know? Maybe you're right. It could have been me, what I did...'

'Please, wait for me. Don't tell them a thing, Anna.'

'They're knocking. I'm going to tell the truth, Elodie. You have already lost too much. If what they say about the cause of death is right, it will be okay, maybe.' Anna hangs up, and Elodie screams with rage into the silent handset, the screen now empty and dark.

Next to her, Fabien unclenches his teeth. 'What the hell have you done, Elodie?'

Soon afterwards, Elodie and Fabien burst through the gatehouse door to find Lottie being comforted by PC Helen Phillips, who has managed to get in on the action for once, while DS Griffin Grant reads Anna her rights and PC Atkins takes notes. Her hands are cuffed in front of her.

'Stop! Stop right this instant!'

Grant has finished reading the rights anyway, though they do turn to see what Elodie's next move is.

'It's fine, Elodie. I'm so sorry for what I did. I deserve to be punished.'

'No! It wasn't your fault, it was me! Take me instead,' she shouts in PC Atkins' general direction, and then to Anna, 'You don't deserve this. All you tried to do was help Mila. Like you help everyone. After everything that life has thrown at you, and still you put others first. I know what Mila meant to you.'

'It's no excuse, Elodie! I had no right.'

'Would someone like to tell me what you're talking about before I lose my shit?' Fabien's words were level and delivered slowly, but there was a hint of hysteria creeping through, like ivy in an old stone wall.

'I double dosed Lord Knutsworth.' Anna hangs her head. 'I'm so sorry, it was my fault. I just wanted him to feel more tired than usual, go to bed, and nod off early that night. After you left to warn Mila that he knew too much, that he planned to expose her, I just wanted to buy you some time, buy Mila some time.

'I knew she was another casualty of war, of displacement, but I hear what people say around the village. Like they used to say about my mother, before the hatred and the loneliness and the sense of never belonging made her lose the will to fight. I couldn't watch it again. Fabien, I knew you'd help her. But your father was raging when you left; he was going to call Harrop and disinherit you, call the police about Mila, and the Wilsons. He wasn't himself.

'I often brought him his night-time medicine, the pills mixed into his Ovaltine. But I put an extra sleeping pill in his drink that night, so he'd fall asleep before he had a chance to act. I just hoped that by the morning, you would have been able to warn Mila, tell someone who could help reveal the whole truth – whatever it was – before the mob was formed, and opinions set in stone. I acted alone. Elodie knew nothing.'

Double-dosed? One tablet extra? Elodie thinks, head spinning.

'Right, enough now. Save this for your statement at the station,' Grant instructs, showing Anna the door with his arms.

'Now hold on,' Fabien says, 'my father was not killed by an extra sleeping pill – he was found in the pool having suffered a heart attack, related to an underlying condition, which had precisely nothing to do with sleeping medication. What are you arresting Anna for, exactly?'

'Section 23 of the Offences Against the Person Act 1861 makes it an offence to unlawfully and maliciously administer to, or cause to be administered to or be taken by, any other person any poison or other destructive or noxious thing so as thereby to endanger their life or cause grievous bodily harm,' Atkins informs his audience. He'd looked it up as Anna relayed her story.

'GBH, PC Atkins? She just wanted him to sleep off his rage before he mindlessly destroyed the life of a wonderful, innocent young woman,' says Fabien.

'The innocent woman currently wanted for murder?' PC Phillips asks, but nobody answers.

'Section 24 of that act is amended to injure, aggrieve, or annoy any other person,' Atkins adds for clarity.

'Thank you, Atkins.' Grant starts to lead Anna towards the door, 'Now please read Ms Knutsworth and Ms Beard their rights. You will both be questioned over the not so minor matter of perverting the course of justice as you clearly ordered the repeat pills to cover up what you believed was possibly a lethal spiking at the time.'

'I'll let Mr and Mrs Beard know their daughter is safe,' offers PC Phillips.

Lottie starts to cry again. Elodie folds her arms and scowls.

Harrop lets himself in. 'What did I miss?'

'These three incompetent fools have once more taken an unfortunate set of unrelated incidents and turned them into a conspiracy theory. They should be put on traffic duty for the rest of their careers,' Elodie informs him.

'Just the next few weeks at least for me,' mutters Grant, 'probably preferable to this.'

'And where have you been, anyway? You could have put your foot down. This is an emergency!' Elodie says to Harrop.

'Listen, all of you. Harrop, especially. I'm hearing this for the first time myself,' Fabien announces, choosing his words carefully, 'Anna gave my father one extra sleeping pill, crumbled up into his milky drink as usual. That isn't a lethal or harmful dose, just something to make him sleep better as he was very upset. Right, Anna?' Anna nods. 'My sister, far from perverting the course of justice, was simply under the impression that a prescription needed to be filled, and sent her little helper to do so. The fact that Lottie collected it on the day my father passed is irrelevant. Why on earth would Elodie think that one extra pill could have been lethal? Admittedly she is no Einstein, but really... There was nothing for her to cover up. Look, I believe the report was clear; our father's heart showed signs of a serious cardiac episode, resulting in a fall into the pool, where he tragically died.'

'We have all read the post-mortem, Lord Knutsworth, but drugging someone is still a crime, and Lottie has already admitted that Elodie's instruction came the day of Lord Knutsworth's death, which is, quite frankly, very suspicious. Intent to harm is still a likely factor in the spiking, and a cover up seems probable, regardless of the suspect's understanding of the dose's effect. And the bruising on Lord Knutsworth was never accounted for satisfactorily.' Atkins takes a breath.

'I'd suggest it was,' Harrop interjects, 'given that the case was closed, and that the bruising was put down to general bumps and lumps of a man known to be overly active for his age.'

'Thank you, Mr Harrop,' says Grant, 'But answer me this: unless it was a cover up, why would Elodie instruct Lottie to collect additional pills, no doubt used to disguise the fact too many had been used from the existing packet, on the morning her father's body had been found?'

'She got it wrong,' Elodie tells them quietly, and looks at Anna. 'I told you she's an idiot.'

Lottie, despite her floods of tears and snot and general dramatics, takes a moment to pause and harrumph in indignation.

Elodie's smile starts slowly. 'Check your texts, Lottie. In fact, check mine, Detective. I think you'll find I texted Lottie to run the errand the night before my father was found.'

'So,' Fabien says, 'my sister's request for Lottie's help was innocently issued before my father died, and certainly well before anyone knew he had gone to meet his maker. Which, I think you will find, can only lead us to conclude that our boys and girls in blue here,' he gestures theatrically to the three officers in the room, 'have made a rather unfortunate miscalculation. Would you say that was a fair assessment, DS Grant?'

CHAPTER FIFTY-FOUR

'If you weren't weeks from retirement, I'd consider sacking you for this, Grant.' DI Payne sits behind her large desk. She has drawn the blinds, though anyone in the open plan office outside will still clearly hear the bollocking Grant and Atkins expect to receive.

'Ma'am, it was me who followed up on the prescription discrepancy, not the boss.'

'Yes, and you were right to do so, PC Atkins, and as a junior member of staff with more enthusiasm than a Labrador puppy, I would expect you to jump to conclusions. That's why you have a boss: to reign you in.'

'To be fair, the boy did uncover a spiking by the housekeeper.'

'DS Grant, it is perfectly safe to take two of those mild sleeping pills. Should she be in charge of how many he takes? No, she was out of line, and that she has admitted, but her actions were done with good intentions: to help Lord Knutsworth relax enough to sleep after a falling out with his son. There's no way the CPS will agree to take this forward. How on earth would it possibly be in the public interest?'

'She said she intended to knock him out to buy Mila time to get away from the accusations he planned to make!' Hoppy Atkins can feel justice slipping away, and it isn't fair.

'Ms Anna Kowaski's statement says no such thing.'

'Harrop's statement, with Fabien as creative director, more like,' Grant grunts, no longer interested in the repercussions of his big mouth.

'The statements corroborate with one another.' Payne casts her eyes down the printed statements from Anna, Elodie and Lottie on the desk in front of her, then looks up, ready to paraphrase. 'Lottie was given a wildly exaggerated story from Mike that she was wanted by the police, and ran to Elodie. Elodie didn't know her parents were looking for her and told her she could stay there, but said she was sure she had the wrong end of the stick. She was planning on finding out what was going on, and then you two rejects showed up causing a fuss, so Lottie hid, and you took Elodie away. At that point, she was unaware that Lottie had been reported missing so didn't mention it, particularly as you were, in her words, "*aggressively questioning based on a far-fetched conspiracy theory with no grounding in facts or reality.*"'

'Anna was desperately upset to have found a distraught Lottie in a priest hole and proceeded to get a garbled version of events, in which Anna became convinced that somehow Elodie was in trouble because of the sleeping pills, but at that stage had no idea what was going on with the farcical repeat prescription errand... and honestly, it's hardly a mystery worthy of investigation, even for you, Atkins – but she was scared that somehow her own misdemeanour was the root of the issue, and could be the key to putting everything straight. She came clean straight away to ensure her innocent partner was released, and no longer under any suspicion, and so that the misunderstanding could be put to bed.'

'A regular Juliet and Juliet,' Grant mutters.

Raising an eyebrow in his direction, Payne says, 'Problem with their relationship, Grant?'

'Don't make it about that, course not. But that family, including the housekeeper, are tight as thieves. It's all very convenient.'

'With a lot of coincidences. I don't believe in coincidences,' Atkins adds.

'As much as I would love to learn more about the intricacies of your personal philosophy, Atkins, may I continue?' Pausing for the requisite *Yes ma'ams,* Payne goes on, 'It is suggested more than once in the statements that undue speculation and pressure was used to *"corner"* a young woman in fear of losing her job, her home, and her relationship.'

'I only asked her about the nature of her relationship with Elodie. There's a half nude painting of her in the living room!'

'PC Atkins, you told her that Elodie was being questioned over suspicions she was involved in a cover-up regarding discrepancies surrounding Lord Knutsworth's death.'

'That was stupid, Hoppy,' says Grant.

'You give him too much rein, Grant,' says Payne.

Atkins says nothing.

'Learning that Elodie might be in trouble for covering something up, she felt she had to shoulder the greater burden, so she admitted to things she could easily take back in the cold light of day – intent to put the lord out of action for the evening, which has now been rephrased significantly, but regardless, as you have known for weeks, hence my instruction to close the case, the PM was clear on the cause of death. The sleeping pills, whether he took one or two, is entirely immaterial.'

'What she did *was* against the law.'

'It was, but it really is a matter of giving someone one or two harmless tablets. He was never in any danger from the extra pill.

It was his heart that did him in, that's what the evidence shows, clearly and without doubt. So, what do we gain by pursuing this? Anna will be punished enough by the guilt, and the fall out. She's no danger to our communities. And as for Elodie and Lottie, we have some apologies to make. There's no evidence the two of them weren't doing exactly what they told you all along. The fact neither of you thought to check the phone records, which would have demonstrated that Elodie had in fact asked for the errand to be run before she knew her father was dead, is beyond me.'

'Lottie did say–'

'Grant, don't interrupt. I *know* what she said. She's sixteen. Teenagers are not known for attention to detail. But because of PC Atkins' rather gung-ho interview technique conducted in front of one of Lottie's old school friends – the hapless intern, Mike – in a surgery waiting room, no less–'

Hoppy raises his hand to correct her – after all, they had been in the office-come-store cupboard – but Payne glares at him. He puts down his hand.

'Lottie got it into her head that the police wanted to speak to her in connection with a suspicious death. She'd only just been told off for her part in Chloe's pranks on Facebook, and she knew she was on pretty thin ice. She went running to Elodie, who, rather foolishly, said she could lie low there – they're sort of friends, though Lottie's more a hanger-on, from what I can see.'

'There's something very strange about the way Elodie handled it. Why didn't they just come forward, as it was all so innocent?'

'Elodie has explained she planned to get in touch about the rumour mill powered by the surgery reception, but was distracted with arrangements for the funeral. Lottie jumped in the priest hole when you lot turned up to speak to her, in a silly panic, fearing her parents more than anything. She thought you were looking for her, and she told Elodie she was frightened. Elodie figured she would find out what was going on, and should be able to get home quickly to reassure Lottie all was well. Young Lottie was hysterical about being in trouble for wasting police time with her runaway tactics, and afraid she would be grounded for life. From what I've heard, the latter is fundamentally true.'

'And the former?'

'PC Atkins, I appreciate your precious time was wasted in your search for a perfectly safe sixteen-year-old, but seeing as she ran away because of your indiscretion and lack of professionalism, I think we can call it quits.'

'Elodie must have known it would be easier to just tell us the truth, if that's what it is, rather than hiding a girl, driving her parents mad with worry. The printing costs alone for the missing person posters must have been astronomical.'

'Her mother was suffering, her brother was away, and they just wanted to get the arrangements completed. She says she took the easy path of agreeing to let the girl hang out for a day, two at most. She had no idea what the parents were going through, and hadn't seen the posters.'

'Wouldn't she be in Honduras when the funeral she was so painstakingly organising took place?'

'Grant, I know you and Atkins just won't let this go, but the one-way ticket was apparently the cheaper way to do it. Elodie does live on a budget, you know? Aside from the gatehouse, her income is from her art and private art tutoring alone. She was waiting for the cheap return flights to go on sale. She said the funeral was planned, she was getting away for a couple of days, and then would come back to face the future.'

'Long way to go for a few days...'

'I've spoken to Lady Knutsworth, who is more than happy

for no charges to be brought against her housekeeper; she will deal with that privately.'

Atkins winces, knowing what that means, feeling terrible for Anna despite his hunger to see justice done. He is fond of her, and only wishes she had seen sense and acted in accordance with the law.

'Lady Knutsworth has agreed that no complaints will be brought forward by any of the family, so long as this is the last we all hear of your amateur detective work. So, count yourself lucky. As your DI, if you'd ruined my career with your careless, under the radar shenanigans, I'd be just as happy as the rest of this bloody community to take the law into my own hands. However, this all stops here. Now. Understood?'

CHAPTER FIFTY-FIVE

The smell of the Chinese takeaway hits them before the secret knock to Monty's flat. They let A.J. in, who is now trusted to work alone, albeit with simple tasks such as collecting food from down the road.

As Peter creates algorithms to sort the masses of information they have gathered around Janos' finances, and all the faces of non-existent companies paying him to do who knows what, but definitely nothing loyal or good, Chloe patiently proofs and checks, and gets things in order. Nikolai dips in and out of the task, exhausted, drained, and emotional.

'The last supper,' Mila says.

'Before the big reveal,' adds Xristina with a smile, 'The answer to our prayers, and I hope the return of my son.'

'What time do you pick up the infamous Monty?' asks Peter.

'I'll leave straight after dinner,' replies Fabien.

As they tidy up, Fabien manages to catch Mila in the hallway, away from prying ears. 'Before I found you the first time, I just wanted to save my business. After that, I wanted to save you.'

'I don't need saving, Fabien.'

'Oh, I know. When I lost you, I realised it was you saving me. That I'd give up everything to find you.'

'I don't expect that.'

'I started to form a plan, to use the house for good. It needs to earn its keep, quite frankly. I thought we could set up a charity, to support those displaced by war... rent out rooms to partner charities, that sort of thing.'

'How would that work? I mean, earn money to pay for itself?'

'I don't know. As you can see, business isn't my strong point,' his words break into a half laugh. 'But then I found you a second time. Since working on this, with you, I see it could be even bigger than that. It could be an investigative practice: for you, for Peter, for the whole crazy little group you've created here. For campaigns to fight for justice, find people, solve problems just like this one. We'd all work from Farlington. We could live there. I think it could be charitable *and* profitable.'

Mila doesn't jump up and hug Fabien, like he had imagined. 'I don't know, Fabien. What about your mother?'

'I have a feeling she'll come round. Besides, Farlington Hall is mine now. She'll keep her quarters, but I'll bet we can't keep her out of ours. She's going to love you, just as I do.'

'We'll see.' Mila's mind is focussed on one thing, still: getting Janos, and finding the children.

The rain pours from the dark sky all the way back from Manchester Airport, and the atmosphere in the car is strained. Fabien squints out of the windscreen, wipers barely keeping up with the onslaught of water hitting it, gears low, as he tries to stop the car from aquaplaning. He is beginning to accept it is not an optimal vehicle for most occasions.

'I'm so sorry, mate.'

'Really? That's it?'

'I panicked. They sold me a pup too, all of them. They're all connected, and when it blew up, well, that was the first I knew of what I was into with those firms. The opportunities had come in fast, one after another. I thought I was rocking it, man. They lied to me.'

'Why did you up and go?'

'Figured it was all on me.'

'It wasn't. Quite the opposite, in fact.'

'I see that now.'

They travel in silence for a while, the streetlights taking turns with oncoming traffic to blind them.

'They tried to get in touch when it all started coming out. They wanted to make sure I hadn't left any evidence of connections. I didn't have any. They were too careful. They gave up on me quickly, then I chucked my phone before they changed their minds. Guess they knew I was a fool who couldn't hurt them.'

'You can hurt them now.'

'I don't know.'

'You owe it to me to try. You owe people like Mila, Nikolai, their families. These people you got into bed with hurt them. You're going to help us put it right.'

'You know I'll try. Mila's kind of terrifying. She said you could sue me.'

'I could.'

'She threatened me with all sorts, as it goes.'

'Nothing you don't fully deserve, Monty.'

Monty nods, eyes closed. 'Will you sue me? Send me down?'

'I won't. So long as you do everything in your power to help us. Now shut up and read the stuff I gave you. You need to know enough to react to whatever they say. We need them to admit Janos was in their pay, while Peter records the line. Mila has made notes on what to say and to ask to lead them into saying more than they might usually. She's a lawyer. She knows how to get stuff out of people.'

'You sure *she* shouldn't do this?'

'You have to tell them your business partner is involved with a woman on the refugee programme who is looking for Janos Byros; she's digging and your name came up. I asked you about it, because I recognised the name. You haven't said a word, but you wanted to warn them. They need to trust you, and to think you are after a bigger piece of the pie. My business is dead, and I'm liable. You're free to walk and help them make new contacts in the UK, just like you did before.'

'Fabien, I...'

'They're not gangsters, Monty; they're greedy businessmen.'

'Who *know* gangsters. Didn't you say they're all involved with traitors in the war? Murderers?'

'I'm sure your contacts don't get their hands dirty.'

Monty exhales, tries to feel better.

'I mean, your guys probably give the orders, though.'

'Shit, what?'

'Maybe, maybe not.' Fabien is enjoying himself a little.

'Right.'

'You have to do this, Monty... and once you do, and we have what we need, we can go to the police and we will all be safe. Mila can locate the children, and apply to bring them here. And Anton can come home.'

'Who is Anton?'

'Anton is Janos' son, Xristina's, too. They are the ones who collected all the evidence. Xristina is Janos' ex-wife. Mila found her through letters hidden amongst her sister's belongings.'

Monty does a few mental calculations, and thinks he is keeping up. 'And what about the rest of the crew I'm about to be held hostage by?'

'Mila leads the charge. She hasn't always known what she was looking for, but she knows at each step how to move forward. Peter has the tech; he finds people,' Fabien explains.

'He didn't find me.'

'He would have done, but A.J. got there first,' says Mila.

'And so where did you find Peter?' Monty asks.

'Tech wizard, and son of Nikolai, who Mila met on the plane. She ran there when she thought she was being set up back in Farlington, and would possibly be sent home before she'd had a chance to find Xristina. He was the only person she knew who might possibly be sympathetic. He's massively sped things up for us, with his clever apps and what-not.'

'And Chloe's here... why?' Monty asks, having spent a great deal of time in Farlington over the years.

'Long story, but give her a chance; seems she's turned a corner.'

'Hey, I'm in no position to be withholding second chances.'

Fabien pulls up outside Monty's skyscraper. 'You ready?'

'I'm ready.'

Peter has set up a line from his computer masked with Monty's old number, ready to source the owner and location of any number it connects to.

'I'm not sure my contact will still answer though,' Monty complains. It feels like a very precarious set-up, in which he is the only one with a name and a face they recognise.

'Apart from me,' Fabien had reminded him, crossly. 'They probably saw it in the papers when you destroyed my reputation.'

Monty had wanted to point out that Fabien's photo used to be in the minor celebrity nightclub columns all the time, alongside fawning write-ups in glossy magazines, but he decided to leave that until after he had somehow got through this.

'No real reason why he wouldn't,' Peter tells him. 'He's covered the tracks of his different businesses very well. His name isn't linked to them anywhere. As far as he is concerned, he is squeaky clean. Just makes money in dubious ways.'

'He's certainly not the first,' Nikolai joins in, darting a look at Fabien, and a worse one at Monty.

Mila squeezes Fabien's hand. 'Without you both, we couldn't do this. Thank you.'

'And now she's a diplomat too! Clearly spent too much time away from home,' says Xristina, winking at Mila.

'He will simply claim any connection to Horton Fawcett was purely an investment, and anything they did illegally abroad or otherwise was their problem. He won't be expecting you to be recording the call.'

'Here, look,' Mila gestures to the written prompts she has prepared. 'You have lines for every eventuality, and we will signpost you if you're getting lost. He'll know Janos killed my sister, no doubt has helped him cover this up, amongst other things, or at least knows those who did. He needs to say it, Monty. He needs to confess it all, and this is how you'll make him.' She stars key points with a pencil.

'All chummy, I suppose, as he and I laugh about how we were both in bed with the big bad wolf but, woo hoo, got away with it – so let's jump into the next adventure together? And by the way, do you mind implicating yourself in covering the tracks of a murderer?'

'Any better ideas?' Chloe injects, arms folded, looking fierce, 'because these people around you have worked tirelessly for justice, and it would seem to me that this is the only way you have a small chance of disentangling yourself too.'

A text beeps, and Xristina squeals. 'Oh God, oh God, I can't believe it! 'My Anton! He has them – the children! Janos is dead!'

'What? How?!' Mila roars with relief, hugs Xristina, hugs everyone. The questions, the disbelief, the screams, the thudding hearts make the room feel like a storm, as Monty looks on, trying to keep up.

'Oh, Mila! The children, they're hiding with Anton. But he's afraid he won't get out of the country with them, that the Byros family is looking for them, and looking for blood, too. I don't know who did it, but if they suspect Anton, he's in real danger now. They all are. He's ditching the phone, just in case. Promises to be in touch when it is safe.'

Mila wants to wail with relief, but fear and urgency compete for her attention. There is no time for complacency, not yet. 'Okay, this is more important than ever now, Monty; we need to get them all out of there. Do not fuck this up.'

Monty nods, and they take their positions. He puts on the headset. Peter connects, and the phone starts to ring.

CHAPTER FIFTY-SIX

Anna and Elodie lie naked in the sheets on Elodie's messy bed. Anna strokes Elodie's arms, feels her tears on her shoulder. Offal is curled up on his bed in the corner of the bedroom, noisily tearing a small fluffy animal to shreds.

'I still wish you had just told me you'd seen me crumble the pills into the drink, Elodie. Then you would have known it was only one extra; you wouldn't have had to get involved. That you could think I'd kill your father, and then still not say a word, just to protect me. I don't know whether to feel loved or to want to scream at you for being so foolish.'

'Oh Anna, I didn't realise at first. I'd tried to soften Daddy with a game of Scrabble by the pool. He always used to let me win, and we'd chat about school and I'd tell him little secrets. I thought if I talked to him in there, while we played, I might be able to talk sense into him. I knew how upset you were that he might be about to get Mila into hot water. It didn't work; he was adamant. I went to tell you where he was for his evening drink, and to tell you I was sorry I couldn't change his mind. I'd said goodbye, but as I walked away I just wanted to kiss you. But when I got back you were finishing up the drink. I saw you add white powder from the pestle, but I didn't quite think about what you were doing with the drink until later.'

'But you went back to the pool room...'

'To try one more time to make Daddy see reason.'

'Oh, my poor love! I had no idea what you went through.'

'When I saw him lying face down in the pool, you adding what looked like quite a bit of powder to his drink flashed into my mind. I acted without thinking, as always. I thought I had to replace any missing pills before he was found. I had no idea how many should be there, so I figured if I just swapped out the open pack with a brand new one, nobody would look any closer. As soon as Lottie had fetched them the following morning – I'd told her to do it first thing the following day – I was going to raise the alarm. But Mummy came home early.'

'I'll never forgive myself for being the reason you had to leave him there all night. You must have been so afraid for me, until the post-mortem revealed it wasn't due to sleeping pills at all. But still, you said nothing.'

'By then I knew I'd messed everything up. Made your actions look much, much worse. I thought you'd blame me. Be angry...'

'I'm sad you thought I could have killed him. I'm sadder you couldn't confide in me. But your mother is right. What I did is unforgivable, and although they say it did not cause his death, I still think sometimes, maybe it did. Maybe he was too tired to fight the heart attack.'

'It wasn't that, Anna; we know that now.'

'I don't want to make you sadder, Elodie, darling, and I will. You know deep down that your father's death will always be linked to my meddling. And it will haunt us, and eventually it will destroy us. Let us be this forever, in our memories and in our hearts.'

'No,' Elodie says, in a whisper. 'No,' it's louder now. 'NO!' Offal stops disembowelling his toy. His ears prick up.

'Yes,' Anna tells her gently. 'It is for the best. Besides, I've been given my P45 today; I've been sacked, and I don't blame her Ladyship one bit.'

Elodie storms into the main house.

'Mother! How could you?' She slams the drawing room door behind her and stands in front of her mother's favourite armchair.

'I suspect you're talking about your girlfriend, or my housekeeper, are you?' Lydia's voice is icy.

'Is that why? Because we are in love?'

'Do grow up, Elodie. You can't marry the housekeeper. It's bad enough that she's female, but the help?! It's unthinkable.'

'Seriously? I know you're old fashioned, but I didn't have you down as a bigot.'

'I'm not a bigot, darling. I helped organise the Pride banner on the Old School House last year. I led the war refugee committee. It was my idea! I welcomed Mila. I liked her. And I've always looked out for Anna.'

'Shame you can't do more than lip-service. Put your money where your mouth is. Committees and banners don't mean a thing if you can't accept difference in your own world.'

'I never batted an eyelid at her lack of references. I could tell she needed us. She was only seventeen when her mother died, and she needed to support herself. *They*,' Lydia continues, gesturing around, indicating a wider community somehow from the confines of her own favourite room, in which the wider community is rarely entertained, 'can marry who they like. And good for them. It's different for us. For you. You have duties to uphold. As does your brother. Your father was right on one count at least: I have been too soft on you both. And you can forget about me reinstating Anna as staff here.'

'Why? She has been so loyal, so good, and she loves it here! At least give her proper notice to find something else.'

'Why?' Lydia repeats, voice rising, standing from her chair, almost knocking over her gin and tonic on the side table. 'She damn-well poisoned your father! And no matter how liberal a person is, no matter how much I like the woman, spiking my husband is not something I can overlook in a member of staff.'

'Father died of a cardiac failure, Mother! Anna just gave him something to help him rest better.'

'I will not have a housekeeper in my house who is happy to medicate me or my family, and if I were you, I wouldn't have her in your bed!'

'That's none of your business.'

'On that matter, you are correct, Elodie.'

'What?'

'Anna will not be working at Farlington Hall any longer. As I say, I will not be able to employ someone who has done something so sneaky to serve their own interests, noble or otherwise. Nor will I have my daughter marrying our housekeeper. I assume given your crass sentimentality a few moments ago, you think you will want to marry her, someday?'

'Yes, Mummy,' Elodie replies, confused.

'Well, then, you had better invite her as our guest for tea, so we can talk about your future plans. I recall Anna having dreams of becoming a teacher.'

Elodie closes her eyes and considers the true meaning of her mother's actions. She smiles, starts to cry, and hugs her mother for the first time in years.

Lydia stands stiffly and extracts herself. Looking into her daughter's eyes, she says, 'I'm still angry and hurt, Elodie, because of the lies, the secrets. It's almost too much to bear. There's a long way to go for all of us.'

'We'll do the work, I promise, both of us. You'll see, we will earn your trust again.'

CHAPTER FIFTY-SEVEN

DS Griffin Grant and PC Hoppy Atkins are surprised to get the note from Fabien, handwritten on thick, handmade writing paper, the family crest in the corner.

> *I would be most grateful if you would do my father the respect of attending the funeral. St Luke's Church, Farlington, Friday 28th October, 11am.*
> *Yours truly,*
> *Lord Fabien Knutsworth*

Griffin Grant and Hoppy Atkins have been waiting in the library at the wake for twenty minutes.

'This is odd,' remarks Atkins.

'Indeed,' replies Grant, and then they resume their uncomfortable silence.

The door opens, and Fabien walks in, followed by Peter.

'Peter Popov!' Atkins exclaims.

'What the...?' Grant begins, remembering the interview in the big open plan kitchen in Cheshire in their search for Mila

Kiss. The case long since filed away, the Home Office team is now liaising with the local force in her home country, who still wishes to question her over the death of her sister.

'Nice to see you again, gentlemen,' Peter says.

Atkins and Grant start to rise, as Grant says, 'My sincere condolences.'

'Please stay seated,' Fabien says, as he and Peter take the opposite armchairs. 'We understand you have been castigated following the botched investigation into my father's death.' Grant clears his throat, as Atkins wrings his hands at the unfairness of it all. 'PC Atkins, your hopes of rapid promotion are vastly weakened. DS Grant, your final weeks after years of service are to be spent under scrutiny, and without the respect of your colleagues. Your career will be ending in a cloud of amusement and derision.'

'Did you bring us here purely to gloat, Lord Knutsworth?'

'I brought you here because I think we can help one another.'

Peter takes out his phone, and swipes.

Fabien continues, 'We have a recording. This recording exonerates Mila Kiss from the crimes she is accused of. It implicates a firm my business invested in, in what we believe to be a large-scale conspiracy to undermine the defence efforts against the war the whole world is united against. It demonstrates that Janos Byros, the man behind the accusations against Mila, is a traitor of the highest order, as well as being the true culprit in the murder of Mila's sister following years of abuse. After that, we can play you the testimony of this fake war hero's ex-wife Xristina, whom he also beat. His ex-wife who lost her son at his hands. His ex-wife, whose only other son is in danger now, because of Janos Byros and his associates.'

'You found Mila?'

'Of course,' Peter says, without looking up.

'What is this about? Why bring us here, Fabien? Why not hand it in at the station, at Scotland Yard, even? What exactly do you want?' Grant asks.

'Immunity. Anonymity. For the other voice on this recording, and for everyone who you work out may have been involved in our investigation, and in looking after Mila. You will tell them this recording, and this evidence,' Fabien walks over to the desk and pulls a large cardboard box file from a drawer, 'was delivered to your home address.'

'Why didn't you just deliver it to my home address?'

'Because, as much as we respect your audacious attitudes to crime-solving, we weren't entirely sure you would be able to, um,' Fabien glances at Peter.

'We assumed you wouldn't understand the connections, even after my algorithms and Mila's words have greatly simplified the picture from the mass of evidence and data we collected.'

'Right,' Grant sniffs.

'Fair enough, I suppose,' says Atkins, as Grant rolls his eyes, 'I mean, Peter Popov is a genius. Even a top scorer in college like myself couldn't be expected to keep up.'

'Quite,' says Fabien, pleased. 'Don't take it personally; we thought Scotland Yard would be too slow to work it out as well. We will explain it all, you will pretend to have worked it out. You will deliver the outcomes we will discuss, and will be hailed as heroes. You'll be promoted in no time PC Atkins, and you, Detective, will be remembered as the rural sergeant who surprised everyone by exposing an international crime syndicate.'

'Bloody hell,' Grant says.

'Yes please,' Atkins adds, images of award ceremonies popping into his mind, PC Helen Phillips watching on in admiration. Later, their first kiss...

'First, you must contact the authorities looking for Mila and ensure she is no longer wanted. Then, you will help expedite her mixed-up documentation, which you will conclude is down to wartime administration problems. You will ensure that anything in her or her sister's name related to Janos' crimes is understood to be solely of his doing. Then you must ensure Anton and the children are safe, and can travel home to the UK. We trust you will ensure this is taken seriously by your superiors and partner organisations. After all, you didn't give up on trying to arrest most of my family, and annoying as that was, we admire your determination.'

'Thank you,' says Atkins.

'You better explain it all to us then, and slowly does it,' says Grant.

'Excellent!'

Peter and Fabien spread out their papers and photos and arrange them on the floor, telling their story from the beginning. They play the tape of Monty and his pal from Horton Fawcett, who, low-level and bolshy, had happily boasted his way through the call with his aristocratic contact Monty, guided expertly by Mila's inspired conversational strategy. He'd given them more than they ever could have wished for in his quest to hob-nob with the elite – with a man like Monty – whom he perceived as connected and powerful.

'Wow,' says PC Atkins afterwards, 'So Horton Fawcett had a hit on Janos Byros? Because he cheated them too?'

'Exactly,' says Peter.

'Once a cheater, always a cheater,' says Fabien.

Peter elaborates. 'Horton Fawcett employed Janos as their eyes on the ground so that they could exploit the war for financial gain, but he was essentially playing for the other side too, which they found out about as they had more than one pair of eyes – and Janos' were not the sharpest of the lot.'

'Greedy, corrupt, and rather stupid to boot,' Fabien adds.

'He knew too much about Horton Fawcett's operations and could no longer be trusted not to blow the whole thing, so, you know...' Peter mimes a gun to his head and pops his cheek for the sound effect.

'No honour amongst thieves, and all that,' Fabien concludes.

'And Mila was innocent all along?' Atkins adds, reddening.

'Thought as much,' says Grant, who feels vindicated for the first time in ages.

Peter hands over a piece of paper with a map, name, and number on it. 'This is the source of the call to the Horton Fawcett associate. It tells you where he was, and who the number is registered to. And this is where we believe Anton is hiding out with the children.'

'Godspeed, officers; help us get our friends home and keep them safe,' Fabien tells PC Atkins and DS Grant.

CHAPTER FIFTY-EIGHT

Anton is used to hiding, and he thinks he has got pretty good at it.

The knock on the door in the middle of the night startles him. His little cabin in the woods hasn't seen a passer-by in days. Only one person knows how to contact him, and that is only if there is news from his mother, news that will mean he is safe to come out of hiding. He's nestled away from his father's comrades, fellow-traitors and foolish acolytes; he's sure both lots think he killed the man. They think he knows too much.

He gets up. The children stir in their bunkbeds. 'Shush, go back to sleep,' he tells them, and their eyelashes flutter.

Anton opens the door. It is not his mother's aunt. It is a man in a suit. He curses himself for letting down his guard. He cannot run; he cannot abandon the children now. He trusted only himself to keep them safe, and he has failed.

'Anton Knight?'

'Who are you?'

'British Embassy. We are here to escort you safely home. You have some very good friends back in the UK. I'm Frederick Bailey.'

'Who is it?' a child asks, sleepily.

The man in the suit raises an eyebrow. 'Are they who I think they are?'

In the car, while the children sleep peacefully in the back seats, Mr Bailey quietly explains the intervention by UK police, who had an anonymous tip-off leading to the arrest of a businessman with links to an underground network seeking to sabotage the war effort for financial gain.

'I'm sorry to tell you that your father Janos Byros is dead.' The man says it in a low voice, so as not to wake the children.

'I'm not sorry to hear it,' Anton replies. Janos had been shot around the back of a pub, half-drunk as usual, left in the gutter. On hearing the children were missing, his awful family was telling the whole city it would be *'That bastard son – just like his faithless mother, no loyalty.'*

'I'm also sorry to inform you that your father Mr Byros is no longer considered a hero in this country. He has been stripped of his medals and awards, charged posthumously as a traitor and for the murder of his estranged wife, Ms Kiss. The investigation into his associates is ongoing. They won't get away with it.'

Anton lets his head loll backwards against the soft leather headrest, closes his eyes and exhales. It's over. They did it. They are safe.

CHAPTER FIFTY-NINE

At Farlington Hall, the banners are up. Anna and Elodie finish blowing up balloons, while Mila and Fabien bring plates of food to the large dining table in the formal hall. Later, the whole village will be here.

Mila and Fabien have been preparing for days. Mila is softening, but still cautious.

'Could you stay here, with me?' Fabien had asked her as they lay in their bed the first night they came home. 'My mother adores you. I told you she would, once she knew the truth. She's oddly right-on, deep down, and hugely admires you. She told someone the other day she was planning a WI talk on brave women in history: from Joan of Arc to Mila Kiss.

'So you're definitely not going to turn the hall into flats for a quick profit?'

'It feels different with you here, everything does. I meant it when I said this place could do some real good. Do you still long for home?'

'I'm not sure – maybe one day I'll go back, when the war is over. But for now, I think this feels like home enough.'

'Just wait until the children get here. This will be a haven for all of us,' he tells Mila with a smile. 'I really think this could work.'

Mila frowns; she still can't believe they are safe. Not until she sees them in the flesh.

The whole motley crew is busy today, and they are all making themselves at home. Lydia is being oddly accommodating, finding that to her surprise, she quite enjoys the rabble and the noise and the life being injected into the big old house, which no longer feels at all musty or stuffy. She misses Gregory, but his departure has also given her a freedom she had forgotten was there for the taking.

Xristina paces. 'I just can't believe it,' she keeps exclaiming to anyone she passes, butterflies dancing in her belly as she thinks of seeing her son again.

Nikolai is sitting with Lady Lydia, delighting her with largely fabricated stories about his youth, as they sip gin and tonics.

Peter and Chloe are tying ribbons to the front door.

Monty and A.J. are in the yard, sneaking a quick joint.

The car pulls up.

'They're here!' Chloe shouts. Xristina is first out, running down the steps, tears of joy already streaming down her face, although she can't believe it, still. Everyone else follows quickly, except for Monty and A.J., who saunter in slowly, having heard the excited shouts from a distance.

'I can't wait to meet him, Xristina,' says Mila. 'He's a real hero.'

Fabien squeezes Mila's hand, willing the reports to be correct, for the children to have been allowed to leave with Anton, with no paperwork.

The car pulls to a stop. The driver gets out and opens the back door, but it isn't Anton who emerges first. Two small children, crumpled from travel and yawning from snoozing in the back seats, appear on the driveway. A little girl clutching a dirty teddy bear with a missing eye. A boy, staring at the big group of people and taking in the enormous Victorian hall behind them.

'Konstantine? Karlie?' Mila stops dead in delighted shock, and then it all bursts forth. 'You're here!' she shouts, overwhelmed with such emotion she drops to her knees, arms outstretched.

'Aunty!'

The children run into Mila's arms.

'I was so worried! I thought I might never see you again.'

'We were scared, Aunty,' Konstantine tells her.

'But our big brother saved us,' Karlie adds.

'I'm just sorry I couldn't save your sister,' Anton, having been released briefly from his mother's embrace, is now standing above her.

Mila stands up, not letting go of the children in her arms, squeezing, squeezing. 'Oh thank you, thank you for bringing them home!' Mila twirls the children, and so does Fabien. Offal jumps up and licks the children's faces with affection, and in seconds there are tickles and squeals of delight, and promises of cake and fizzy drinks and comfy beds and story times.

Everyone celebrates all afternoon, welcoming the new residents of Farlington. Mary plays the piano, and Harry, the muck-spreading farmer, dances with Mrs Bentham. Unlike the welcome party for Mila Kiss at the Old School House, there is no stilted conversation or awkwardness. Jenny has brought homemade cakes, and they are not dry in the slightest. Councillor Beard makes a short speech, only to be outdone by Lydia, who makes a much longer one. There are tears, but so much warmth and laughter, as the fires burn and the music plays. Eventually, the last guests bid goodbye and meander, sated, out into the cool evening air, walking home beneath the night sky.

Mila is tucking the children up in bed, smothering them with kisses.

'Mummy used to kiss us like that,' says Karlie.

'You miss her?'

The children both nod from their single beds, side by side.

'Me too, and we won't ever forget her. We will look after you now, this will be our home, for now. Do you like it?'

'Yes, Aunty, it's like a castle,' Konstantine says, happily.

'Are you going to keep Mummy's name, Aunty?' asks Karlie.

'I like to think of it as borrowing it, to keep her close, but only if you don't mind?'

'We like it,' Karlie tells her.

'And big brother Anton and Uncle Fabien can stay,' Konstantine adds.

'I'm sure they will be very happy to hear it. Good night, my sweet babies.' Mila switches off the light and pulls the door, leaving it just slightly ajar. As she walks down the landing corridor to the stairs, she can hear faint laughter and music, and the clinking of glasses below. She smiles, as she goes to join the rest of her new family, to start the rest of her life.

THE END

Mother Rebel Misfit Sleuth

In a world of lies, who will fight for the truth?

In this gripping second instalment of the Mila Kiss series, justice hangs by a thread, and one wrong move could cost everything.

AUTHOR'S NOTE

I would like to say an enormous and heartfelt thank you to Olha Badornra-Zhuranska.

Although Mila's country of origin is a fictional Eastern European country, intentionally unnamed, the *Homes for Refugees* scheme that enabled Mila to arrive in Farlington was inspired by the UK scheme to support Ukrainian refugees following the Russian invasion of Ukraine in 2022 and the subsequent, ongoing war.

Olha, who came to live in the UK as a result of the war in Ukraine, kindly gave me her time and told me a little of her story. It is through speaking with Olha that I learned so much more about Mila Kiss than I could possibly have known without her. Olha helped me to understand how Mila might perceive certain aspects of (rural) British culture, how she may respond to particular scenarios, as well as how her communication and behaviour could confound her hosts at times. Olha brought Mila to life for me, and I am forever grateful.

Olha, I only hope that I have managed to create a version of Mila that you like and find believable. Thank you so much for all your help.

ACKNOWLEDGEMENTS

Thank you to everyone in the amazing team at Bloodhound Books. And most special thanks to Betsy Revley for taking a chance on me and my story, Rachel Tryer for bringing the magical editorial combination of rigorous attention to detail and genuine care for my characters and their crazy antics, and to Tara Lyons for always making sure everything comes together perfectly. I feel very lucky to be part of the Bloodhound gang.

Thank you to Gemma Chadwick for answering all my questions about rural policing. Your explanations were brilliant and incredibly useful, and so I can only apologise for letting Hoppy run amok and for almost certainly getting things wrong. Thank you to Sally Clifford for sharing her experiences of being a host for a Ukrainian refugee; your insight was invaluable. (And thanks to Ellie Clifford for making the connection). Thank you to Zosia Wand for introducing me to the wonderful Olha Badorna-Zhuranska.

And thanks to JJ Flames, Paul 'Carps' Carpenter, Jake Doherty, Graham Preston, and Rob Slade and their band Inver, for giving permission for Mila to be a huge fan and allowing me to reference their songs.

A huge thank you to my writing pals. Kirstie Pelling and Danielle Owen-Jones – thanks for being my cheerleaders and for all the sage advice administered over coffee and, that one memorable time, over fondue. Thanks to my Lancaster University Creative Writing MA gang: Claire Gray, Suzi Nelson, Geoff Cox, and especially Phil Murray for all your help with digitally visualising Mila. I will always think of you as a tech guru however many times you tell me it was a piece of cake. And thank you to my tutor Dr Ines Gregori Labarta for recommending that I submit my work to Bloodhound Books in the first place.

And finally, but always most importantly, a huge thank you to my wonderful family. Thank you Mum and Dad for reading my work and telling me it's brilliant, whatever state it is in at the time, and for spotting millions of typos before I send it out into the real world. Thank you Cade and Ellie for being the best step-kids anyone could hope for. And thank you Steve for everything. It is only with your support and love that I get to live out my writing dreams.

ABOUT THE AUTHOR

Lisa Nicholas lives with her husband and two big, daft dogs in a rural hamlet in Lancashire. Other than curling up in front of the fire with a good book, she enjoys long walks, yoga, and travelling to warmer climates.

A NOTE FROM THE PUBLISHER

Thank you for reading this book. If you enjoyed it please do consider leaving a review on Amazon to help others find it too.

We hate typos. All of our books have been rigorously edited and proofread, but sometimes mistakes do slip through. If you have spotted a typo, please do let us know and we can get it amended within hours.

info@bloodhoundbooks.com

www.ingramcontent.com/pod-product-compliance
Lightning Source LLC
Chambersburg PA
CBHW050545190726
48283CB00007B/2016